The
Green
Horse

I0662305

~Full Bifta Books~

The Green Horse
Caballo Verde

**Historical Thriller,
Fantasy, Love.**

'I haven't been disappointed.' – H.

'Classic tale.' – P.

'Intrigued and enthralled me.' – LN.

'Pick this up, and you won't put it down.' – MF.

'This gripped me from start to end.' – IW.

By Stuart Roberts

All Time Lowe:
Supernatural Thriller

Hand of the Beast:
Supernatural, Detective Thriller

The Green Horse:
Historical, Mystery Thriller

Alien Stealth:
Sci-Fi, Thriller
Out Spring 2026

Thinking of Detective Bob.
A legend.

It is only from the heart that you can touch the sky.

PROLOGUE

The evil jinni cast its shadow across the Jalon Valley. Unbeknown to the innocent villagers, the poison of hatred, contempt, and wickedness had already begun, not that they would know anything about it. Their way of life was honest, simple, and straightforward. Hard work, Christian beliefs, and strong family values formed the foundation of their all-encompassing community spirit. Little did they know a malevolent force was about to disrupt their peaceful coexistence.

The shapeshifting jinni, capable of good but with a strong tendency towards wickedness, revelled in fiendish behaviour.

Señor and Señora Morales had retired early on a cold November night. Luis Morales was first in bed, shivering and cursing the raw cold and his aching bones. As his wife turned in for the night, she set the candleholder down on a rickety bedside table, said her prayers, kneeling at the side of her bed and quickly got under the covers. Soon, their joint body heat would kick in, giving some well-deserved warmth. Her last action was to blow the candle out and snuggle back under the bedclothes. However, as she leaned towards the meagre light to blow out the flame, the candle holder rose a few inches off the table and rotated to the side, suspended in mid-air. Señora Morales lay there wide-eyed, heart racing, frozen with fear, watching candle wax drip on the table. As she conjured up the courage to scream, the candle holder fell to the floor and set light to a cheap, threadbare rug. Within seconds, the rug was ablaze.

In the middle of complete panic and a worsening blaze, the two elderly folks made it out of bed, down the stairs in their nightwear, grabbed overcoats, and spilled out onto the street, shouting for all they were worth. By the time neighbours had reacted to the kerfuffle, it was too late. Their home was on fire. A kindly neighbour took them in, sat them in front of an open fire and gave them a drink. Señora Morales repeatedly voiced what she saw: the candle holder rose, tipped over on its own, and fell to the floor. Recounting the spooky incident, she crossed herself and kissed the crucifix hanging around her neck. However, nobody believed her account of the events. The only witness knowing the truth was the evil jinni.

Days later, on a cool but sunny day and out of public sight, a small wisp of smoke transformed into the look of an underfed, flea-ridden black cat. Looking around, it made its way towards civilisation and a local market. The cat walked unnoticed through unsuspecting assemblages of people chatting about the severe fire at the Morales' home. Harassment was deeply ingrained in its mind. Ahead, the cat saw its quarry and source of mischievous fun. Sidling up to a group of gossipers, the cat approached and bit the exposed ankle of Señora Molina, drawing blood and creating a great commotion. In a flash, the cat fled only to stop by an area of rocky scrub; out of sight, it changed into a Horseshoe Whip Snake, a symbol of danger and deceit. With evil written all over its face, flicking its tongue, sensing the air, the serpent scurried away in the undergrowth.

For millennia, the jinni deceived, dominated and ruined all in his path without fear of consequence. Nobody knew when the dark, devious jinni had infiltrated a family's domain or begun an insidious scheme of cruel, torturous behaviour upon individuals or families. Deceit, disruption, and dismay featured in the jinni's twisted mind. His was the realm of darkness and eternal despair. Now, his sights were set on more fun in the sleepy, unsuspecting village of Murla.

ONE

The Year 1609.

Juan's Finca, known as Finca Poeta (Poet's cottage), was three miles outside Murla, a quaint village in Spain's Jalon Valley. Like many Spaniards working off the land, he had gone to sleep that night weary, aching and unaware of the passage of itinerant Moorish people moving across his land. Under cover of darkness, they headed for the sanctuary and seclusion of the countryside. The first he knew about it was when he was noisily woken early the following morning by Spanish troops who had surrounded his home. As they hammered on the old wooden door, it nearly fell from its hinges, convincing Juan that his home was being broken into.

"Open in the name of the King, you swine," raged an impatient general.

Juan complied immediately. Soldiers stood with swords in hand, ready to engage anyone who showed dissent or noncompliance during questioning or instructions. However, he had no fear of being mistaken for a Moorish refugee or a sympathiser. He was local, born and bred in Murla, of pure Spanish descent.

Showing openness and compliance with their instructions was paramount if he hoped to live.

General Miguel Cabrera Arroyo held his Toledo

steel sword to Juan's throat. "Name?"

"Juan Martinez Alonso, Señor," said Juan, visibly shaking and mumbling through trembling lips.

Standing at the door of the Finca, he backed off so that the general and two of his troops could enter. He knew that compliance and a show of fear were what the general would expect. The fear aspect came easily to him. Juan put his hands together in a beseeching manner. "Ple...please, señor; I am a humble farmer. I live by myself and have nothing, but anything I have here is yours. Please don't kill me, please, I beseech you?"

Disregarding his plea, the general instructed his men to search the Finca, which did not take long, as it was a mere three-roomed hovel. They reappeared, shaking their heads, to indicate that nobody else was in the building. The general lowered his sword.

Juan had an idea. If it worked, he would emerge from the confrontation alive and unscathed.

"Please, Señors, take a seat," he gestured towards the rickety table, "and I will find you food and drink."

His clever notion was precisely the right thing to say under the circumstances. The men had not eaten in a long time, and food in their bellies would appease their aggression and mollify their macho behaviour. The general sat and stabbed the point of his dagger into the centre of the table. Juan could not be sure whether this was a warning to anyone who stepped out of line with him or just a typical outward display of aggression from the general, affirming his status as the alpha male. His two comrades sat. As quickly as he could, Juan brought wooden plates loaded with bread. The plates rattled on the table with nervousness as he set them down. A jug of olive oil was placed by the general, who liberally soaked his bread. The men followed his lead. They talked as Juan laid the fire using dry kindling.

Being very shrewd, Juan called to mind the rumours he had heard about Moorish inhabitants of Spain fleeing their homes, ousted by cruel, insensitive troops; many were caught up in disagreements with the soldiers, effectively ejected from their homes and out on the streets with nothing and nowhere to go – their crime: being descendants of Moors.

King Phillip III of Spain decreed the expulsion of all Moriscos (Moors) on the 9th April 1609. Unfortunately, the treatment of every Moor was dispensed arbitrarily – long-standing feuds and hatred were acted out under the royal decree. Any treatment was acceptable towards the Moorish population. Bodily harm, torture or death was commonplace. Complete households and family possessions were taken in the name of the King and divided between those forceful enough to commit heinous acts of cruelty towards the Moors or those fortunate enough to be around at the right time to be the recipient of someone else's property. Experience, life, or social standing meant nothing in the 1600s when the Moors were expelled; it did not matter to King Felipe III's soldiers what happened. Rules were interpreted on the spot and at a whim, depending on how the officials felt. The Iberian Peninsula was in a state of flux and would be so for many years to come.

Juan recalled a recent conversation with his friend Santiago Moreno, who was savvy and well-informed. It appeared that the population of Muslims living in Spain objected to their religion being outlawed. In addition to two major Morisco revolts, accompanied by demonstrations and pressure on local and general governments, it all became too much for the king. Internal problems within the Spanish Empire became the breaking point. In response to advice, a royal decree was introduced to purify the population of the Iberian Peninsula, quell further dissent, and demonstrate strength and determination in controlling the problem at large. According to his good friend, getting rid of the interlopers meant removing the Moors from society and sending them back to North Africa. Any dissenters would be killed. Additionally, torture was commonplace when the royal troops needed answers to questions or merely wanted to mete out heinous acts of cruelty on innocent people.

Juan was shocked at the total disregard for life. The thought dominated his mind, unsettling his basic but honest, paltry life. He was doing all he could to live for another day. Farming and earning a sufficient income to support himself were his first priorities. Secondly, he hoped to see his brother in Castilla-La Mancha one day before he died.

By now, the general and his soldiers had eased back from their austere behaviour. They ate ravenously, washing the bread down with red wine, which mellowed their minds. Juan knew his clever approach was working and working well.

Meanwhile, some troops outside, fed up with waiting, questioned why the general was taking so long to search such a small hovel. An assault could have befallen him in the decrepit Finca, and no one would have known.

One imaginative soldier listened at the Finca's door and heard the soldiers talking inside; he caught references to cheap wine and instantly knew they were filling their stomachs. To be sure, he spied through a crack in the door and saw for himself. The men outside were hungry while the privileged general and his men sat inside, filling their bellies. Despite that, they would not complain about their unjust treatment for fear of retribution or possible death at the hands of an out-of-control, irate general. The troops had witnessed many questionable judgments by the general and knew it was wise to hold their counsel. Even so, hunger and the injustice of the situation drove some men to search the land and ramshackle outbuildings for any sustenance they could find. Anything would do so long as it filled their bellies and sated their hunger.

Fire lit, Juan stepped back with his hands behind his back in a subservient stance. He watched and waited for the general and his men to satisfy their appetites. There was no further inquisition from the soldiers, particularly given that signs of his meagre crops had been taken, indicating that the Moorish fleeing hordes had passed that way last night.

"A little more wine, general?"

"No, enough; we have many swine to kill today. We must go."

Juan gulped. He was glad to be on the right side of the general and not falling foul of dubious, inconsistent decisions or even momentary aggressive whims.

The general looked to his next in command. "Vamonos! (We go)."

He did no more than get up from the basic seat, belched, tossed a gold coin on the rickety old table and was gone.

Juan was in shock. His passive handling of the situation had kept him out of harm's way. Thankfully, he was still alive and grateful for his quick thinking, which played out very well. Besides that, he had earned a gold coin to make up for any loss. However, with his main crops on the land ravaged, life would be challenging towards the end of the year, and he would go hungry for many days in the depths of winter. Just last year, in a similar situation due to severe drought, crop failures became commonplace in the valley. In desperation for food, Juan climbed the mountain of Caballo Verde, searching for anything to fill his belly. Noticing some birds descending to the ground from nearby bushes drew his attention. Upon investigation, he found the carcass of a gruesome, half-eaten wolf. There, he tied some string (which he always kept in his jacket pocket) around its remaining front legs and dragged the lupine back to his home. He prepared a stew from the remaining carcass meat and a few vegetables and slept well that night, feeling full and satisfied. Yet, he suffered from a bellyache, diarrhoea, and vomiting the following day. For ten days, Juan lost a stone in weight and was close to death, but for the care of a compassionate neighbour.

Behind the Finca, two soldiers had discovered an injured Muslim male hiding amongst fruit trees and long grass. They pointed their swords at him. He stood holding a cloth bag to his bloodied ribs. Speaking perfect Spanish, he begged for mercy. They seized the bag from around his neck and immediately thrust a sword into his gut. He fell where he stood. Blood soaked the earth. Juan would find him later and have to deal with the atrocity. His death was senseless; the bag contained a few personal belongings, no valuables and no food. The most precious item in the bag was a lock of his wife's hair, wrapped in silk and secured with a ribbon.

Unable to find food, the soldiers drank some of the well's cool, clean water to put something into their bellies. With a feeling of belligerence, one of the soldiers picked up Juan's wood axe and deliberately smashed the well housing. He cursed the war, cursed the Moors, but most of all cursed the time away from his home in Valencia. Amidst anger and loathing, he threw the stupid bag belonging to the dead Moor down the well, followed by the axe, and joined the rest of the troops as the general emerged from the Finca. Their pangs of hunger would spur them on to wild killings when they found any Muslims.

Astride his horse, the general called for his troops' attention.

"Men, we have come a long way, and the end of this

conflict is in sight." The soldiers cheered with joyous enthusiasm, pleasing the general. Although he was a no-nonsense general who gave unequivocal orders which were never challenged, he also liked the admiration and respect his men paid him. "We are awaiting supplies and reinforcements – knights and pikemen, who have eliminated the devilish Moors in Denia and the surrounding area, so we will camp in Jalon tonight and wait. That is all."

TWO

Carlos Alvarez Tobin (Carl to his friends) had an affinity with Spain, probably because it was in his blood. Isabel Tobin married Luis Alvarez García in the Sixties. She met her only love on holiday, on a sunny June afternoon in Benidorm, Spain. Two years later, Carl was born. He grew up in rural England as a typical English boy. That said, his fluent Spanish and swarthy good looks were a hit with all the girls.

Every year, Carl and his friends, Theo, Lawrence, and Carrie, took turns arranging a surprise summer holiday for all, on the understanding that it would be somewhere unique, diverse, and adventurous.

Last year, Carrie organised a trip to Disneyland in Paris. Nevertheless, it seemed like a good idea at first, but the trek around Disney was overly busy and tiring. The holiday was aimed mainly at youngsters. Too many children screaming, shouting, and generally getting in the way was too much for Theo, one of the four friends, who was a serious, no-nonsense character. The trip turned out to be only just okay. Unsurprisingly, Carrie and her husband, Lawrence, thoroughly enjoyed it. However, this year was Carl's turn to organise the holiday, and it was special, life-changing special.

Clambering out of the taxi at John Lennon Airport, Liverpool, Carl took charge of the proceedings, barking orders, aware that time was slipping away and the flight deadline was looming.

"Come on, Carrie, we'll miss the flight!"

Carrie, model-like, with long blonde wavy hair, pretty but a little scatty, was more concerned with her vanity case's contents than keeping to a flight schedule. Like a film star, she alighted from the taxi and primped her luscious, wavy hair.

"Carl, I can't do this. Look at my hair and my clothes. I need time to prepare. Look at me; I've ..."

He cut her short mid-sentence. "Carrie, move your lovely little arse, or we're going to miss the flight. Theo, get two trolleys. Lawrence, help the driver with the cases." Fumbling in his wallet, he paid the taxi driver.

They rushed towards the departure lounge, suitcases and hand luggage secured on two trolleys. At speed through the entrance door, they stopped and stared in disbelief at the empty check-in desks in the departure lounge. The only person visible was a maintenance worker changing fluorescent light tubes at the top of a mobile tower scaffolding. He looked down at them in astonishment and jovially said. "They're all gone, mate. You've missed your flight."

Carl was in shock. "What the hell?"

He had booked the holiday with a local high-street travel agency and agreed on a flight and holiday to Spain. Some time after making the booking, the flight time had changed. Nevertheless, due to a technical glitch, contact with Carl never happened. He did not receive an updated flight time. The oversight was more than apparent as they stood and stared at the vacant departure lounge and blank departure boards.

"Didn't you check seventy-two hours beforehand to make sure all was well and that there were no changes?" said Theo, an obsessive character who did not indulge in guesswork or uncertainty. His world was constant and exacting. The look on Carl's face said it all. Theo was less than impressed with the apparent poor organisation. "If there's one thing I can't stand, Carl, it's bad planning, and this takes the prize."

Yet, although his reprimand was cutting, it did not provoke lasting hostility. Their relationship had endured for many years, and jeopardising an otherwise enduring friendship would require something far more significant.

"Well, better see what we can find out," said Carl apologetically.

Carrie and Lawrence took the *faux pas* in their stride. The holiday had already begun for them, and the excitement had started. Both enjoyed duty-free shopping, but first they would look forward to a leisurely breakfast and to spending quality time together. Following breakfast, Lawrence would have a pint or two under Carrie's watchful eye.

Theo and Carl ambled around the duty-free shops, bought a paper, had a coffee and decided not to have breakfast in favour of an in-flight lunch, which, although not lavish, was more than enough for the two of them.

To the delight and relief of all concerned, the flight

took off early in the afternoon and on time. Carrie and Lawrence sat behind Theo and Carl on the plane, billing and cooing, enjoying the holiday feel and excitement. The flight was going well; Lawrence felt tired after his early morning indulgence in beer, but everyone was in good spirits. At least Carl had the seating correct, remarked Theo with a wry smile. Having forgotten the earlier debacle, all four chatted happily, wondering what the forthcoming holiday surprise would bring and what it would hold for them. All they knew was that they were flying to Pamplona Airport in Spain, but Carl would divulge no more.

Carrie tested some in-flight duty-free perfume while Lawrence sat arm outstretched, admiring a new duty-free quartz movement watch that would allow him to dive to a depth of one hundred metres. However, it was much deeper than he would ever consider attempting, but in his mind, such a timepiece was well worth the cost. Like a Magpie, he had chosen the watch for its bright blue dial and fashionable shape and size.

With a glint in his eye, Carl stood up in the aisle and looked at his friends. He raised his can of beer above his head and elevated his voice over the drone of the airliner, announcing. "Ladies and gentlemen, boys and girls – a toast to my excellent friends, Carrie, Lawrence and Theo. Happy Fiesta to you all, and hello, you gorgeous señoritas."

Lawrence forgot himself and smiled agreeably.

However, Carrie quickly pulled her husband back into line, digging him in the ribs.

"You're with me, Lawrence, remember? I'm your

señorita."

Always the joker, Carl put his beer down, clasped his hands over his mouth and nose to deepen and distort his voice and mimicked a Tannoy announcement. "Ladies and gentlemen, boys and girls, this is your captain speaking. We are now flying at an altitude of 35,000 feet and ..."

All three seated stared over Carl's shoulder in shock and embarrassment. The flight captain stood behind Carl, winking at them. "It's 32,000 feet, actually. We have clear skies ahead, and it would appear a full complement of happy holidaymakers."

They burst into laughter as the captain strolled down the aisle, smiling and nodding to passengers.

Passing through European Customs was usually uneventful, but not for Lawrence. An overzealous immigration official scanned Lawrence's passport and viewed him as if he were a suspected terrorist. He spoke to Lawrence in pigeon English: "You here for holly day, no?"

Lawrence was a little baffled by the question. "No, sir, err, yes, sir. I mean ..."

Carl stepped forward to help his friend. In perfect Spanish, he explained that they were in Pamplona for the Fiesta de San Fermín and that his friend Lawrence was a little tired from the flight. In reality, he was mildly intoxicated. Seeming to ignore Carl's explanation, the immigration officer waved them on with a wave of his hand. "Pasar."

Still confused about the entire episode, Lawrence

tried to make sense of what had happened.

"What was it with that Customs guy, Carl?"

"Oh, you know, just an over-enthusiastic official doing his job, take no notice, Lawrence."

However, Carrie felt most put out. "Well, I think he was a nasty man. My poor Lawrence didn't even get a chance to practise his Spanish when he was rudely dismissed."

Lawrence and Carrie looked at each other adoringly as Carl and Theo, with their backs to them and in laddish behaviour, gestured, putting their fingers down their throats, implying that Carrie's doting was sick-making.

The airport concourse bustled with people milling around, trying to find their way to waiting coaches and the taxi rank. Excited children confined to the flight ran around, chasing each other, squealing, shouting, and generally letting off steam. The sheer number of suitcases and trolleys interrupted the flow of passengers trying to leave the airport, causing disquiet and frustration. Overall, it was mayhem. Carl pointed out to his friends that the hustle and bustle they were experiencing was an unintended but significant clue to their holiday surprise. Eventually, after finding a taxi in the chaos at the airport taxi rank, Carl instructed the driver to take them to the Hotel Presidente. With agility and practised skill, the taxi wove in and out of traffic at suicidal speed towards Pamplona City centre. Worryingly, in a laid-back, carefree manner, the driver casually conversed with Carl, taking his eyes off the road for more than the usual second or so. His one finger on the steering wheel was particularly troubling.

"Here for Fiesta de San Fermín, no?" said the driver in Spanish.

Carl took up the conversation enthusiastically. "Yes, we're here for the Fiesta. We want to run with the bulls".

"Really! Can you run fast?"

"Of course," was Carl's reply.

"Be very careful, my friend; many people run, and some die. The bulls are powerful beasts. Treat them with respect."

Lawrence was intrigued listening to the Spanish conversation.

"What are you talking about with the driver, Carl?"

"Oh, you know, just passing the time of day." He stared out the window, hoping to bring closure to the questioning. Carl had planned to announce his holiday surprise later, when they were settled in at the hotel and in a relaxed, receptive mood. Maybe, having imbibed a drink or two, he could sell his very unusual idea much better. Only time would tell.

The Hotel Presidente was busy with many new arrivals. At the check-in desk, the receptionist greeted Carl and his friends. "Hola! Can I help you"?

"Hola!" said Carl. "Party of four in the name of Tobin."

"Your passports, please?"

Carl handed all four over.

"Yes, I have you here for ten days for the fiesta.

Señors Carlos Alvarez Tobin and Dr Theodore Andreou. We have a room with two single beds and a balcony for you.

"Correct."

"Señor Lawrence Doy-lee and Señora Carrie Doy-lee. We have a double bedroom with a balcony for you in the honeymoon suite."

"But we are already married and have been ..."

Carl interrupted the conversation. "I thought you two lovebirds would like something special, so I have treated you."

Carrie blushed at the thought of being regarded as a newlywed. Conversely, with his mind focused on their surname, Lawrence attempted to correct the receptionist's mispronunciation of their surname, which irked him greatly. "That's D O Y L E – Doyle," he spelt it out to correct her mispronunciation. "You didn't say it correctly."

Ignoring Lawrence's lesson in English, the receptionist pushed four cards across the counter. "Please fill in the forms."

Carrie felt annoyed with the receptionist's brusque attitude and took Carl aside. "Carl, it happened again! This is the second time today that my poor Lawrence has been disrespected. And it isn't good enough." People who knew Lawrence and Carrie knew that she was overly protective of the love in her life. Deep down, she had a very caring nature and, having found her soulmate, she was determined to shower him with affection and motherly love. Maybe a tad overdone, yet Lawrence treasured her caring nature and, as such, was committed to her and her loving ways. Theo, a clinical psychologist, had been heard saying to Lawrence on more than one occasion that he was getting too many warm and fluffies. Nevertheless, Lawrence would not hear a word spoken against her; she was the love of his life, and he always chose to reject any criticism of her.

Theo smiled at Carrie as he slid his card back to the receptionist.

"What time is the restaurant open?" enquired Theo.

"It opens at six in the evening, señor."

"Good. And breakfast?"

"Seven in the morning, normally. But, tomorrow, Friday, the day of the Fiesta de San Fermín, breakfast is at six in the morning if you want to run." At that point, she crossed herself and touched a figure of the Virgin Mary, set to one side of the reception desk.

Listening to the conversation, Carrie was intrigued. "What does she mean, Carl, if you want to run? I'm not sure what she is talking about."

Carl gestured towards the lift. "Let's go! I will tell you later."

As the lift doors opened, Carl kept the conversation to a minimum. "We'll leave you two lovebirds to get settled in and see you in the restaurant at six-thirty. If you're not there, we'll send food to the honeymoon suite." He put his hand over his heart and gave a wink.

Carrie blushed again. "Carl, stop it!"

Leaving her to deal with one of her hot flushes, Carl and Theo continued up to the seventh floor.

"Okay, let's give the rooms a once-over, Theo,

freshen up, and then we'll head to the bar for a local beer. I believe San Miguel is amazing, especially on tap." He salivated at the thought. "Then we can head out of the hotel and check the local bars, unless of course you have any other ideas."

"Carl, I'm here on holiday. Right now, I have no better idea than one or two beers."

"So, you're not just a boring, sensible doctor of psychology; you're just here to pickle your liver."

"Mmm... you could say that, but could we stop chatting? I'm having withdrawals."

THREE

As the four strolled along the crowded streets of Pamplona city on a beautiful, warm evening, locals and visitors danced and sang; fireworks exploded in the night sky, popping and sizzling, twirling and spiralling, forming flower-like shapes in various colours. The air was electrifying with the joyful festivity. Drink flowed, and so did the hospitality. Strangers invited them to take a glass of wine and offered tapas (tasty food items). They each took one of the bite-sized delicacies and moved on. The party invitations to join the fun were endless. On one occasion, a beautiful señorita threw her arms around Lawrence; he looked as if he might be dragged away from the group of four until Carrie intervened, showing her displeasure. The cordial, inviting atmosphere was unique in its openness and sincerity, something they had never witnessed before on such a grand scale.

A local bar off a side street seemed a good place to stop and relax. They found a table and sat down, taking in the atmosphere of the fiesta. It was a great surprise to find revellers enjoying themselves without being stupidly drunk or silly – a sense of occasion was their excitement. Carl had done well with his planning; the sense of occasion was why the four were on holiday in Pamplona – to enjoy and appreciate the people and culture of another country. The hubbub around them in the bar and on the street was captivating, verging on sheer euphoria.

As he took a sip of his drink, Theo fired a question. "Right, Carl. Let's have it. I know you have something up your sleeve. You've been pretty quiet about the arrangements since we left the UK, so what is happening, where and when?"

Carrie looked on, surprised at the no-nonsense, searching question; Lawrence was only mildly curious, still thinking about the gorgeous señorita who nearly whisked him away from the group.

Carl took a sip of his drink, and with everybody's attention, he set his glass down and explained his amazing holiday idea.

"Has anyone heard of the book '*The Sun Also Rises*' by Ernest Hemingway?" He looked around the table at blank faces, except for Theo.

"I read it ... ooh, many years ago at University."

"Okay, that's a start," said Carl. "In his book, Jake and his friends travel to Burguete in France on a fishing trip and then on to Pamplona, Spain, for the Fiesta de San Fermín." He held his hands up in a here-we-are moment, signifying, this is it. Faces remained deadpan.

"Okay," he said, knowing he needed to sell his idea a bit better. "The fiesta is spread over many days and features bull running, amongst many other things. As the name fiesta suggests, we, my friends, are recreating the whole party thing out of Hemingway's book here in Pamplona and having a great time joining in with the fun, partying, and indulging in the culture. I'll read a short passage from the book over our evening meal, and we can talk about it."

Lawrence was confused, but a growing look of enlightenment was spreading across his face. "This thing, bull running, Carl. Has it got anything to do with the white shirts, pants and red neckties you asked us to bring along on holiday?"

"Got it in one, Lawrence. Tomorrow morning, we get dressed in our cricket whites, put on our red neckerchiefs, have a few wines ..."

"Wine in the morning!" Poor Carrie was perplexed. The conversation was going too quickly, and her understanding would take a bit longer. She was still trying to work out the Cricket White's part of the conversation.

"Yes, it's a fiesta, Carrie – remember?"

"I don't think wine is good for my Lawrence so early in the morning."

Carl pushed on for fear of losing momentum. He knew his idea would be a difficult sell; now, it was beginning to look like it was in jeopardy. "So, whites and red neckties, a few wines. Happy, happy, happy. Then we join the others for ..."

"Others?"

"Yes, Carrie, others. After breakfast, we join other men in the Plaza Santo Domingo and wait until a rocket is fired, which tells us the bulls have been released."

"Bulls?"

Carl was becoming mildly agitated with the

constant interruptions, which were adversely affecting his account of the planned bull run. "Why do you keep on repeating what I say, Carrie?" His look of annoyance and frustration was plain for all to see. Once again, he gathered his thoughts and calmed his emotions.

"Sorry, Carrie, it must be the heat getting to me," he said, sipping his wine. "So, when we run ahead of these decrepit old bulls down through the cobbled streets to the bullring, we..."

"Wait! Let me get this right," said Theo, trying to clarify it in his mind, but in reality, feeling sure he knew what Carl had intended. You're saying we dress in our cricket whites and a red scarf around our necks, drink wine at breakfast with our cornflakes, and join others waiting for whatever the signal is..."

"A rocket."

"Okay, a rocket. And then we run ahead of ..."

"Six, tired old bulls," said Carl, trying to trivialise the hazardous bull running event. He failed to reveal that past events had sometimes ended up in death or injury. Not a good basis for selling the idea to his friends. So, he decided to keep it simple.

"Six bulls, all the way down to the bullring ...?"

"Eight hundred and seventy-five metres, not all that far, mate!"

"Eight hundred and seventy-five metres?" Theo shook his head as if to say crazy.

Meanwhile, Carrie looked at Carl, bewildered and unsure of what he was alluding to.

Theo's logic kicked in. "No chance, Carl. You've

had some wacky ideas in your time, but this ..!"

Carl saw his biggest ally's support slipping away and piled on the reassurance. "No, Theo, it's not what you think. You and I have been training hard for some time now, right?"

"Yes, but ..."

"We're so quick on our feet; we meet ourselves coming back–yeah?" He looked at Lawrence. "You'll give it a go, won't you? You're not troubled by a morning run." In desperation, he focused intently on his mate. "Come on, Theo, it's a walk in the park – truly."

They sat in awkward silence. The holiday surprise Carl had given so much thought, time and effort to had gone down like a lead balloon. The atmosphere around the table became awkward. His friends seemed to be giving up on him and his harebrained idea. In total disillusionment, he gazed around the bar area; everybody else seemed so happy, enjoying the fiesta and anticipating tomorrow's bull run. It was all going so well, yet just minutes after his announcement, he felt low and despondent.

At that moment, he gazed over to the other side of the bar area and saw the most beautiful vision of loveliness – a young Spanish señorita – Olive-skinned, trim, above average height, long dark hair tied back, brown eyes and an exceptional model-like figure. Carl gave one of his cheeky smiles, but it was not returned. However, it did not surprise him; she could have her pick of any of the hot-blooded men who stood around her, and she knew it.

Carrie spoke up, breaking his reverie. "Carl ... Carl ... Lawrence and I have talked it over, and he's definitely not doing the bull run thing. It's too dangerous. Besides, my Lawrence has to watch his blood pressure."

His emotions were awry as he listened to the holiday surprise reaction. He felt thoroughly disheartened because of all the planning that had gone into his amazing idea. Yet he felt, at the same time, incredibly besotted by the mysterious Spanish señorita; her vision of loveliness transcended everything. He would do anything to be a part of her world. He was utterly smitten. From across the room, she casually looked in his direction and smiled. He had not imagined she would be interested in him for a minute, but there it was, a definite indication of interest. However, he was caught off guard, missing the opportunity to return the smile before she looked away. He reprimanded himself for his folly. Later, she looked across the room again and then continued talking with her friends. Over the next few minutes, Carl could see her taking the occasional sneaky look at him; he knew there was chemistry and hoped for the chance to engage her in conversation and learn more about her. However, the group and the Spanish beauty left the tapas bar, which disappointed him greatly, but not before she glanced back, smiled, and exited with her friends.

"Carl, are you listening to me?" said Carrie.

He tuned into her conversation and listened, but realised he had lost the argument for the bull run. Nevertheless, Carl was not the sort of person to take no for an answer. He needed to take a different approach in selling his idea; he had to discourage their negativity, but how? Subterfuge was called for.

They emptied their glasses and ventured out into the warm evening air. Walking his friends through the streets of the bull run route seemed a clever way of selling his idea. He had not given up on his plan yet. It needed more work. Perhaps his two running mates would see how short and easy the course was as they meandered the streets. With luck, maybe he would catch sight of the gorgeous señorita again.

Additionally, seeing the security barriers en route might give Theo and Lawrence confidence and alleviate any safety concerns they may have. He would try to convince his friends that the bull run was safe and achievable. But it would take careful management.

The party atmosphere filled the air with melodic, happy sounds. Dancers lined the streets. Musicians played to anybody who wished to listen. Excitement flowed through laughter, cheering and shouting against a background of joy and positivity. Flamenco music, fireworks, alcohol, and excitement combined to create an enthralling evening atmosphere. They strolled on to the bull's release point near the Plaza Santo Domingo, then through Plaza Consistorial, Calle Estafeta, and down to the bullring. En route, again, strangers invited them to join in and offered wine, tapas and the promise of a good time. However, saying no to the wine was unacceptable. It was going to be a long and boozy night.

Carl felt ecstatic with the warm, hospitable

atmosphere. He recalled Ernest Hemingway's accurate account of the nightly fiestas. Now, he and his friends were immersed in the very same scenario. Despite the earlier problem with selling his idea, the evening's fiesta was, in his estimation, out of this world.

"This is how it all happened."

"What was?" said Theo, trying to catch his drift.

"The book! Ernest Hemingway's book! Jake and his friends wandered the streets, taking in the atmosphere. Strangers invited them to the celebrations and offered them wine and food. My God, this is so amazing."

Just like all good things, the evening came to a close. Despite the ongoing celebrations, all four felt it was time to head back to the hotel and rest after the evening's excesses.

The morning of the bull run, the Hotel Presidente's dining room was a hive of activity. Sporting his whites and red neckerchief, Carl sat at a table by himself, nibbling on a piece of toast and sipping coffee. He looked around the dining room and considered the day's events. His hopes of selling the plan to his friends had failed. How he wished they could have seen it his way. It would have been a sense of adventure and achievement, maybe even a modern-day rite of passage for three close friends. Then they would have agreed it was a great idea. Carl buttered another piece of toast and took a sip of coffee.

"Well, is that the best you can do? Where's the wine and the pretty señoritas?"

He looked up to see Theo and Lawrence standing

side by side in their whites, each sporting a red neckerchief. Carl stood up excitedly, making a loud screech as the chair legs scraped the floor, hardly able to contain himself. "You're going to do this?" he said, so delighted that his raised voice turned heads.

Lawrence smiled. "Well, we couldn't let you have all the glory. People might think we were pathetic English wimps unworthy of such friendship. Now let's grab some breakfast. I'm starving!"

"Where's Carrie?" enquired Carl, looking around, yet not seeing her.

"She's still in bed, sleeping it off. I've sent breakfast to the room, but she looked a little green after all that wine and tapas last night."

"Does she know?"

"About our bull running escapade?"

"What else?"

"Well, I did tell her, but I don't think she took it all in; she had her head down the toilet pan at the time. Right! Cereal first, then egg, bacon and toast with gallons of tea."

FOUR

Following breakfast, the three lads discussed their game plan for the big event; in many ways, talking about the bull run helped allay their fears. Carl thought they should stay nimble on their feet and run way ahead of the bulls while keeping together. The only addition was Theo's comment that they should not take any risks. They should use the high wooden barriers to duck behind and take cover if anything untoward happened or if the bulls were too close. Other than that, they were good to go.

Lawrence looked at his new watch. "I think we should be making our way, mis amigos (my friends)."

Carl smiled at his appropriate and accurate use of Spanish. Now, with reality kicking in, their stomachs felt as if they were full of hyperactive butterflies fluttering away. Although it was merely the body's release of adrenaline, preparing them for fright or flight, it was a natural bodily process that Theo was familiar with due to his medical training. However, the seriousness of the bull run kept reminding them, despite their attempts to push the unsettling thoughts away. With the immediacy of the moment, they mustered up the courage to join the testosterone junkies, who made their way down to the starting area. Never having endured such dread before, Carl, Theo, and Lawrence all felt an emerging sense of foreboding. It was a strange, unpleasant emotion not to be repeated ever again. Now, they felt mildly nauseous, and although nobody mentioned it, they began to question whether they had made a serious error of judgment in running with the bulls. Still, now they were committed. Theo's advice was to take deep breaths. Yet, feelings of fear kept pushing to the fore, dominating their minds. In reality, they wanted to turn around and head back to the hotel for safety and normality, yet no one admitted it. Theo wondered if this was how soldiers felt before battle, recalling that his grandfather had been part of the D–Day landings, which brought the reality of war to his emotions.

In the real world of Pamplona, Spain, their clash with danger could result in injury or even death. They knew this well but also knew they could not back out. The three focused on sprinting, staying out of trouble, and completing the course; however, they had not considered the mass of runners intent on doing the same thing, all with a similar game plan.

As alcohol-fuelled chatter filled the air from the mass of white-clad bodies waiting for the start, Carl looked at the macho horde gathering, waiting to fulfil their crazy, virile fantasy. Older youths and mature men chatted and drank their final hit of alcohol or merely crossed themselves in a profoundly religious way, hoping for divine intervention to keep them safe. Others worked out strategies for a secure run. Some wanted to back out of the bull run but felt ashamed for even thinking it. Others stood silent in contemplation.

However, nothing could disguise the look of sheer terror on their faces. In a very unpredictable, adrenaline-charged dice with death, nothing was certain, and everything was to play for in the macho world of bull running. Fear, apprehension and exhilaration hung in the air. Yet, all fears and worries faded as the runners sang a stirring Benediction – a prayer before the bull run, asking Saint Fermín for his blessing and protection in the up-and-coming run through the streets ahead of six bulls. The Benediction concluded with Spanish runners and a few non-Spanish shouting, 'Long live Saint Fermín.'

Carl, Theo and Lawrence looked at each other, moved by the stirring, emotional blessing. It was similar to singing Land of Hope and Glory at the Royal Albert Hall.

To shake off their charged emotions, they focused on limbering up, stretching their legs, shaking their arms and loosening stiff neck muscles, moving their heads from side to side like boxers before a fight.

The event was imminent. The stage was set. All three friends wished each other good luck again, and although trying to hide their fear and apprehension, their smiles of 'I'm okay' belied the look in their eyes. The occasional wiping of clammy hands on their thighs, elevated breathing, and dry lips gave the game away to the trained eye. Their bond of friendship was palpable. They hugged each other in turn and wished each other good luck. In reality, this could be the last time they saw each other in the mortal world.

Lawrence glanced at his watch. "Not long to go

now." His focus on time produced a sudden rush of fear; his heart palpitated, only heightening it all the more.

Lawrence searched the crowd, hoping to see Carrie, and there she was. There was no mistaking her long blond hair standing out amongst the Spanish Moreno types, both arms waving high above her head. She was trying to say something above the cacophony of sounds from the hysterical crowd, but hearing her was impossible. Lawrence removed a pair of Carrie's briefs from his shirt pocket and waved them in the air for her to see, with a loud cheer from the runners nearby. He stuffed them back into his pocket with pride.

"We have a knight in shining armour with us, Theo," said Carl. "The lady hath bestowed her favour on Sir Lawrence." They laughed hysterically, helping divert their attention from the seriousness of what was about to unfold.

Held in a temporary corral, bulls bellowed, snorted and madly rushed the substantial wooden barriers of their confinement. Leaning over the protective wooden fence of the enclosure, men prodded the bulls with sticks to enrage them all the more, causing them to buck violently. The dangerous action could, if continued, provoke a pre-emptive stampede or a barrier collapse.

On cue, men took charge of the sturdy gates to release the bulls. A rocket flashed high in the sky with a loud bang. Moments later, a second rocket indicated that the bulls had been released. Mad panic ensued as a sea of white bodies pushed forward, mindful that the bulls would be upon them very soon. So began the run, with substantial focus on the crazed bovines appearing from behind. There were no instructions for the run; participants automatically ran for their lives. Their mission was to run ahead, avoid danger, and prove their courage and skill in outwitting the aggressive stampeding bulls.

Like greyhounds out of the traps, Carl, Theo and Lawrence sped off, trying to stay together in the adrenaline-charged melee of man and beasts. The din of the cheering crowd was deafening. Along the way, men stumbled, slipped and fought for their feet. By their very nature, the cobbled streets made it difficult to keep one's footing. Crowded bodies searched for clear pathways ahead to gain an advantage over the stampede. Yet, the mass of bodies all heading in the same direction created bottlenecks, making it difficult for the runners to implement their would-be exit strategy in the event of a crisis. Colossal, wooden safety barriers stood high and erect at strategic points to prevent bulls from entering side streets. Some runners headed for the wooden barricades for sanctuary, although most tried not to, as it revealed a lack of courage in their minds. Lawrence was forced to slow down by the tightly packed bodies ahead of him.

Carl shouted to his friend above the din of the melee. "Lawrence, keep up!" However, the narrowing bend in the street ahead had caused gridlock for the runners and a field day for the wild bulls. He lost sight of Lawrence but kept running and dodging. Amid the chaos, Carl looked over his shoulder to see men parting like an ocean wave as a bull broke free from the leading group of six. He became aware of a loud snorting behind him, which curdled his blood. He felt queasy; hair stood up on the back of his neck, yet running was the only course to avoid imminent danger; he could not stop and look around for fear of slowing down. The conveyor belt of men headed in the same direction sped as fast as possible; there was no stopping to take a breath or feel faint. Adrenaline-filled bodies charged along. Carl's legs cramped, giving rise to pain. The baying crowd's noise made it difficult to concentrate; he felt confused. Ahead, a wooden safety barrier, to escape the perceived threat. Fear carried him forward, yet, at that precise moment, approaching the wooden safety barrier, a Red Cross medic trying to move behind the barrier away from the same peril tripped and fell in front of him.

The narrow entrance was blocked, and the medic was in danger of being trampled by the bull or worse. Carl could have jumped over the medic and headed for safety, but he realised the medic lying on the floor was a lady. In a split second, he made a decision that would change his life forever. The bull was about to exact revenge on both of them. Carl feared for the young female – she could be injured or, at the very worst, gored to death by the beast's horns. Without thought for his own life or personal safety, he threw himself across the medic in a selfless, heroic act to protect her from the raging beast. The scene turned ugly. Like a hot knife through butter, the bull's horn punctured

Carl's rib cage. Unceremoniously, the beast flung Carl up in the air; he fell in a heap near the safety barrier. His white shirt, having turned crimson, matched the neckerchief. But for the fact that the nurse was picked up bodily and carried behind the safety barrier, she could have been gored as well. The scene became desperate as people endeavoured to distract the bull from its manic onslaught as it toyed with Carl's body and his precious life. However, brutal revenge was in the beast's mind; Carl was tossed around the street like a puppet. The tirade was vicious, and the bull determined that the plaything lying on the street before him would be gored and pummelled some more.

People tried shouting and slapping the beast to distract it. The bravest individual tried pulling its tail, turning the bull's head away from Carl.

The lifeless, crumpled body lying on the street showed no movement. All was lost.

Diverting its attention away from Carl, the beast looked at the provocateurs around him and then ran off, searching for its next victim. As it bolted down the street, its bloodied horns warned – do not mess with me; and indeed, the runners did not mess with the bull from Hell.

Time passed – everything was deathly silent. Carl could see people, streets and buildings around him. He turned his head to see a crowd of runners in white and red milling around. In the distance, the herd continued its charge along the cobbled street, around the corner and out of sight. However, he was perplexed by the complete and utter silence. Minutes ago, the crowd was deafening; now, nothing. He felt bewildered. What was happening? The weird feeling made him believe he was dreaming about the bull run. Nothing made sense. Then, it all became frighteningly apparent.

He was dead, floating over the tragic scene at a height of about ten feet, where he saw a likeness of himself face down on the stone cobbles, his shirt soaked in blood. Medics covered him with a blanket and rolled him carefully onto his side with the open wound exposed, stemming the flow of blood.

Police, seeing the situation, stood by, guns at the ready in case the errant bull decided to venture back and terrorise some more. Carl lay like a rag doll, motionless and defunct. First-aiders tried to revive him as the young nurse stood nearby in shock.

FIVE

Emergency department medics at the hospital worked frantically to revive Carl. He had already been declared clinically dead once at the scene; however, at the female nurse's insistence, Carl was worked upon in the ambulance; fortunately, his heart started beating. An intravenous line inserted into a vein to administer life-giving drugs played a vital role in his treatment. An oxygen mask was also placed over his nose and mouth. Now he was back from the brink, and they did not want to lose him again. His heart began to beat erratically – fibrillating, which raised concern. Shocking the heart on two occasions brought about a steadier heart rhythm. However, his condition was critical, and it became vital to move him to intensive care at speed.

Theo, Lawrence and Carrie sat in silent vigil in the hospital waiting room. Carl's breathing improved slightly with the medical emergency team's professional intervention, yet his vital signs were weak; moreover, he had not regained consciousness. Nevertheless, the signs were slightly encouraging from the tempestuous morning when he died. The next phase was to stabilise his condition.

Carl lay in a coma in a hospital bed for two days. His body was transfused. A chest drain inserted in his rib cage trickled blood into a receptacle hanging beneath the bed frame. He remained critical, kept alive solely by the medical staff's skill and professionalism. In the late afternoon of the third day, his eyes half opened, and his blurred vision cleared slightly. Before him, he saw a face.

"Hola, Carl. Welcome back," said the voice.

He was unsure what was happening and tried to focus, yet confusion reigned. His eyelids were leaden, and his mind a blur. Trying to make sense of the image before him, he blinked his eyes, mustering up the energy to speak. "Hello, are you an angel?"

Alicia, a Spanish nurse, took his hand and leaned in close. "You are safe; now you must sleep."

He focused on her accent. "Are you a Spanish angel?"

She smiled sweetly. "You must rest. You have a serious accidentay. You will be soon better, I am sure." Although her second language the nurse spoke basic, but understandable English.

"Where am I?"

"In hospital, in Pamplona."

"Not in heaven?"

"No, not in heaven." She smiled again. "You are in hospital. We make you better. No talk now. You must keep your energy."

His memory began to return. "I've seen you before."

"Yes, in the bar in Pamplona. I am Alicia," she said,

her heart warming to the moment. "Now, you sleep."

All became clear in Carl's mind – the vision of loveliness surrounded by friends. That was where he saw her.

Alarmingly, the audio/visual monitor readout of his vital signs suddenly became erratic. He lapsed into sudden unconsciousness; monitor lights flashed, warning sounds filled the air, indicating an emergency. Alicia shouted. "Heeelp?"

The following afternoon, Carl regained consciousness to find his friends sitting around the bed. In the night, he had been given the last rites, indicating the seriousness of his fragile condition. He had been close to death. But with his friends around him and with effort, his voice became a little stronger.

"Hello, you lot." He tried to sit up, yet it was impossible and not recommended.

Theo, usually reserved in such matters, placed a hand on his shoulder. "Don't move, Carl. Stay nice and still. How are you feeling?"

"A little bit stiff and sore, but not bad."

Lawrence tried to lighten the moment. "That's what happens when you try to stop a raging bull. Not a good idea, you know."

"Bull!"

"You don't remember? Just as well, I suppose."

"No, I don't remember."

"Hey, you made the local papers," said Lawrence, continuing his input. He was so pleased to see his good friend back from the brink of death and hoped to jog his memory.

"What do you mean by papers?" Lawrence held up an edition of 'Diario de Navarra' at close quarters so he could read the headlines.

MAYOR'S DAUGHTER SAVED.

"Yes, it seems you're a bit of a hero."

"Let me, Lawrence," said Theo with mild frustration. The idea was to keep Carl calm and relaxed, rather than getting him worked up. "We'll get there a bit quicker if I explain." In reality, Theo was experiencing deep emotional feelings for his friend, who had thankfully been brought back to life. He tried to explain the situation simply, without making Carl excited. "Do you remember anything at all, Carl?" He thought that if he talked to Carl gently, it would be good for him. In reality, he feared Carl slipping off into a coma and then dying before his eyes. At all costs, he wanted to do everything possible to see his dear friend return to full health. However, his own emotions were all awry.

"I remember the rocket, and we ran ... the rest is ..."

Theo continued. "Do you remember us running ahead of those crazy bulls?"

"No, I don't."

"Well, we separated, and I was running ahead of the bulls with you. I looked back and saw you, but with a bull right behind. I tried to turn back to help, but it was like fighting against a tsunami. Everyone was running towards me, trying to keep ahead of the danger. Then I saw it happen." He paused for a moment to control his emotions. "You were in its sights, but it was too late. The crazed beast was ... well, it wasn't good."

Carrie became upset at the thought of Carl being set upon. Tears flowed. She sensed the whole conversation was becoming too much for him. "No more, Theo, Carl's still very weak."

Lawrence continued, to her displeasure. "It wasn't really after Carl; it was just mad at everybody, and poor Carl got in its way."

Carrie rounded on him. "Lawrence, now that's enough of the horrible experience!"

"Yes, well, the bull is now beef burgers."

Carrie kissed Carl on the cheek. "Well, I think you were very courageous, Carl."

"You sure were," Lawrence agreed. "We'll tell you more about it when you feel stronger and can hold a glass of wine." Lawrence looked at Carl, feeling belligerent towards the bull that had caused his friend so much harm. "Then we can celebrate the return of our very good friend and thank God you are alive and that the bull is well and truly gone."

"We're so happy to see you feeling better, Carl," said Carrie.

Nurse Alicia approached the bed. "Doctor, he says a lot of sleep for Carl."

Lawrence was back in his corrective mode. "You mean rest."

However, Nurse Alicia was unsure about the correction. Although she had a reasonable understanding of English, certain words and phrases still eluded her.

"It's good to see you guys again," said Carl, positively wilting – his voice trailing off. "I'm going to be fine. I'm in good hands."

Lawrence looked towards Alicia and winked at Carl. "Yes, I can see that."

"What about Mum and Dad? Do they know?"

Theo, as usual, being the organiser, had communicated with his parents. "Your Mum will be here later today, but your Dad can't fly at present because of his Asthma. Still, they know you are safe and out of danger. Alicia's grateful family will be looking after your mum, and she will stay at their home. Carl was relieved that Mum knew about the trauma, but worried that she might be overly concerned for his well-being when she saw him.

His voice was quieter now. "Thanks, guys. Now go, get out of here, and not too much wine without me."

"If you drank right now, Carl, it'd come out of the hole in your chest," said Lawrence, cracking a silly, childish joke, having watched too many mindless cartoons.

Carrie looked scornfully at Lawrence. "Goodbye, Carl. Take care." She leaned in and kissed him again.

In a rare display of emotion, Theo kissed Carl on the forehead and smiled. "See you tomorrow, superhero."

All three left feeling reassured that their heroic friend, Carl, was out of the woods and on the mend.

Later that evening, the ward routine changed, reflecting the winding down of procedures for the day and preparation for the night shift. After a lengthy sleep, Carl looked a bit brighter. Lying still, deep in thought, he searched his mind for more answers to his forgetful recent past. He looked at Alicia as she straightened his bed.

"Alicia, what did my friend mean when he talked about the hole in my chest?"

Alicia was a little perplexed. "I not know this hole. You rest now. You tired."

Carl did not give up. "But also, why is my mum staying with your family?"

"They show gratis... greatit ..."

"You mean gratitude."

"Sí. They show gratitude for you, save me from El Toro."

Carl was puzzled. He did not ask any more questions. With heavy eyelids and a disconnect from the real world, he drifted off again.

Dr Gonzalez reviewed Carl's treatment with Nurse Alicia and a junior doctor the following morning. "Carlos is much better today. There is no bleeding from his lungs, his blood pressure is within normal limits, and his breathing is fair." He looked at the nurse and asked if the patient was generally okay. Her answer was affirmative.

"So, we can remove the drainage tube. But we must keep him under close observation."

Later, with help from Alicia, the junior doctor removed Carl's chest drainage tube and stitched the chest wound's opening, making his patient feel more comfortable.

"Okay, Carl. It is looking good. I give you a clean bill of health – well, nearly," he said, enjoying his little joke. Surprisingly, although Spanish was his first language, he spoke English with a cockney accent. He had trained as a junior doctor in one of the London hospitals and picked up his cockney English working and living there for three years. Following the procedure, the nurses straightened Carl's bed and made him as comfortable as possible.

"The doctor speaks good English, Alicia."

"Yes, he is doctor in London." Carl was enchanted by her English and concluded that her speech was very alluring and sexy.

"Are *you* going to keep me under observation all night, Alicia?" he said with a cheeky smile.

She looked over her shoulder at a large Spanish nurse making beds. "She take care all night, and she no have lip from you."

His face was a picture of disappointment as he played along with the fun moment. Alicia smiled, countering his cheeky, familiar behaviour. Secretly, she enjoyed his warmth and beautiful nature.

"I'm feeling much better already," said Carl.

"That is good. I happy."

"Alicia, what my friends were saying about the raging bull, I don't understand. Do you know what they were talking about?"

She struggled with his question but knew he wanted clarity; however, she did not want to reveal too many gory details early on in the recovery phase.

"To top it all, I keep on getting horrible flashbacks," said Carl.

She misunderstood the word in his sentence.

"Thrash backs?"

"No, flashbacks. It's like having strange pictures in my head, but I don't recall what happened when I ran down the cobbled streets of Pamplona as the guys were telling me."

Alicia took a moment and sat on his bed. "So, I tell you. Me I am there. We help a man through a wooden barrier; he is not well. Then I see bull; he chase you. I turn for go and fall, and somebody fall on me. It was you. You stop the bull for me. My father is, how you say, he love you forever; you save my life."

"So it was you! I protected you from the bull, but if I am correct, he stuck me with his horn."

"I think is what you say. Now you sleep. Tomorrow, friends and girlfriend are coming to see you. She very preety."

Carl was a bit puzzled by Alicia's comment. "I don't have a girlfriend."

"She kisses you, I say me, she is your girl."

Carl understood. "Oh, you mean Carrie. No, she is lovely and a good friend, but she isn't my girlfriend; she is Lawrence's wife." Just then, he stopped talking and grimaced. "Aaargh!"

Alicia looked on with concern. "Is problem?"

"Just pain."

"You see, it is too much early. I get doctor."

Carl held his chest with both hands. "No, it's alright. Maybe it's just my heart."

She became even more concerned. "Your heart?"

Carl smiled at Alicia. "Yes, my heart is aching." If you put your hand on my chest, maybe it will make me feel better."

Alicia understood the joke with a smile, which paid her back for her earlier trick on him with the nurse.

"I theenk you are much better now," she looked around. "Oh, here is your Mama."

Señor Romero, Alicia's Dad, escorted a very emotional Isabel to Carl's bedside. After a few words with Alicia, Señor Romero left, but not before walking up to Carl's bedside, shaking his hand gently and declaring his heartfelt thanks.

"Oh, Carl, my love. How are you?" Isabel leaned in and kissed him.

"I'm fine, Mum."

She stroked his head and kissed him again. "No, you're not. You nearly died; Señor Romero told me everything that happened."

"But I saw the doctor this morning, and he said I'm recovering well."

With all the worry and pent-up emotion, Isabel broke down in tears. "Thank the Lord."

"Come on now, Mum, it's not that bad," he said, holding his hands up, moving them around, demonstrating his vastly improved health. However, in doing so, he experienced pain in his chest. His pretence of feeling well told him he had a long way to go yet, to full recovery. "Look, see, I'm fit and healthy. Never felt better."

She ignored his silly statement about his health.

"Just what possessed you to do such a foolish thing as running in front of bulls?"

"Oh, you know."

"Yes. I know, just like your dad, impulsive and prone to moments of madness." She leaned over and kissed his forehead.

"I'm going to be alright, Mum. They took the chest tube out earlier, and I'm feeling so much better now."

"Chest tube?" Obviously, she had not been told about the lifesaving procedure.

"Mum, I'm fine and feeling good. Stop worrying ... please." He tried to move the conversation on to stop her from dwelling on the negative aspects of his condition. "Is Dad okay?"

"Yes, he's okay, just going through a nasty bout of Asthma, though. You know how he is. The last time he saw the consultant, he said his asthma was well controlled with his inhaler, but that changes depending on his stress levels. By the way, he sends his love and looks forward to seeing you soon, fully recovered. Perhaps when you're up to it, you could call him and have a chat. Put his mind at ease, so to speak." In reality, his dad had reacted badly with an Asthma attack when given the traumatic news about Carl. Nevertheless, it was essential to remain positive and focus on Carl's recovery rather than dwell on the ordeal and how it had occurred.

"Carrie and the lads have been so good visiting me. I wish I was out of here enjoying the holiday with them."

"Well, right now, my lad, it's rest and relaxation for

you. And do as the doctors and nurses tell you."

Carl looked at Alicia and winked.

"Señor Romero and his wife have been so good to me. They met me at the airport and insisted I stay at their home. Isn't that kind of them, Carl?" Isabel leaned in close and lowered her voice. "They're very big around here. He's the Lord Mayor of Pamplona."

Carl's strength began to wane. He felt tired. His eyes became heavy, and his voice drifted in and out as he spoke.

Alicia intervened. "He is good, Señora Tobin. You not worry. He is ... umm, I learn this. He is very ti-red. Maybe you have time tomorrow with him. I see you tonight at home for dinner and tell you how he is repairing."

Isabel smiled to herself, thinking about how the nurse used the word "repairing." However, her compassion and genuineness shone through, and Isabel appreciated her devotion.

The following day, with exemplary care from hospital staff, Carl was able to sit up in a comfortable chair beside his bed. His friends popped in to visit and were pleased to meet up with Carl's mum. Having visited as often as possible, she felt reassured by his progress. Discharge was imminent, and unsurprisingly, Alicia's parents insisted that Carl convalesce at the Romeros' substantial property, on the outskirts of Pamplona.

Days later, following a positive assessment and discharge by the consultant, Carl sat on the veranda in a comfortable chair; Mum fussed around as Alicia prepared drinks.

Unable to contain her thoughts, Isabel lowered her voice." Carl, what a lovely girl."

He sensed that Alicia could hear what his mum had said, but he liked listening to her approval, even if it was a bit embarrassing.

"Yes, she is very special," he said in a low voice, sufficiently loud enough for her to hear his approval. Mum held Carl's hand as they sat quietly, looking at the spectacular mountainous views.

Isabel broke the silence. "Did I tell you? Señor Romero wanted me to stay longer, but now that I know you are on the mend, I should be getting back home."

"I know ... Dad needs you."

"Well, he does."

"And, you have your jobs – the dog will be missing you, and the Women's Institute can't manage without you," he said, knowing his mum very well.

"Something like that. I've got a ticket for a flight late tomorrow morning."

She showed Carl her ticket. He reached for it to check the flight time, remembering his screw-up on the outbound flight at the beginning of their holiday. Without warning, he suddenly felt weird. A trancelike sensation came over him; a sense of sheer foreboding ran through his mind. He experienced darkness and felt deep despair.

"Mum, don't fly back tomorrow; it isn't right! I have a strange feeling."

Isabel could not understand why he had spoken so vehemently about her flight. "Why, Carl? I don't understand what you are saying."

Alicia put the drinks down in front of them, listening to Carl's strangeness. She had never seen this in anyone before, and it troubled her.

"Mum, I have a bad feeling. Please don't fly back tomorrow." He became agitated and tried to stand even though he still felt weak.

Isabel calmed him. "Well, if that's what you think, Carl." She saw the look of consternation on his face. This was unlike him, but she knew he would calm down if she agreed to his strange request. "I'll have to phone Aunty Grace and let her know. She'll be expecting to pick me up from the airport."

By now, Alicia's concern was front and centre. "You alright, Carl? You look white."

Isabel stared at him. "As if you've seen a ghost."

"Sí, is what I theenk. You must rest now. We take care of you."

SIX

By the following day, Carl started to find his feet; he slowly walked around the villa with Alicia's help, a perfect excuse for close contact.

"Carl, you not tell me why your Mama must not go home. She can stay forever if she want. That is not a problem."

They sat down as Carl searched his mind for a plausible answer. "I don't know. I just had a terrible feeling of foreboding that something bad would happen."

"This bad thing. You have before?"

"No, never." A moment of reflection ensued as Carl sought a straightforward explanation for the incident involving the flight ticket. "Alicia, did I die when the bull got me?"

"What you mean?"

"Did I die? Did my heart stop?"

"I not know how to say." Alicia wanted to protect Carl from the traumatic experience's stark reality, but realised it was becoming too difficult to conceal the truth from him any longer.

"It's alright, you know. You can tell me what happened. I won't get upset or collapse in a heap on the floor."

Alicia took Carl's hand and spoke slowly. "You die two times, that I know. The first when bull get you, and again in hospital. The doctors are good and save you a lot of blood you lost."

"I see. So that's why I felt so weak." A wave of sentiment came over him as he looked into her beautiful, dark brown eyes. Alicia, I want to thank you so much for helping me. I don't think I could have got through this without you."

She looked into his tearful eyes and saw a sincere, vulnerable, tender person. "There is no need for thank … I thank you."

His feelings were all off balance. Unknowingly, Carl was reacting to the horrors of the trauma in Pamplona, which was, in reality, post-traumatic stress. He had never experienced tremors before, yet his body shook. Images flashed before his eyes. He felt anxious enough to make him hold onto Alicia's hand tightly. With time and patience, the awful feelings abated.

"No, I want to thank you, Alicia. Being ill like this, I feel so much better having you with me. The horrible events pale into insignificance, knowing I saved you from danger. I would do it all over again in an instant." Alicia did not quite understand every word Carl uttered, but instinctively knew he spoke from the heart. They looked at each other longingly. Then, a smile followed by a hug. Both were caught up in an intoxicating moment of desire and love.

Breaking the moment, they heard a shriek from another room and parted abruptly, feeling awkward about their moment of passion. Isabel and Señora

García left the kitchen to join Carl and Alicia.

"Carl! Carl! We've just heard it on the radio. There has been a nasty accident at the airport. A coach with passengers heading for a plane on the runway bound for Liverpool hit a barrier and flipped onto its side. I would have been on that coach today if you hadn't stopped me from getting that flight." Isabel could hardly contain herself. Carl and Alicia looked at each other in utter amazement. In a freaky sort of way, the airport incident answered the question as to why Carl had such a strange reaction when he held Mum's flight ticket. It indicated he had precognitive awareness of the event – an ability to see into the future. However, it posed many more unanswered questions. The biggest conundrum was how and why Carl had developed the ability to foretell future events when he did not possess it before arriving in Pamplona.

That evening, the Romero family laid on an impressive meal for Isabel; she was due to depart the following day for her flight back home. There was a party atmosphere; Carl's friends had been invited, making it a delightful get-together. Despite that, Carl and Alicia spent most of the evening in each other's company. They were on an emotional rollercoaster like two lovers on their first heady date.

That evening, Carl met Alicia's brother, Antonio, a tall, slim man who looked the epitome of a young, lithe bullfighter. As a good judge of character, Carl was not overly enthusiastic about their first meeting; however, he kept his counsel, and the conversation was very polite and hospitable.

"You haven't mentioned much about your brother," said Carl, curious to know more.

"He is matador and very famoso. I do not see much; I work, and he is in Spain. When we together as a family, he tell stories of bullfights."

"So, does he travel all around Spain?"

"Sí."

"And is he fighting in Pamplona for the Fiesta?" said Carl, reflecting on the book by Ernest Hemingway, which cited a matador, Pedro Romero, who had an affair with Lady Ashley, a main character in the book.

"Sí. He is, how you say? He is people popular. They love him."

With a devilish look in his eyes, Carl tantalised Alicia. "His name isn't Pedro Romero, is it?"

"No. Is Antonio Romero García. Why you say this to me?"

"Oh, it's just silly nonsense."

"Please, you say?"

"Well ... I'm Jake Barnes; my friends are Robert Cohen, Bill Gorton and the lovely Lady Brett Ashley."

"I confuse; you joke, no?"

"Yes, I joke. An American journalist, Ernest Hemingway, wrote a book describing these four people who came to..."

"Deescri." Yes, I know this word.

"Described. It means to tell you about something. Ernest Hemingway's story is of friends Jake, Robert, Bill, and Brett. They holiday in Pamplona and join in with the Fiesta de San Fermín."

"Ah, you read this book and see in Pamplona?"

"That's right. And the bullfighter in the story is Pedro Romero."

"Yes, I hear my son he say this."

Carl chuckled. "You mean your brother."

"Yes, my brother, he tell the family many stories of Romero and others. Come, I show you something in other room."

Alicia excused herself and walked with Carl towards the building's rear, where a room was set out with her brother's bullfighting memorabilia. On display were suits of lights and bullfighting jackets in various colours, draped around mannequins. Posters adorned the walls. Capes, ceremonial swords, and Monteras (bullfighting hats) were accompanied by many pictures of her brother, creating an imposing display.

Carl looked closely at a family picture hanging on the wall. "Is this you in the picture?"

"Yes, I am eighteen years." She pointed. "Thees is my brother, and thees is Mama and Papa."

"Wow! You look absolutely stunning," said Carl, genuinely enthusiastic. Even now, he found it hard to believe. He was in her company, and she had strong feelings for him.

"Can I have a photograph of you?"

Alicia loved his charm and loving compliments.

"You are very nice, Carl. I like it in you."

"Well, mum always says you should say what you feel."

Alicia linked Carl's arm and walked him around the room, aware of their blossoming relationship. She pointed to a vivid suit of lights. "This is especial. My brother fight for King Juan Carlos."

"What! King Juan Carlos was at a bullfight when your brother was a matador?"

"Sí is special honour." Carl moved a bit nearer to the display, picked up a matador's hat and put it on. "Is this the hat that he wore in front of King Juan Carlos?"

"Sí, is Montera. But I don't think you put on. Is not good."

Suddenly, Carl felt strange. The room swirled, unusual shapes materialised in his mind. Dark, foreboding images appeared, heightening his apprehension. He held his head in pain. Alicia was shocked at the sudden change in his demeanour. "Carl! What is it? Oh, Carl, you alright?"

Just then, Antonio, nicknamed 'The Rage' in bullfighting circles, entered the room. He had not disguised his feelings towards Carl at their initial meeting, and now he had good reason to show his contempt. In essence, he was overprotective of his little sister and disliked Carl, possibly because he was of English descent. The fact that his sister had feelings for Carl annoyed him greatly.

"What you do? Get out NOW!" Antonio snatched the Montera from Carl and pushed him out of the room. Poor Alicia could not believe what was happening, and Antonio had not finished. "Get out, and don't look at my room again. Do you hear me? Get out!"

Alicia tried to help by defending Carl, but that only made matters worse. "No, Antonio, he is ill. Stop,

Antonio."

The cosy, informal atmosphere in the dining room ceased; everybody stopped what they were doing. Señor Romero excused himself and left hurriedly to find out what all the commotion was about. He entered Antonio's room and immediately began to remonstrate with him. Aggressive behaviour towards a guest in their home was unforgivable and, in Señor Romero's eyes, the height of bad manners. Unfortunately, the altercation became a tense, out-of-control situation. All three family members raised their voices, adding to the unfortunate altercation. Carl headed for a chair and sat down, holding his head in his hands. After a few minutes, a furious Antonio stormed out of the room, leaving home in a foul temper. With Alicia and her dad's help, the patient hobbled back into the living room.

Señor Romero and Elena felt embarrassed that such an argument occurred in their home. All the same, Carl was troubled about the situation, which appeared to be unintentionally of his own doing. He offered an apology: "I'm sorry if I offended Antonio or did something wrong."

Señor Romero, mortified by his son's behaviour, tried to explain the reason for the disrespectful outburst. "Please, Carlos. It is no problem. My son is ... how you say, quick-tempered. He has been like this for many months. He is a good man, but sometimes he is like a mad bull himself."

"I know why," said Carl.

Everyone in the room stopped and looked on,

intrigued and amazed.

"You know why he is angry?"

"Well, I think so. For some reason, and I don't know how or why, but I seem to have developed some psychic power." The mere act of saying that made Carl feel self-conscious. He wondered if they would think he was losing his mind. However, he pushed on with it, committed to his tell-all, bizarre news.

"When I touch an object, I associate with that thing. Feelings and thoughts flash through my mind." His voice trailed off as he felt eyes upon him. "It's a bit like having second sight."

"What you mean, Carl?" said Alicia, even more confused.

"I'm not sure, but I get an unusual sensation when I touch objects. It is like I feel what the object feels or has felt."

His thoughts were a conversation stopper; nobody spoke, but Isabel broke the silence. "Is that why you didn't want me to travel to Pamplona airport with that flight ticket?"

"Yes, I believe it was." Carl looked around the room at blank faces. "Now, this is going to sound really wacky."

"Wacky?" said Alicia.

"It means to sound strange or weird."

Frustrating the moment all the more, Alicia said.

"What is weird?"

Her dad was irritated by the constant interruptions at such a tense moment and said something to her in Spanish, which she quickly understood, and sat back quietly to listen.

Carl picked up the conversation. Señora García crossed herself and uttered a few words.

"Well, the wacky bit is this. When I put the montera on my head earlier, I experienced intense pressure and pain in my skull, which was unbearable. I just knew that this was what Antonio was feeling." He held his head, which amazingly contorted his face, sensing the awful pain that Antonio had experienced earlier. To his amazement, just thinking about the event gave him agonising discomfort. He pushed the thought away, and the pain diminished.

Señor Romero was concerned. "My son has headaches. He takes tablets, but the doctor says his life is stressful because he is an important, active man with great responsibility."

"No, Señor Romero, this is different. This isn't just stress; it's more than that."

In stunned silence, they struggled to comprehend the implications of it all. However, Alicia wanted to know more. "Carl, what you mean this is different?"

"This is such intense pressure and pain. I think ..."

"You think what?"

"Well, I think your brother could have a problem in his brain, maybe even a brain tumour or pressure inside his skull. At any rate, he should have it checked out as soon as possible. "

Señora García closed her eyes, reeling from the shock of Carl's revelation.

Carl looked around the room for inspiration. "Señor Romero," he pointed across the room to a silver crucifix on the sideboard. "Is the crucifix yours?"

"No. It is ..."

Carl held his hand up. "Please, don't tell me! Would you mind if I touch it?"

Señor Romero handed him the cross. "No, I don't mind at all. But I can't see why you want to hold the crucifix under the circumstances."

He hoped to prove to the Romeros that he had a special gift and that his hunch about Antonio, although a recently acquired skill, was genuine and relatively accurate.

Carl held the cross as if mindfully searching for something. A curious tingling in his fingers spread to his hands and wrists. Strange, fleeting messages from the inanimate object flowed. Then, as if out of nowhere, images flashed through his mind. His newly acquired gift fed him basic information, which he had to interpret and articulate. "The cross isn't from this house. I get a feeling of distance. And there's a connection with an elderly Spanish lady."

Señora García looked on in amazement. "Dios Mío, mi madre." (Good God. My mother.)

Then, his exclusive insight changed. Colour drained from his face. His eyes became fixed and staring. His mind plunged headlong into something that shocked him to the core. A slash of a sword and something falling to the ground. If he did not know better, it could have been the thud a limb falling to the ground. This paranormal experience he was dealing with was by far the most dramatic, gory and painful he could ever have imagined. His heart raced. Carl wiped his forehead with his sleeve. The experience was becoming too much for him to endure. Just as he was about to put the cross down in fright, the image in his mind's eye changed. Now, he saw green mountains, a blue sky and trees. Although deeply disturbed by what he had just experienced, Carl continued with the spectacle. He shifted his focus to the cross's rudimentary history, which focused on the Spanish lady. "I see a tiny cottage nestled in the lee of a mountain. Yes, the elderly lady lives there. The cross belongs to her, although..." he looked at Alicia. "It now has a new owner – just a minute!" He held the moment. "The mountain has something to do with a horse, and it's ... a green horse."

Isabel did not quite understand. "Now you're really losing it, Carl. A mountain and a green horse?" said Isabel. Although the horse and mountain may have sounded strange, Carl dared not divulge everything he saw in his mind's eye; the other images were far too gruesome. Then fleetingly, he experienced images of a witch's broom and cauldron. Carl would undoubtedly have been ridiculed if he had mentioned that aspect of his vision. He began to believe it was necessary to channel the information, say only the most pertinent and realistic points, and defer the rest. It became evident that it would take quite some time to understand, recall, and interpret information accurately in order to deliver it successfully.

Alicia could not contain her enthusiasm. "No, he is right. It is Nana's crucifix, and it was given to me. She live near a mountain."

Señor Romero, although stunned, filled in the remaining information. "That is correct. My wife's mother, Señora Rosa García, lives many miles away in the tiny village of Murla, in Alicante. The mountain you mentioned is Caballo Verde, which means Green Horse."

"If you don't mind me asking, why have you got the cross here?" said Carl.

"My Nana gave it to me when I was little girl. She is supersticioso and thinks I need protection.

For his mum's benefit, Carl explained that Nana Rosa was superstitious.

Just then, the telephone rang, breaking the silence. Señor Romero went into the next room to answer the call. Alicia and Carl talked while Isabel consoled Señora García, who appeared troubled by the strange proceedings around her.

Phone call over, Señor Romero entered the room, looking a ghastly colour and visibly shaken." That was the hospital. Antonio has been taken to the emergency department. He collapsed in the street with a severe headache."

The unwelcome news was prophetic. Fearing that Carl's prediction could be correct, everyone hoped it would not be. The mood was sombre. However, Carl saw a glimmer of hope.

"Señor Romero. Do not waste any time. Tell the hospital it is vital that they do a scan of Antonio's head."

Señor Romero stared at his wife, who was in tears and beside herself with concern.

Alicia knew that Carl was right. "Papa, it is right. Carl, he knows."

"Trust me, señor. You must act fast if you want Antonio to recover (he chose his words carefully, not wanting to alarm the family). There is no time to waste."

Señor Romero and his wife conversed with each other in rapid Spanish. Alicia joined in. Convinced that this was the correct action, Señor Romero agreed: "I will do better. I know the surgeon; he is a friend of mine. I will ring him at home now."

Amid the drama and upset, Carl's friends sat quietly nearby. It was akin to watching a film scene unfold before them, yet they were unsure of where the plot was leading.

The next few hours were deeply troubling for the family. They sat around trying to do everyday things to distract their minds, but all they could think about was poor Antonio and the potentially tragic outcome.

The family received a phone call late in the afternoon, requesting that they visit the hospital.

With urgency, the family sped across the city to the medical centre and met their surgeon friend.

"Felipe, Elena, Alicia." The surgeon smiled assuredly. "I have operated on Antonio and removed a brain tumour. The operation went very well, and he has an excellent chance of making a full recovery. The tumour appears benign (non-cancerous), but we will not know for certain until we receive a pathology report. It was pressing on a part of his brain, causing the symptoms you described. Unfortunately, this is all too common. I have seen this tumour many times before, and I say this with reservation: the prognosis is good."

Señora García wept with relief, took the surgeon's hands, and kissed them as if they were the hands of the Holy Father. Undaunted, maybe even enjoying the grateful display of gratitude, he continued.

"Antonio will be unconscious until tomorrow; then, if his signs are good, we will wake him up from the drug-induced coma. It is necessary to rest his brain from the operation. He is young and fit, and all the signs are encouraging. I have done all I can, and now we must wait and pray."

The surgeon and Señor Romero walked away, continuing to talk, as the nurse beckoned the family. "You can see Antonio now."

Although lying immobile in intensive care with a mass of tubes and wires around him and a nearby machine beeping, which indicated his positive health, Elena and Alicia felt optimistic about his recovery. His colour was good, and according to Alicia, reading the notes and checking his vital signs, all was going well.

The following day, Alicia and Carl's friends sat on the Romeros' veranda, talking and laughing. They had come to better understand the Spanish way of life and culture by sharing the Romeros' family home and experiencing it firsthand.

Theo scanned his English newspaper while they sat on the veranda; Carrie and Alicia talked about clothes and fashion.

"So, one day of our holiday left, hey Carl," said Lawrence, feeling sad that his best friend had missed so much of the planned holiday. How cruel life could be. However, it was Lawrence's turn to choose the holiday next year, and he was already working on an idea.

"Yes, it's gone too quickly."

Lawrence wondered how Carl felt about going home. "Are you ready for the return journey, or are you staying on for a bit longer?"

"I'd like to stay, but ... I must get back. I have a job and commitments. Alicia and her family have been so good to me here, and I would love to stay, but it's impossible right now."

Although talking to Carrie on the other side of the room, Alicia tuned into the conversation. A rare talent that females often possess. "Well, you stay. My family, they like you stay," she said aloud.

"Carl looked at Theo. "What would you do, Theo, my personal therapist?"

In one of those rare humorous moments, he looked at Carl. "Don't ask me. I'm a psychologist. I only listen to people; I don't give advice."

Amidst laughter, Señor Romero stepped onto the veranda. "Good news. Antonio is awake, his condition is good, and he is well."

The holiday appeared to be ending on a high note. Señor Romero took Carl's hand. "I thank you from the bottom of my heart, Carl. First, you saved my beautiful Alicia, and then you saved my son, Antonio. I am deeply, deeply indebted to you."

"Señor, please, there is no need to thank me."

"Yes, I must. You are like family, and my family means so much to me. Now we celebrate. Oh, I nearly forgot. Antonio wants to see you before you go home, Carl. He wants to thank you and express his sincere apologies for the trouble he caused. Now, then, shall we open a bottle of champagne? Spanish Cava, of course."

The event became a bittersweet moment. The sweet part was Carl's recovery, and it would seem he had found the love of his life. Additionally, Antonio was recovering well and hoped to be home soon. The downside was that Carl had to leave shortly and head back home, which would make the parting miserable.

Later on, Carrie and Alicia had a girlie moment in the bedroom, experimenting with hair and nails. It was an excellent opportunity to discuss life in the UK and, of course, Carl. The conversation even broached the topic of cultures and names. Alicia was intrigued when asked if she had ever shortened her name. She was even more surprised by the suggestion that her name, Alicia, could be shortened to Ali, Al, or Aly. She was beginning to see that immersing herself in the English culture and way of life was great fun. Carl and his friends had to leave an hour later and return to the hotel to pack and prepare for their late afternoon flight. Unsurprisingly, Alicia would find it challenging. Saying goodbye to Carl would be the worst day of her life.

The Romero family and all four good friends sat around the first-class departure lounge at the airport–

compliments of Señor Romero. The Tannoy system announced the departure of the Liverpool flight as they chatted excitedly, except for Carl and Alicia. Parting was looming, which seemed so unreal following all that had happened.

"Passengers on flight 1129, bound for Liverpool, England, please make your way to boarding gate five."

Theo looked at his friends and the Romero family. "Well, that's us guys. Good old Blighty, next stop, whether you like it or not."

Carl's friends got up, shook hands with the Romero family members and prepared to depart, picking up their hand luggage. Embarrassingly, Lawrence put on a floppy Mexican sombrero, an acquisition from the poolside shop. However, the purchase proved a great buy, shielding his sensitive face and neck from the intense Spanish sunshine. Alicia turned to her parents and said something. They both nodded in a gesture of agreement. She took Carl by the arm and guided him to a quieter part of the lounge.

Sitting close to him, she became emotional. "So much has happened, and I ... I try to practice what I say, Carl, and I not know how to tell you I am sad you go."

He held her hand. "I know Alicia. I feel the same. No one has ever touched my heart so much as you. I haven't said this to you before because I wasn't sure how you felt about me." He stopped to control his own emotions, although a tear appeared in the corner of his eye. "I love you so much and can't bear for us to be parted. When I look at you, I see an angel, but more than that, I see the love of my life – the love I want to spend the rest of my days with."

She leaned forward and kissed him tenderly. "I want to say so much, but I cannot. My heart is sad, I don't want you to go," said Alicia, wiping away tears.

Carl was trying to hold onto his emotions. "Do you feel the way I feel?"

"More," said Alicia, now crying, which shocked Carl. He did not like seeing her cry because, in this instance, it meant she was sad. Unknowingly, in the short time he knew her, he had pledged to treat her with respect and love and always to make her happy.

"More than me would be huge ..."

From across the lounge, Theo's voice boomed.

"Carl! We must go, or we'll miss the flight."

"Okay, coming now."

Carl looked back at Alicia.

"Right, must go." Knowing he needed to move, he stood up, yet his feelings told him to throw his arms around her and agree to stay in Spain forever. Yet, despite that, he knew it would be the wrong thing to do. Right now, he had commitments that needed to be addressed; once they were taken care of, he would be in a much better position to make a rational decision, along with Alicia.

With time becoming critical, Alicia reached around her neck, removed her Gold crucifix and chain and put it around Carl's neck. She kissed him one final time. At that moment, a myriad of thoughts, feelings and images raced through his mind. "Your nana gave you this for Christmas," he said assuredly.

"How you know, Carl?"

What he did not tell her was that the crucifix and chain, in addition to revealing their source to him due to psychometry, also focused on Nana's life. Unbelievably, this was a similar reoccurrence of the time he held Alicia's silver cross, given to her by Nana. There seemed to be a great significance in Nana and the area of Murla.

By now, Theo was frantic, given the blatant disregard for the need to head to the departure gate. Carl's indifference was causing Theo significant problems. "Carl! It is urgent! We must go now!"

Later, in private, he would have the opportunity to touch the chain and crucifix and see what else he could discover about the parting gift which held so many secrets.

Carl took a small box out of his hand luggage and gave it to Alicia with one final gesture. "Not to be opened till you get home," he said. Handing it to her, he turned and departed with haste, leaving Alicia alone.

Carl and Theo ran as fast as they could.

Nearly out of sight and causing Theo more angst, Carl turned to see Alicia waving wildly. He took hold of the crucifix around his neck, put his hand on his heart and beamed a loving smile.

SEVEN

Arriving back in the UK, Carl found it difficult to settle; even so, he continued in a humdrum manner. The love of his life was one thousand and fifty miles away, which could have been the other side of the world as far as he was concerned. Alicia felt equally devastated, as her mother had confirmed on many occasions when talking to Carl or his parents, either by mobile or FaceTime. There was a void in Alicia's life, and it felt devastating. She had considered working as a nurse near Carl and his family in the UK. Unfortunately, her English was not up to the standard required to be accepted as a nurse in the UK, so it was a non-starter. Carl would have to move to Spain if they were to revolve in each other's worlds again. However, the only problem for him was leaving his family and home. Yet, he knew he had to be back with Alicia, but this time permanently.

The gang of four met weekly for a meal or maybe drinks in a wine bar, sometimes at each other's homes. Occasionally, they would watch a film at the local cinema and eat at a nearby restaurant. They regularly discussed the highs and lows of the Spanish trip, as well as their love for Pamplona and the Spanish people. Nevertheless, the conversation generally centred on Carl's plans. They knew he was besotted with Alicia and often saw Carl in a state of disillusionment. On one occasion, Theo sat him down and talked about his dilemma. It was as if Theo were talking to one of his patients, who had overwhelming social and personal problems. Help from his best friend clarified his mind and generated a much clearer sense of judgment. Ultimately, Carl decided to move to Spain, but the prospect of leaving his parents and friends behind was challenging, to say the least. The dilemma was a tremendous psychological tug-of-war for him until Theo, with calm logic, argued that he should follow his heart. Mum, Dad and his friends could always fly out to Spain, or in turn, he and Alicia could come and stay with family or friends in the UK. Besides, communication between people in today's world is easy. The session with Theo ended, which greatly helped Carl. Theo's humour came to the fore when he said, "That will be £60 for the consultation, and I don't take cheques." They parted that evening with a massive hug of appreciation and deep fondness for each other.

Lawrence, a computer technician, had taken to researching the bull run in Pamplona and had amassed hours of footage from the web relating to the Fiesta de San Fermín. As Isabel put it, plenty of event footage showed Carl, Lawrence, and Theo running with the other crazies, doing stupid, irrational things. However, the footage of Carl gored by the bull was particularly harrowing and, in some cases, unwatchable. Seeing him as he lay lifeless on the cobbled street in Pamplona was challenging to deal with, for Theo and his friends, let alone Carl. In reality, it showed a bloodied, dead body, similar to a victim of a nasty car crash, lying there immobile. Videos also showed people around him trying to distract the bull and save Carl from further onslaught. It demonstrated man's humanity to fellow man and highlighted the courage of some brave individuals in the face of danger.

Carrie continued life in her inimitable way. The salon where she worked was a short bus ride away from home, where she spent the day beautifying women, preparing them for weddings, parties, and special occasions. Her holiday version of events enthralled work colleagues, especially when she showed them a photograph of all four in Pamplona. That said, every woman who saw the picture wanted to know who the Latin hunk was. Of course, it was Carl. He had the same devastating effect on every hot-blooded female when they saw him. Carrie contacted Alicia regularly using FaceTime and enjoyed many moments discussing fashion trends, makeup, and other girly topics. The subject of Carl always came up, and a lot of time was spent assuring Alicia that he was well and, of course, missing her terribly.

Working at a local NHS hospital, Theo settled back into his job as a clinical psychologist. Referrals for his type of work were constant and never-ending. Significant numbers of people in society appeared to have problems and needed help, whether from a counsellor or a psychologist. He handled the day-to-day pressures of hospital life without difficulty and remained upbeat, enthusiastic, and ready to apply his mind to more challenging referrals.

Ten days had elapsed following Carl and Alicia's parting at the airport in Pamplona, Spain. His farewell present to her was half a gold heart on a chain. He wore the other half on his chain and cross from Alicia. Carl thought it was very symbolic of their present plight. Parted, they were incomplete; together, they were as one. Both regularly spoke on their mobile phones, texted, and sent voicemails, usually several times a day. Occasionally, they used web-based video conferencing. Interestingly, communicating online only made their plight more challenging to cope with – seeing each other but not being able to kiss or touch one another was difficult to endure.

Carl was passionate about his work and was regarded as a great teacher with a BA in French and Spanish. He worked at a secondary school, helping many children to understand and speak another language. He enthusiastically carried out his duties as a professional but continually reflected on and reran his first meeting with Alicia. Her remarkable beauty and poise, the first time he saw her in a Pamplona bar, were so unforgettable.

After days and weeks of wavering, Carl came to a decision. He intended to live in a rental flat near Alicia in Pamplona, find a job to support himself in the short term and see how it all worked out. However, his abiding obsession was to be near Alicia and part of her world again. Alicia always spoke positively about their future whenever they conversed by mobile or occasionally by conference call. She had shown commitment and waited for his decision. Nevertheless, she knew it was a big ask of him and did not exert any undue pressure; she waited and hoped Carl's move would come soon.

One memorable night, Carl sat his parents down, explained his dilemma at length, and proposed moving near the love of his life. In essence, he was looking for their approval. Although saddened by the thought of their son moving away from home, Isabel and Luis knew the decision was inevitable and, of course, the right thing for him to do. They gave him their unequivocal blessing, knowing it would make the family parting easier if they put on a brave face.

The eventual news sent Alicia into a spin. Her family offered Carl a room in their home. However, he graciously declined, opting for a flat in the town centre. Alicia's Dad even pulled a few strings to get Carl a job in a local secondary school, teaching English to the pupils. Amazingly, it was a reversal of his teaching job in the UK. There, he taught Spanish to English students. In Spain, he would teach English to Spanish students. How strange life was, he thought.

After a lot of planning, the penultimate day was upon him. To celebrate the move to Spain, his parents laid on a party the day before his flight. Yet, unknown to Carl, Mum and Dad had arranged a big surprise for him. Secretly, they had arranged with Alicia and her parents for her to fly to Liverpool to be with Carl on his final day back home. The cloak-and-dagger arrangements were so secretive that Carl had no idea what was about to happen.

As usual, he got up at seven o'clock, washed, shaved, dressed, and went downstairs for breakfast. As he opened the kitchen door, Alicia was sitting at the breakfast table, beaming the biggest smile ever; she jumped up and ran to Carl with arms outstretched. The embrace was unlike anything they had ever experienced, and the surprise was the best present they had ever received. And, of course, they would travel to Spain together, billing and cooing all the way back to Pamplona.

The day belonged to Alicia and Carl. They were inseparable, talking continuously and embracing whenever they had the opportunity. Seeing the young couple madly in love was so enjoyable for his parents. Unsurprisingly, it transported them back in time to when they first met in Benidorm – so long ago, but as if it were only yesterday.

Carl's dad enjoyed speaking with Alicia in his mother tongue. That evening, there was a party for Carl with his friends, immediate family and of course, the stunning Alicia. All the heartache, missing each other, and moments of feeling low paled into insignificance. They were together, now, and the future was theirs to determine as they wanted.

The day of the flight came too soon for Isabel and Luis. However, it was inevitable that their son would someday meet the love of his life, get married, and start a family. They were continually filled with joy and delighted with their son. His thoughtful, caring nature was precious to his parents, one that they often proudly spoke about with others. In many ways, Carl's maturation and subsequent severing of the umbilical cord turned out to be a bittersweet moment. The move to Spain was a significant turning point in his life, and it tempered his parents' sadness, as it was what Carl had wanted. They looked to the future with optimism, knowing it would mark the beginning of another chapter in their lives. Carl would undoubtedly be with Alicia for the rest of his life, and who knew what the future had in store?

However, an unimaginable enchantment had been cast unbeknown to the adoring couple. Carl was destined to meet with a long-dead friend if everything went as planned. Thereafter, they would face an epic challenge to rid Caballo Verde (The Green Horse) of evil. Dark forces would be released, intent on killing and destroying all in their path. Carl, Alicia, and their newfound friend would require all the strength and power to prevail. But would that be enough?

EIGHT

The flat in Pamplona was perfectly adequate for Carl. It was a one-bedroom property with a living room, kitchen, and bathroom above a restaurant off the main street in Pamplona. Although basic, it was satisfactory as a single-person accommodation. When they first viewed the flat, Alicia dismissed it out of hand, deeming it to be dirty and desperately in need of attention; however, because of its location (near the school), where he had secured a job, and with its cheap rental status, Carl persuaded Alicia that it was more than adequate for his needs. It became evident that she wanted better for him, which he understood; however, Carl was practical and saw it as merely a step on the ladder of life. The contract was signed, and with the benefit of a long weekend, both set to work on cleaning and making minor repairs to the front door lock, the loose bedroom window, and addressing a toilet issue. All of these were repairable by Carl, much to Alicia's surprise. Still, the most challenging job was painting over a garish red living room wall with a neutral colour. One redeeming feature of the flat was a balcony overlooking the main street, which allowed sitting out on evenings when it felt warm and oppressive. With the occasional breeze, it felt so welcoming.

Additionally, with many fiestas in Spain, they had a great vantage point for the processions in Pamplona. Although it was unlikely that Carl would ever watch a bull run again. Both enjoyed watching the world go by from the balcony in the busy metropolis. However, there was a problem with Carl that Alicia needed to address, and she had to choose her time carefully.

Over the coming weeks, she spent less time at her parents' home in Pamplona, spending more time with Carl. Her parents did not object; they could see contentment on her face and happiness in her general demeanour.

Time permitting, Alicia would occasionally pop around to the flat and do what most practical females did – clean and tidy. However, it had to be said that he was a savvy bachelor who tidied and generally cleaned up after himself. Sometimes, Alicia prepared an evening meal, allowing them to enjoy time together and discuss the day's events over a glass of wine. Yet, Alicia never stayed overnight. She always got a taxicab back to her parents' home and regaled them with all the latest news.

Late Sunday afternoon at the flat, Alicia encouraged Carl to go for a stroll. Hand in hand, they wandered about the streets, taking it all in. Nevertheless, the problem she had foreseen needed to be addressed, and Alicia had a secret plan she hadn't shared with Carl. Linking arms, they meandered the cobbled streets of the bull run where Carl, on the day of the fiesta, was gored by a raging bull, suffering traumatic injury and death. Fortunately, the dire outcome was averted; Carl was resuscitated by medical professionals and quickly taken to the hospital.

Weeks later, Alicia wanted to ease the ghosts of Carl's traumatic past. She witnessed evidence of post-traumatic stress disorder in her loved one and wanted to help him overcome the ordeal that he had buried deep in his mind. Carl did not discuss his innermost feelings while recovering in the hospital or later at the Romeros' home. Flashbacks of terror, nightmares and heightened anxiety were all so real to him, yet he kept them to himself. However, one day, the images in his mind worsened to the point where he sat alone in his flat, quivering like jelly – his life in turmoil. He genuinely thought he was going crazy.

Even so, Alicia knew something was wrong when he avoided discussing the bull run and its painful, deathly experience. Ingeniously, her walk encouraged Carl to tread the cobbled streets of Pamplona, some of which were near the bull run route, while others intersected the bulls' course. Although not without concern, they made slow progress, as Carl kept a tight hold of Alicia's arm. In an instant, if left to himself, he would run away from the scene. At all costs, Alicia did not want him to flee; in truth, she wanted him to face his fears and deal with the stress disorder. She showed great fortitude and smiled lovingly throughout the walk, encouraging and helping ease the fear-provoking images that came out of the blue, which fed inaccurate sensations and triggered horrifying flashbacks in his mind.

A small tapas bar located near the incident site on that fateful morning was a good place to stop, have a drink, and reflect.

By now, Carl was aware of Alicia's endeavour to help him, which he cherished dearly, for this was his love, his very own Spanish Angel. Although a clever idea to expose Carl to fear gradually – walking the cobbled streets to dispel fears of the past, it was more thanks to a Spanish psychologist at the hospital, who advised Alicia on how to help Carl overcome his fear of the streets, nightmares, and avoidance.

Sitting it out and chatting with the beautiful Alicia beside him, Carl began to settle. His breathing calmed, and his mind, although still racing, slowed down appreciably. He had to agree that reliving the events of the fiesta, sitting tight and letting it wash over him, was a difficult thing to do, but a good idea, as it allowed him a means of gaining control over his fear. Accepting and discussing his problem (which he thought was a secret from Alicia) was the first step on the road to recovery. The only thing he impressed upon Alicia was that she had to agree to keep his stress disorder a secret, known only to them.

One final step was for Carl to agree to visit the same café on various occasions over the coming weeks, to ensure that, over time, he would overcome the fear-inducing situation that had been created in his mind. With courage, determination and his Angel's help, he would overcome the stress disorder.

Later that evening, Carl called for a taxi and walked Alicia to the pavement outside the flat to wait for it to arrive. She embraced and kissed him tenderly. "I am so happy to help you, Carl. I want you well again," she said, feeling mildly emotional, probably due to revisiting the awful sight herself and experiencing all that she had tried to forget.

He smiled at her sincere and heartfelt feelings. Her adoring nature brought him immense happiness, and this, in part, would help him overcome the trauma's horror. He smiled, brushed her cheek with the back of his hand, and kissed her again.

"I think you like me," she said.

"No," said Carl. "I absolutely adore you."

At breakneck speed, the taxi pulled up by the kerbside, bringing their precious moment to a close. Incredibly, it was the same taxi driver who had taken the four friends to the Hotel Presidente all those weeks ago at the beginning of their holiday. The driver demonstrated excellent memory, recalling the group well. He even recounted the conversation. Carl was reminded of the prophetic warning by the taxi driver. 'Be careful, my friend; many people run, and some die.'

Although challenging culturally, Carl's job at a local secondary school proved rewarding. It was why he got up in the morning, enthusiastic and ready for another day at school with eager learners. In addition, he achieved celebrity status within the school. How incredible it was to be an Englishman who spoke perfect Spanish yet taught English to Spanish children. Additionally, his good looks made him a hit with all the girls, who ogled him longingly. Amongst the pupils, he was known as El Salvador – the teacher who saved the mayor's daughter from death. However, he did not talk about the savage attack by the bull on that fateful day for fear of creating more terror.

His stay in the flat was okay, but incomplete without Alicia by his side. It seemed every minute together, they spoke about their future. Yet, they wanted more – far more. Their ultimate goal was to get married and live in their own home, but they needed financial stability to achieve that goal. There were no obstacles to marriage or Carl's acceptance into the Romero family. The major problem was their self-imposed need to do everything correctly and in their own way. Alicia's dad would gladly loan the couple money to buy a home. Nevertheless, it all had to be of their own doing and under their control. Secretly, Señor Romero admired them for their independence, yet he was always there to help if they changed their minds.

However, little did they know that an unseen force would take them to the edge of Hell, looking to obliterate them for good.

NINE

The diaphanous figure looked on as a lone climber made his way up the rocky escarpment of Mount Caballo Verde. An air of mystery and fear had shrouded the mountain for hundreds of years, giving rise to rumours of fearsome beings roaming wild and attacking people, which caused untold disquiet among the community. The Devil's Chair, a unique rock formation high on the uppermost elevation overlooking the village of Murla, stood imposing, never changing, dominating – a fearful reminder of malevolence and danger to the villagers and beyond. The chair's name hailed back to Roman times when troops, situated miles apart on mountainous outposts, signalled events by brazier fires from one post to another. The mountain fires struck fear into the hearts of villagers in the valleys below, who firmly believed the devil was at work. Thus compelling locals to lock their doors, secure windows, and shut out the dreaded evil at night.

The climber paused his ascent, his step uncertain; rough, calloused hands gripping a jagged rock to steady himself, tentative and unsure. He stared to his left. Mental acuity faltered. He thought he observed an Arab-like figure, minus an arm, moving away into the distance on the lower slopes, now hidden behind scrub and rocks. The climber screwed his eyes up, trying to clear his vision. The area of his brain responsible for threat arousal spiked. His sixth paranormal sense peaked. His initial thought was to make his way back down the mountainside as quickly as possible to safety. However, ashen-faced with a quivering chin, his mind went blank; something held him frozen to the spot. His 20/20, eagle-like vision, did not fail him; yet he doubted what he had seen. For the moment, he was speechless, unable to concentrate on anything. His remaining free hand covered his mouth in shock and fear. There again, he thought, it would be foolish to react by shouting out in fear; he was courageous, a man of the world, or so he thought. What if he had heard a reply or a gut-wrenching, eerie response if he had called out? What would he do then?

In the local Bar Papa in Murla, the day before, he overheard a conversation about strange happenings on the mountain. There was even a mention of a peculiar translucent ghost wearing a long robe. Looking at the gossipers sitting in the corner of the bar holding court, he dismissed their silly nonsense out of hand as foolish boloney – finished his pint and left to get an early night before the following day's adventure climbing Caballo Verde. Like most climbers, he was elated at the thought of scaling the mountain's South face, yet nervous about being alone on the climb. Still, he had his mobile for emergencies, and the weather was forecast to be suitable for the day. What could go wrong?

Despite all the rumours and the gossip, here he was on the mountain, and he had just witnessed the ghostly figure described in the bar the night before. Fleetingly, he thought of the well-known documentary footage of a Yeti in the mountains of California as it wandered into the treeline and disappeared out of sight. Closer to home, rumours of the mountain's ghostly figure he believed to be mere gossip from ignorant people. Having considered the local blather, his mind tried to make sense of the disturbing moment he had just experienced, but he could not. It was an image that would stay in his mind for a long time. His only regret was not having a photo of the spirit on his mobile. He concluded that all the rumours he had heard in and around Murla were genuine. If only he could have produced a picture of the ghostly apparition, he would have achieved notoriety with evidence of the phantom on his mobile. He would undoubtedly have been regarded as a clever, daring, and intrepid spirit hunter, and a rich one at that.

However, coping with the initial shock and trying to rationalise the moment was useless.

Within that moment, his mind went blank; he became caught up in a dreamlike state, noticing a white orb in the near distance, floating between the trees in the morning breeze. Frightened and yet mesmerised, his mind struggled to cope with what was happening. Trepidation took hold.. Absorbed with the weird anomaly, his heart raced. The nightmare continued unabated as other orbs arrived on the lower hillside and, frighteningly, began to move up the mountain, like bees to honey; scarily, he saw himself as the honey. By now, the orbs were fifty feet away as he clung to the rock face. Looking around, he saw a plateau he could reach and be safe from falling; however, it brought him closer to the orbs. He had to muster all his strength and courage and move to safety.

The orbs multiplied, coalescing, nearing him, pulsating, controlling his mind, rooting him to the spot. In the short distance remaining, they flew at the stranger with lightning speed, enveloping his body – terrifying him. The figure he had seen earlier advanced towards him, its arm outstretched. The orbs backed off.

He didn't pray very often, and at times in his life wondered if he was really a non-believer, an atheist. However, at that moment, and with such gravity of mind, he prayed frantically and loudly. Loud in the hope that God would hear him in his time of need, yet conveniently ignoring life's little indiscretions in his degenerate world. At that moment, he needed divine intervention. Nothing else could or would save him.

The forces of good and evil were teetering on the brink.

TEN

At the age of seventy-eight, Alicia's Nana, Rosa, who lived near the village of Murla, was in her usual morning routine at home when she tripped and fell, sustaining a fracture of the hip. It took many weeks of recovery and intensive physiotherapy before she could walk again; however, Rosa was not the active person she used to be due to muscle wastage and an understandable lack of confidence. She walked with a stick and vowed to throw it away at the first opportunity. Yet, the shock to her system knocked her confidence. Fortunately, at the time of her accident, she had her mobile with her and was clear enough of mind to call for an ambulance and alert the family. Regretfully, seeing sense, she agreed to move in with her daughter and son-in-law in Pamplona and sell her Finca on the outskirts of Murla. Yet, the thought of selling her home played heavily on her mind. She had lived in Murla with her husband for most of her adult life, and even now, after her personal trauma, it was difficult to say goodbye to the home of her dreams.

Locally, Rosa became known as Gaia Madre – (Mother Earth), a name and reputation that she rather enjoyed. Her understanding of natural medicinal remedies for treating illnesses and obscure conditions helped many locals with health problems long before health clinics became commonplace. Rosa was a blessing to the locals and was considered very knowledgeable. She was well-respected and highly esteemed for her skills in understanding life's ailments, but more than that, she had many natural remedies at hand and sought out herbs and plants locally for this purpose. Often, there would be a knock on her door at some obscure hour by someone needing her help, which was always forthcoming, never declined and always free. However, after receiving her help, locals would leave eggs, a chicken, or vegetables and fruit as a gesture of gratitude for her kindness.

In trying to sell Rosa's Finca, time permitting, the family would drive from Pamplona to Murla to meet with the estate agent and verify that everything was in order with the property. The journey was long and arduous, so they turned it into a long weekend break, staying in a hotel in Jalon for two or three nights. This gave Rosa a chance to catch up with friends from the village of Murla. However, seeing her beautiful, empty Finca filled her with sadness. Conversely, she was glad that properties placed on the market for sale in the vicinity were taking a long time to sell. This meant a final decision on her property's sale could be many months away, maybe even a year, thus delaying the inevitable. Yet, she could not bear the thought of her Finca being on the market, let alone sold to a stranger. Besides, she did not like the idea of people traipsing around her beautiful home, maybe even disrespecting it with odd comments or causing damage. The fabric of her life was within the four walls, creating an intensely personal sanctuary that she, in reality, did not want to sell. The troubling saga played heavily on her mind. Then, one night, following a lot of intense thought, she had a eureka moment as she sat alone in her daughter's and son-in-law's study. Rosa knew her plan would work well if accepted and would inevitably keep the Finca within the family's domain.

The following day, she saw Alicia at the family home in Pamplona. Sitting her down with a cup of coffee, Rosa discussed the future and what it meant for everyone.

"How are you and Carlos – still madly in love?"

"We're very well; thank you, Nana, and yes, madly in love." The young couple were undoubtedly in love, planning their future together, so the question seemed odd. Their togetherness was apparent for all to see.

"Do you think he is the right person for you?"

Alicia was mildly curious about the polite but even stranger question. Still, Rosa and Alicia had an extraordinary relationship. Although the questions sounded intrusive, maybe even a tad personal, it was not unusual for them to be openly candid with each other.

"Well, we love each other dearly, Nana, and we often talk about being together for the rest of our lives, so that is a yes; most certainly, we are right for each other. We are saving money in a joint bank account, and as soon as we have enough for a deposit, we will look for a flat in Pamplona and hopefully get a mortgage. Nevertheless, that is quite a long way off.

We believe it is better to get married and enjoy life together in our own home, rather than in a rental. Mum understands our reasoning, but thinks that if we love each other that much, we should marry now and live here. Mum loves Carl so much and would happily have him live here permanently."

"Well... that's a decision only you two can make, and your mum is entitled to her own opinion, of course, but I know what I would do."

Alicia thought the question was strange and slightly off; however, she knew Nana well and believed the conversation was leading somewhere, though she was unsure exactly where.

"Do you like the village of Murla?" said Rosa, throwing another odd question into the mix.

Despite all the oddness, all Alicia could do was try to answer to the best of her ability. "I'm not sure how to answer that, Nana. I mostly remember Murla from childhood, when Antonio and I stayed with you on our summer holidays. However, I haven't been there for a very long time. I imagine it is still the same – country living never changes."

"How very true... On one of those occasions at the Finca, I gave you some pretty pink Rosary Beads. Do you remember?" said Rosa.

"Yes, of course, I do. It was a silver chain and a rose quartz crystal. I thought it was the most beautiful Rosary I had ever seen."

"And, you still have it and pray every night to ask for the Lord's blessing?"

"Yes, the Rosary sits on my bedroom dressing table,

and I pray each night. Do you remember all those years ago when you showed me how to use the Rosary, and often you said prayers with me?" She smiled at the thought. "But, I was unsure why you thought it so important as a child that I needed protection."

Rosa smiled in response. "The world is full of lovely people, Alicia; however, some aren't quite as lovely, so to have the Lord's blessing and protection shining down upon you is comforting and reassuring. I seem to recall you learned to use the rosary very quickly. From then on, I knew you would be clever growing up. Now look at you. Here you are, a qualified nurse, doing a worthwhile job helping those in need with their traumas or physical problems. And you know so much about medicine and people. Carl was fortunate to have you nearby in his time of need." She chose her last remark carefully so as not to talk about the bull run incident. "Who knows what else you can achieve in life? You might even become a clinical nurse specialist. Now, that would be good."

Alicia smiled, knowing she had pleased Nana. Yet, she believed there was more to her guided questioning than was apparent. She also felt a sense of preparedness coming her way in the form of talking up a situation, but what was it all in aid of?

The conversation shifted from Carl to Murla, focusing on Rosary beads and her qualifications. Alicia felt indifferent about Murla; equally, if she thought it essential to embrace the Rosary and pray for God's blessing, then she had always done so. If Nana wanted to discuss her relationship with Carl, that would be okay. However, she was puzzled by the shifting direction of the conversation, the information, and the questioning, which seemed to be culminating around her job and qualifications.

"From what I remember, the people in Murla are very nice, and the hamlet isn't all that far from the coast. On one of our summer holidays, we visited Altea Beach the day before your birthday. Do you remember? We had such a lovely time. I can still remember it now," said Alicia.

"Yes, we did. You were eight years old, and Antonio was ten."

"And the tapas and crème caramel we had at a nearby bar were so lovely. I remember you had tortilla; then after that, you had Flan De Leche Acaramelado."

"You can remember all that from seventeen years ago? What a memory you have."

"Of course," said Alicia, quite matter-of-fact.

They both smiled fondly, recalling the occasion and time spent on that special day all those years ago. Alicia took Nana's hand and kissed her on the cheek, thinking the conversation was over.

Alicia's affection for Rosa was central. With age came the issue of feeling unimportant and a nuisance; it often crossed Rosa's mind, but she said nothing about it. Over time, loneliness and feelings of unworthiness grew. However, her granddaughter was sensitive enough to Nana's needs, constantly showering her with love and affection, and showing a unique understanding of life's challenges and the importance of being such a lovely member of the family and society.

"There is a small hospital four miles away from Murla," said Rosa, "and another fifteen miles away in Denia. And there are many schools close to Murla," she said, intent on continuing the curious conversation.

Even so, Alicia had witnessed scheming from Nana before, and it did not come as a great surprise when she talked about something completely out of context with the moment. It was evident there was more to her curious conversation.

"Now, Alicia, I want to say something to you. It might seem out of the ordinary, even strange. But I want you to hear me out and think about what I have to say."

"Alright – I promise."

"Your grandfather and I, God rest his soul." She crossed herself and touched the crucifix around her neck. "We lived many happy, loving years in our Finca in Murla, and the community took us to their hearts. We grew up in that era where everybody helped each other, and although we lived frugally, we never went short of food or clothes. We gave to our friends or neighbours if they were in need, and we received in return if we fell on hard times, when our almond, walnut, or orange crop developed problems and our profit dwindled, making life difficult. Nevertheless, times have changed in this modern world of Facebook and Twitter – I accept that life has to change and that we must progress. That said, living here in Pamplona, I have moved on from what I knew to another chapter in my life. I'm telling you this for a reason, and I have thought long and hard about you and your future. What this is building up to is that I want you and Carlos to have my Finca so that it may remain within the family. Still, more importantly, you can live and appreciate married life in Murla and be happy for many years to come, just as your grandad and I were when living here." Rosa faltered for a moment, then continued. "Nothing would give me greater pleasure than to see you two lovebirds happily set up in my beautiful Finca. Now, what do you say?"

Alicia was stunned. Her feelings for Rosa were unique and special, but giving her Finca away was an extraordinary gesture of kindness. She thought for quite some time, seemingly troubled by the prospect of answering. Eventually, her answer was forthcoming.

"Nana, I don't think we can."

"Why?"

"Well, it doesn't seem right." She searched her mind for a plausible explanation as to why they could not accept the generous offer.

"Are you trying to say that you and Carl are not worthy of this gift, or are you merely refusing an old lady her wish because she is senile and doesn't know what she is doing, and that people may think I have been duped into giving you my home?"

Alicia took hold of her hand again and looked lovingly into her eyes. "It's not that; I'm just not used to such generosity. Knowing Carl as well as I do, I'm sure he would agree with me. It is like something for nothing. Mum and Dad have always taught me that if I wanted something, I had to earn it. So, although your offer of the Finca is incredibly tempting, I don't feel we can accept it."

Rosa thought for a second, understanding the dilemma but still wanting desperately to give the cottage away to the two lovebirds, as she called them. She needed to resolve the troubling issue.

"Okay, try this one then. What if I ask you and Carl to live in *my* beautiful Finca? You can make all the necessary alterations and turn it into a gorgeous, modern home just as you would like. Look after it and give it your devotion and love, but shall we say it still belongs to me? Now, how does that sound?"

"Well ... I'd need to talk to Carl about it."

"Of course, I wouldn't expect anything less."

"But it does sound very exciting, and it is such a beautiful home," agreed Alicia, smiling at the thought of their own property, ready to move into and be tenants of a lovely and charming proprietor.

Rosa smiled inwardly, knowing her plan had worked and her beloved family home would be cared for and loved just as she would want it. After all her questioning and negotiating, now, she could rest easy knowing that two extraordinary, beautiful people would look after her beloved Finca.

Even if the answer were still no after the conversation with Carl, her next gambit would be to suggest a peppercorn rent, making them feel more amenable to living in the property and more conscious of paying their way. If that were the case, and how it played out, the monthly rent would be put into a bank account and left to the couple upon her death.

Rosa's ingenuity gave her even more satisfaction, as she knew that she would change her will in the coming weeks and leave her home to Alicia and Carl in its entirety. Maybe the spare bedroom in the Finca might see Rosa again for high days and holidays in her own home.

All's well that ends well, especially when she got her way and, with Carl's agreement, it seemed she had found the perfect solution.

ELEVEN

The Finca's offer to Carl and Alicia was wholly unexpected and, upon reflection, a game-changer. They would have a ready-made home to move into whenever they wanted. Of course, they intended to alter and modernise the home to their taste, which was exciting in itself. Additionally, Nana's generous gift cleared the way for their marriage to proceed sooner rather than later.

With pomp and ceremony befitting a mayoral daughter's wedding, Carl and Alicia were married in the beautiful Pamplona Cathedral of Santa Maria la Real in early May. There were one hundred and twenty-eight guests, and a grand reception was held at a prestigious hotel in the city that afternoon.

Following the cordial ceremony, the happy couple flew to Fuerteventura, Canary Islands, to spend a week honeymooning in Corralejo. Their time together away was all that they had hoped for and more. Finally, they were together in marital bliss, enjoying the laid-back lifestyle of the resort area and doing the usual touristy thing – visiting places of interest, Lanzarote, Isla de Lobos and Atlantico shopping centre in Caleta de Fuste, to name but a few. They recorded their honeymoon, which was filled with precious moments, on video to share with their family back home. However, by the end of the week, they were eager to head to Murla and start a new life in their very own finca, which they renamed Casa Azahar (Orange Blossom Home). The house name was chosen because of that area of Jalon, renowned for its extensive orange groves. At blossom time – mid-May, the valley's scent was one of the most stunning features.

Equally remarkable was the total silence of the countryside both day and night. In their lives, Carl and Alicia had grown accustomed to the noise of cities and towns. Therefore, hearing birds, cicadas, and other wildlife sounds during the day, and nothing else, was a complete shock for them. The occasional hoot of owls and howls of wolves in the distant mountain range at night were quite magical. Regular phone calls between Alicia and Nana kept the joy alive. Rosa was even more thrilled to learn that the newly married couple were enchanted with their new home. Talk of renovation and change in and around the Finca added even more excitement and joy for the newlyweds. Essentially, the home felt like their own; they were putting their stamp on it, which felt fulfilling. The occasional photograph of an alteration or paint job to the Finca thrilled Rosa beyond belief. It was as if she were reliving her earlier life in the Finca with her beloved husband.

One of the first jobs Carl wanted to undertake was laying paving slabs to create a patio for entertainment. However, to achieve this, he needed to demolish the old water well's housing outside the back door.

While Rosa and Grandpa lived in the Finca for

many years, they coped very well without mains water and merely used well water. This necessitated carrying water pails from the well to the home on a regular basis. It was a way of life and a necessity for most of their lives. The routine continued, regardless of rain, hail, or shine. Indeed, it could become very cold and icy living in the lee of the mountain, mainly because the mountain obscured the sun late in the afternoon in the winter, which, under normal circumstances, would give low-level sunlight warmth to the home's walls. High mountains in the winter often held clouds; when cold enough, the clouds would deposit hail, sleet, or snow on the surrounding land.

Alicia set to clean and rearrange the kitchen. Later, she took Carl an iced drink and sat with him, absorbing the unique ambience of the land and surrounding splendour. She closed her eyes and held her head up to the sky like a Buddhist monk contemplating enlightenment, and listened to the sound of silence, something she would have scoffed at months ago back in the city. Now, it had all changed. Her love of the countryside proved to be quite a wonder. In Pamplona, she had a large circle of friends and acquaintances. There was always something to do and somewhere to go in the big metropolis. However, her burgeoning contentment in Murla reinforced in her mind that she and Carl had done the right thing in moving to that area of Spain in the Jalon Valley.

Renovation of the Finca continued with occasional

weekend breaks in Valencia or Alicante. Gradually, the early autumnal seasonal change began to take effect. There would be icy-cold days and nights in a few weeks, possibly even frost. Carl had already spoken to a work colleague whose brother ran a double-glazing company. With a small amount of savings, they would replace some of the Finca windows, improving thermal insulation against the winter chill.

Having had her fill of the sun and jobs to do, Alicia caught Carl's look with a loving smile. She returned his gaze with joy and blew him a kiss. "I can't believe this, Carl. It seems too good to be true. Is it for real?"

"Well, you better believe it. This is ours forever and a day."

"Forever and a day. I have not heard that before. Where it come from?"

"Shakespeare – The Taming of the Shrew. I studied it in English literature at school."

"That makes you very clever, I think," said Alicia.

"I suppose it does," he said, smiling, continuing the intended fun. "It makes you very clever, also recognising genius in someone else."

Alicia shook her head as if to say, bighead.

Break over – rolling up his sleeves, Carl removed the rockwork from the water well housing. Some of the stones he touched flashed an image in his mind. He saw the faces of two medieval workers. Along with a mental picture, he felt bodily pain and discomfort. They would have experienced physical discomfort from manual work, but more so, occasional injury to their arms and legs. Life was cheap, and people laboured and died at an alarmingly early age due to sickness, accident or plague. Even so, Carl struggled to accept the newly acquired ability of psychometry. Personally, it had become a nuisance. It was one of those so-called gifts he wanted to switch off from and return to the pre-bull-run days.

A good point in question was when he first met Rosa. As he shook her hand, many images flashed through his mind. Yet, puzzlingly, the most striking impression he had was of folklore and paganism. Even so, he could not comprehend the wild sensations he had detected from her. Carl often pondered that first meeting and tried to determine its meaning. Despite that, no sense could be made of the mental noise he experienced in his so-called Midas mode, as Alicia referred to it.

Carl was mindful of installing a large paving stone to cap the well. Before doing so, just out of curiosity, he dropped the wooden bucket tied to a rope down the well, hoisted it back up and examined the cold, clear water. At thirty feet in depth and at the height of summer, the water from the well always remained cool. Carl cupped his hand, scooped some water from the bucket and drank. Initially, the water was cool and thirst-quenching; then, an extraordinary event occurred. He became detached from his surroundings, experiencing wild sensations and weird sounds. Bizarre thoughts flashed through his mind, just like when he touched Mum's flight ticket and when he wore Antonio's bullfighting hat, the Montera. Drinking water from the well was like receiving an intravenous injection. Sensations coursed through his body at an incredible speed, alerting his senses and stimulating his cerebral cortex.

Although rooted to the spot, Carl envisioned a battle on the mountainside. Spanish troops mercilessly killed Moorish folk trying to escape the fray. Everywhere he looked, Carl could see death on a grand scale. Blood-soaked bodies lay on the ground, some writhing in agony. The smell of death, blood and bodily waste assaulted Carl's senses, causing him to gag, although he was not sick. He raised his hands, pressing them to his eyes, trying to block out the sickening, gory sights.

Nevertheless, it was futile. The images continued with greater ferocity – soldiers from a bygone era killed with repulsive savagery. The visions, sounds and smells refused to abate. Nothing Carl did could stop the nightmare. Like three-dimensional reality, he looked around and saw carnage. The mêlée continued unabated. Bloodthirsty soldiers savagely cut down civilians without a moment's thought; even children were caught up in the vicious slaughter.

Then, as if out of nowhere, a Moorish knight riding a charger in green livery, accompanied by many fellow knights, sped into the midst of the furore. The civilians parted, making way for the spearhead of chargers – their saviours. For a while, the status quo held. The newly arrived heroes fought the Spanish army with adrenaline-charged bravery, aggression, and sheer determination. Thankfully, their actions afforded time for the remaining civilians to flee the appalling, grim scene. The only course open for escape was to clamber up the treacherous, rugged mountain. Weary, tired, injured, and traumatised, the group of displaced refugees helped each other ascend the perilous mountain until they were high enough and sufficiently distant from their oppressors – the Spanish army.

Men, women, and children nursing wounds grouped together for safety and protection in continued fear for their lives. Temporarily safe, they looked at the carnage further down the mountain; however, the tide had turned. The Spanish soldiers had regrouped, re-established their superiority, and fought back with even greater ferocity. The message was clear to the few remaining Moors on foot and horseback.

A mere handful of knights remained. However, their fate was sealed. They fell like dominoes one by one until only two remained – the knight on a green charger and the last remaining foot soldier. With horrific injuries, they fought on with superhuman strength. The horse fell to the ground, injured. The Knight stepped away from his steed and joined his one and only compatriot. Side by side, they fought like wildcats.

Nevertheless, their days were numbered; a pike thrust forward buried itself deep into the brave Knight's chest. He fell to the ground, dead. The bloodied charger tried to upright itself; it scrabbled sideways, lost control, and rolled back over the fallen dead on the ground. From the mountainside, the civilians viewed the sickening scene play out; they were traumatised at the sight of their fallen saviours – the Moorish knight and the final dead foot soldier. All was lost. Yet, as the Spaniards looked on amid all the carnage, the horse in green reared upwards again, startling the troops. Fear and shock heightened the horse's senses. Its green livery, now brownish red, stuck fast to its body. Yet, the stallion was determined to flee the scene. Spanish soldiers parted like a tidal wave in the wake of the charging horse's bid for freedom. The horse bolted down the mountainside in the fading light, never to be seen again.

TWELVE

While Carl was busy out front on the driveway, hearing an English voice in the lane, he stopped his task and looked up to see a stranger intent on making conversation. He waved to Carl and said, "Hello, neighbour." From that day on, it marked the beginning of a perfect friendship.

The evening went well with Jeff and Lynn, their newfound English friends living near Casa Azahar.

For the past two years, they had eked out a living and turned their hands to anything that would make money, which allowed them to survive and live their dream in the sun. Their most significant success in Spain materialised when they purchased their present property, which included extensive land and orange trees producing a substantial yearly crop. They had bought the home on a whim, as it was affordable and located in the country; however, it required extensive renovation. They worked together for many months and brought about substantial changes to the building's structure, making it a pleasant place to live. Although seasonal, a significant amount of money could be made when their oranges were sold to the local co-operativa. They learnt Valenciano, a local Spanish dialect, to an acceptable level, allowing them to communicate with locals. Car boot sales and market stalls generated additional revenue, and purchasing local meat, eggs, and vegetables helped reduce the food bill. They had even tried growing unusual vegetables for personal use and sale on their market stall. Overall, life was good but challenging at times. Yet the joy of living in Spain far outweighed the occasional temporary difficulties they experienced.

The walk from Jeff and Lynn's home to their Finca usually took ten minutes. With a beautiful, balmy evening and enchanting nighttime sounds, the walk became a gentle stroll interspersed with the occasional stagger here and there. At one point, Alicia lurched to the roadside and almost ended up in the ditch as a result of too much local wine.

"This is what it's all about, Alicia," said Carl, lending a steadying hand to his wife as they strolled along the narrow, winding road back to their Finca.

"Yes, is perfect. I felt so happy here."

They stopped and kissed. Even now, Carl found it hard to believe they were so many miles away from the civilisation he once knew. Living in the country was a million miles from reality, and it was perfect in every respect. They were married, in love, and living in a beautiful Finca with a view of the mountain Caballo Verde. To complete the joy, they had found very agreeable English friends nearby. What more could they want?

"Are you looking backwards to your job in local school?" said Alicia, unaware she had made a humorous mistake in her question. Confusion with the English language was one of the many things that made her so endearing to Carl. She was beautiful in every respect and always made an effort to speak good English. Her innate obsessive character compelled her to do everything to the best of her ability, regardless of the task at hand. However, sometimes, her improving English was naively off the mark. He smiled at the gaffe and decided not to correct her mistake. Maybe the wine had mellowed her mind so much that it had interfered with her concentration and recall. They walked on, seeing their Finca and the outside light left on, shining like a beacon in the distance.

"Yes, I am looking forward to the new job. The school is small but perfectly formed, as we say in English."

"I remember perfectly formed. It good phrase."

They meandered along, walking in the middle of the road, not a care in the world.

"I've been thinking, Alicia. There is no immediate need for you to get a job in a local hospital, you know. We can manage on my wage for the time being."

"No, I will get a job. First, I need to get our beautiful home – how you say, shipy-shapey?"

They stopped and kissed again.

"I just can't get enough of you, my gorgeous wife. Do you want to stay with me for the rest of your life?"

Her answer had an edge to it. Even now, Carl's humour was sometimes outside of her understanding. "Of course. Why you ask this? You not like me?"

Carl laughed aloud. "Come on; I'm only tantalising." He pinched her cheek to raise a smile.

As they walked on swinging hands together, Carl

amused Alicia by singing one of his favourite songs, *'When I'm Sixty-Four'* by The Beatles.

The evening had gone well, and Carl was pleased to see Alicia thoroughly enjoying herself. Her English had improved to the point where she felt more confident interacting with English-speaking people. That evening, she joined in with trivial pursuits and quickly coped with the questions. She provided a few surprising answers after translating the question into Spanish; she thought about it and then translated her response back into English. Yes, Carl was very proud of her.

Hand in hand, they strolled along the country road, nearing a long bend that led to their home. It was sheer bliss to walk in the warm evening air. The moon lit their way, crickets chirruped, and an owl hooted in the distance. The joy of being in the country filled them with a sense of *joie de vivre.*

Within view of Caballo Verde, Carl pointed to something in the mid-distance, somewhere between them and the mountainside. He saw what appeared to be a small, misty light. They could both see it and tried to make sense of what it could be. As they watched, the light formed into a clearly defined orb pulsating in strength every few seconds. They stood transfixed.

"What do you think it is, Carl?" said Alicia with a tremor in her voice, standing closer to her loved one for protection. She was not the sort of person to frighten easily, yet the strange spectacle unnerved her. She gulped.

"I don't know. I've never seen such a strange green

light in my life."

"Why you say green light? It is white."

Carl turned to Alicia. "You see it as white?"

"Yes, of course, is white."

"Okay, well, maybe this is a good time to tell you something about me I have never mentioned before. Maybe it will come as a surprise; I don't know."

Fleetingly, Alicia forgot about the weird light, concerned about what Carl would reveal. Could this be a big dark secret, she thought? Should she have known about this earlier in their relationship? "This is big secret?" she said with consternation.

Although he smiled at her disquiet, Alicia was becoming overly concerned about an insignificant matter.

He explained. "I am green/red colour blind."

Alicia was familiar with colour blindness due to her nursing career. Carl explained that he sometimes detected white light as green, particularly at night. She thought this most peculiar but understood his big secret was merely a misunderstanding of the mind. Panic over; she agreed they would talk about it again sometime. Currently, the mystery of the glowing light took precedence over everything else. As they looked back towards the mountain, three more orbs accompanied the original ball of light, and they were nearer. Were they multiplying, like an amoeba cell, or were there many more orbs on the mountain ready and prepared to unite for an unknown purpose?

They looked at each other and then quickly back at the lights, which were multiplying. There were even more now, some white and some silver, growing in number by the second as they watched. In essence, many more orbs from different parts of the mountain had assembled, uniting and appearing to act as one. Alicia gripped Carl's hand tightly. The vision sent shivers down her spine. She rubbed her eyes with her free hand, not daring to let go of Carl's hand. A vast conglomeration of white and silver orbs moved towards them at increasing speed.

Carl thought it could be a UFO phenomenon, but he was unsure about the occurrence beyond what he had read or heard. In reality, he was simultaneously intrigued, concerned and yet very frightened. Then it happened. With extreme momentum, the orbs flew straight at them so fast that there was no time to shout or scream from the shock. White and silver light enveloped them; a strange timelessness held them in suspended animation. They felt hemmed in, encircled by a numbing spectacle. Terror took hold. Carl and Alicia held onto each other tightly. Their fear was palpable. Carl began to pray in that moment of danger, trying to hold onto reality. Alicia joined in with the invocation.

"Hear us, oh Lord, in our time of need ..."

"Are you alright?" A heavily accented Spanish voice broke the moment.

Neither Carl nor Alicia realised that the orbs had temporarily encircled them, protecting them from a malicious black orb trying to invade their auras.

The dreamlike state, pulsating orbs and fear had gone. An older man stood before them. Carl focused on his dog collar, which, although white, had a greenish tint. The tall figure was a priest. For all that, why would he be there on a country road at night? Although Spanish, he spoke pigeon English with a heavy accent.

"I was driving back to Jalon and saw you in the car's headlights. You were standing in the middle of the road, holding each other, praying... Is everything alright, my children?"

"Err, we were walking back to our Finca," said Carl, pointing to their home, "and we saw light, possibly orbs, on the mountain. They appeared to be growing in number and heading straight towards us."

"I see... Are you the new people in Señora García's Finca?"

"Sí, Señora Rosa García es mí nana," (Yes, Señora García is my nana), said Alicia.

The priest enthusiastically shook hands with both of them.

"I am so pleased to meet you. We have all missed Señora García since she moved to Pamplona to stay with her daughter. We all wondered who would move into her Finca. How nice someone from the family has taken it over." His speech was rapid with excitement.

"Thank you, father ...?"

"I am Father Tomás Sanz Bernardo, and this is my parish," he said, standing in the headlights of his car, indicating where he stood to be his parish. "This light on the mountain. I have heard about it before, but never actually witnessed it myself."

"Well, it was terrifying," said Alicia."

He sensed a tremor in her voice. "Get into my car, and I will take you the short distance to your Finca."

Neither Carl nor Alicia hesitated at the offer of safety and protection from a man of the cloth. Carl eyed his beat-up Renault and wondered if it could be reversed. However, they did not wait longer than necessary and gladly hopped into the Renault's back seat. The priest drove his new acquaintances the short distance to their home. They offered him a late-night drink, which he politely declined, but he agreed to take them up on the invitation again sometime.

Negotiating the bumpy lane from their driveway to the main road, with his hand held out of the window, waving, Father Bernardo did not see the orbs in the distance. Little did the couple know that the father had also been drinking that night and focused all of his attention on the road ahead. There would be plenty of time to pay another visit to the two young people at Rosa's Finca and discuss many things, including orbs.

Back in the safety of their Finca, they flopped onto the settee and tried to make sense of their ordeal. With the speed at which the orbs multiplied and gathered around Carl and Alicia, they believed the phenomenon to be malicious. Whatever the bizarre orbs were up to, in their estimation, it was an experience not to be repeated.

Alicia was unaware of something troubling in their strange encounter that evening. Later, when changing into her pyjamas, she noticed three scratches above her left knee across her thigh, yet she dismissed them as probably occurring when she staggered towards the road's edge. Maybe she had scratched her leg on a low-growing, thorny roadside shrub.

Due to an over-indulgence of wine and feeling groggy, Alicia fell soundly asleep, dismissing any further thoughts of scratches. Yet they were substantial and not the result of an innocent stumble. The black orb had momentarily penetrated the wall of protective white orbs. Whatever would have happened without divine intervention coming their way in the form of Father Bernardo was anybody's guess.

THIRTEEN

The work outside the Finca (paving the patio) was temporarily put on hold. Enthusiasm had waned since Carl witnessed disturbing images after sampling water from the patio well. In the unsettling episode, he recalled a peculiar sensation as the water travelled into his stomach. In many respects, the incident had frightened him, and the DIY job only recommenced after Alicia questioned why he seemed to lack enthusiasm for completing it.

It was difficult to shake off the distressing imagery or even understand why it should have happened in the first place. The only sense it made was in its similarity to when he touched Alicia's cross at the in-laws, which had been given to her by Nana. When he handled it, Carl had witnessed killing and cruelty on a vast scale. If there was any sense to be made from the whole scenario, there was a common denominator: Nana and Caballo Verde.

The night of the well incident, he experienced a troubling nightmare centred around Poltergeist II. In the film, Steve Freeling drank whiskey from a bottle containing an insect larva. Tossing and turning, Carl became obsessed with swallowing something dreadful. Eventually, he woke up in a cold sweat, breathing heavily, uncertain of his whereabouts, yet glad to be awake. Feeling jittery, he got up to make himself a drink, still disturbed by the all-too-real nightmare. He put his hand to his stomach as if to relieve his discomfort in some way. Although just as quickly, he wondered why he was doing that. The obsession with something odd in his gut, with something he had swallowed from the well water, did not immediately disappear.

The following day, the horrific scenes were still wandering around his brain. Roast meat that he would generally have enjoyed resembled part of a severed limb. Pouring red wine, he spilt some on the kitchen countertop. The thought of blood grabbed his attention. He had seen a lot of blood and gore in his mind's eye of late, and it did not want to go away. Carl was on edge, his reality distorted. He was preoccupied with the gory aspects of battle, which he frequently envisioned. How could he reconcile the brutality of what he had witnessed and cope with day-to-day life? Maybe he still hadn't fully worked through the trauma when he was gored by the bull and experienced excruciating pain. Perhaps that had contributed to the recent Psychometry images and created a negative association in his mind. He needed to talk to somebody, but who? He did not want to burden or upset Alicia with his freakish, gory visions, but he had to speak to share the worry. Perhaps a private conversation with Father Bernardo would be helpful. He made a mental note to ask for his assistance fairly soon and hoped to end the nightmarish episodes quickly and wholly.

Speaking to a local in the village recently, while shopping, confirmed the little-talked-about battle on the lower level of Caballo Verde Mountain. He looked around the immediate area and speculated that the fighting could have occurred where he stood, or at least nearby, all those hundreds of years ago.

Lately, Alicia noticed a slight shift in his overall demeanour. For all the imagery and horror flashing through his mind, Carl never came to any conclusions about the appalling scenes. It became even more vital for him to conduct research in the school library (time permitting) to understand what had transpired during that time and era, specifically in 1609. Teaching from Monday to Friday at a local secondary school took up much of his time. Maybe Father Bernardo himself was aware of some of Caballo Verde's history and could help by discussing what he knew.

Nevertheless, he had to be careful not to cause alarm or appear obsessed with the strange happenings. He had to continue as usual to avoid worrying Alicia. Yet, even with guarded thoughts, she had observed times when Carl appeared vacant – his mind elsewhere. She guessed he was keeping something from her, or at least preoccupied with something out of the ordinary and was protecting her from undue worry, even disturbed nights.

As it was a Saturday, Alicia asked Carl if he wanted to have lunch at home or go to the local Tapas bar. In a distant mood, he answered 'yes' to her question.

"Well, which you like?" she said.

"Umm?"

She smiled sweetly. "Would you like a Bocadillo (filled bread roll) for lunch at home, or should we go to Orba and sample some of the local cat food?"

He tuned into the conversation and, with stunned incredulity, repeated. "Cat food?"

"Now that's got your attention, hasn't it?"

He smiled at her clever question, aware of how funny the trick was. "We'll go to Orba. Besides, I rather fancy trying tuna cat food. Oh, and I need a bag of mortar from the ferretería (hardware store) for the flagstones, so that would work out quite well."

"Okay, then we'll go soon."

Alicia enjoyed discovering local shops and places of interest. She was building a mental picture of the town (Orba) and its amenities.

The Tapas bar near the town square was busy for a Saturday. Even so, they secured a table, chose their savoury dishes and ordered drinks. Both detected a predominance of Valenciano spoken in the bar, yet they understood most of the conversation. The locals, mainly from farming backgrounds, discussed the cooperativa's prices for oranges, almonds, olives, and goats in the Jalon Valley. In their unique way, the conversation was a delight to hear. It gave Carl and Alicia insight into the local people. To their advantage, they learned where to buy the best-priced wine and from which Bodega.

"Not cuddling today?" Came a voice from behind

them. As they looked, Father Bernardo's distinctive face beamed a welcoming smile. They instantly stood and shook hands.

"Father Bernardo, how nice to see you again," said Carl, mildly surprised to find him in the bar with a large glass of Soberano Reserva 12 Brandy in his hand.

"And nice to see both of you. Alicia, how is your lovely Finca?"

"Good, thank you, Father Bernardo. We are settling in well. Carl's latest project outside is working on the well outside; he hopes to cap it with a paving stone."

"Sounds interesting. I can help you with that." They offered the father a seat at the table, which he readily accepted.

"Have you considered putting an electric pump down the well before capping it? Then you will have access to water for your plants and a few shrubs around your property."

"Not really, I hadn't given it a thought," said Carl. He wondered why he hadn't considered it in the big scheme of things.

"Well, if you need any help, let me know. I have extensive knowledge of water systems, primarily because I own an orchard of oranges and a few olive trees, which I irrigate with well water. You'll find many properties in the area that have wells. Yet, most people fail to use this vital resource. God, in his infinite wisdom, gave us rain to fall upon the land. Why not use it?"

"Why not indeed? Thank you, that's worth knowing, Father."

"And have you recovered from the other night when I met you on the road heading back to your home?"

Carl felt mildly embarrassed when he considered how odd it must have looked. "Oh, that. Yes, fully recovered. We weren't sure what the light orbs were, and I suppose we became worried and frightened of the unknown, particularly when they encircled both of us."

"That is why you were praying. It is good to see that you would want the help of our Lord in your time of need. However, the only white orbs I have ever seen have been in the cemetery at night. People say they are earthbound souls still looking for their loved ones. I'm really not sure. Mind you, I'm not in denial, and don't dismiss the idea of the orbs being souls. But ..."

"Well," said Alicia, taking up the conversation, "we weren't sure what was happening. Maybe we had a bit too much wine," she said, feeling equally embarrassed at the thought of the two of them standing in the middle of the road, hugging each other, praying.

"Maybe," said the father, unconvinced about the alcohol theory.

"Can I buy you another drink, Father?" said Carl, keen to change the subject.

"No, I have to go. Unfortunately, Señor Ibáñez in Benigembla is ill and can't attend church, and I promised to call by and give Holy Communion."

"Maybe again, sometime," said Carl. "You are bound to be busy on Sunday, but would you like to call by our Finca on Monday and have Merienda (afternoon snack at 5 o'clock)? Then we can talk about the water pump idea." Carl hoped he would also have the opportunity to speak to the father privately, but that would require some arranging, given that Alicia was around most of the time. Maybe he could walk the father around the Finca's land and talk to him unhindered.

Alicia's natural tendency was to ask Carl many questions, so much so that he wondered if she had been like that all her life. Although she always had Carl's interest at heart. She was like a puppy dog – overenthusiastic but adorable. Nevertheless, that was fine; he loved and doted on every word she said. Now he knew how Carrie and Lawrence felt and understood firsthand what a pleasant feeling it was. Even so, a quiet word with the father, without his wife joining in with the conversation, would be far better.

"Yes, that would be a good time for me. I shall look forward to that," said Father Bernardo.

"Monday it is then, and we are in for a treat," said Carl. "Alicia is an excellent cook and will produce some fine Spanish cuisine, albeit from Northern Spain." He smiled, knowing that his remark would put her under pressure. Her kick under the table was instantaneous.

The priest left the bar without further ado, crossed the street, and spoke briefly to a local police officer who was visibly checking his vehicle. The priest got into his car and left for Benigembla. But not before saying to the policeman, "God bless you, my son."

FOURTEEN

It took Rosa many weeks to settle into her daughter's home in Pamplona. Her heart was still in Murla, the place she had known and loved for many years. All her thoughts, dreams, life, and love in the home she and Ernesto had created still lingered in her mind.

Rosa had never considered leaving her home after Ernesto's death; however, life had played a cruel trick on her. The sad loss of her husband had cruelly demonstrated the fragility of life, and his passing was a mortal indicator that life was in its final throes. She busied herself in her new surroundings and re-established acquaintances with people she had known years ago as a child in Pamplona. In many ways, the contrast between Pamplona and Murla surprised her greatly. For all its laid-back feel and lack of modern facilities, Murla still came out on top in her mind. Pamplona was too busy, too noisy and too fast-paced for her liking. However, her daughter's home had one redeeming quality: it was situated on the city's outskirts; consequently, it was much quieter, similar to the peace and tranquillity of Murla.

"Have you heard from Alicia lately?" said Elena to her mum as they sat on the veranda, drinking coffee and catching up on the news.

"Yes, I spoke to her two days ago. She passed on

regards from a good friend of mine, Mariela, who lives in Murla. I have known her for many years. We often met up to shop or have a meal out. Sometimes, we would return to her home, and I would help her with housework. She has a large four-bedroom home; unfortunately, it is too big and rambling for her, especially now that she has arthritis. In truth, Mariela should have sold up years ago, but because it was the family home, she was reluctant to leave, just like me, I suppose. Reluctant to let it go."

"Oh, dear, poor Mariela. I'm sorry to hear that. Is Alicia okay?"

"Yes, she seems very happy and contented. I don't think that will ever change as long as she has Carl by her side."

"I'm sure."

"She talked about Father Bernardo. Do you remember him?"

"Vaguely. I only met him once, as I recall, but he seemed to be a kindly sort of person."

"He was our local parish priest. I got to know him well; as you say, he is very kind and caring. His only problem is that he enjoys his drink a little too much. But, I think the pressure of looking after such a large diocese brings a huge burden."

They talked at length about anything and everything until the phone rang. Elena excused herself and went to answer it. Five minutes later, she sauntered back out onto the veranda.

"It's Alicia, Mum. Would you like to talk to her? I've got to go out."

The conversation focused on Alicia and Carl's first meeting with Father Bernardo. Hearing the account of them walking back home from their friends and experiencing the lights that seemed to emanate from the mountain made Rosa cautious about what she said. Talking about the incident again indicated to Rosa that the occurrence was still very much on her granddaughter's mind.

"I think you should talk to Father Bernardo about that, Alicia and get him to tell you what he knows about Caballo Verde. Although he may not have all the answers, he can provide you with some of the history. His local knowledge is excellent."

"We saw him on Saturday at a bar in Orba."

"Oh, really, and...?"

"Apart from the first night, we met him on the road, making our way back home; that was the first time we spoke about the strange occurrence. We briefly talked about the orbs, but didn't want to sound too obsessed with the encounter. I'm sure we'll have an opportunity to discuss the strange event again sometime."

"Orbs, you say?" said Rosa, wanting her to elucidate what she saw that night and talk about her feelings."

"Yes, orbs; although they are green according to Carl, with his colour blindness, they are in reality white orbs, although having said that, I think there were silver orbs as well."

"Huh, fancy that. You see white, and he sees green. Anyway, white or silver orbs will not harm you. If anything, they confirm that loving souls are present on the mountain, and from what you are saying, in sufficient numbers to be noticed."

"Have you seen or known about these orbs, Nana?"

"Yes, I had seen them on occasions. Let's say that mysterious old mountains sometimes have mysterious things happening about them. But there's nothing for you to be concerned about; however, it would still be worthwhile to know what the locals think of the mountain and to ensure you both understand its history. However, as I said, Father Bernardo should be able to tell you a lot more."

"Okay," said Alicia, quite intrigued. He is coming over for Merienda, so I'm sure we'll gossip. He is going to help Carl put an electric pump down the well so that the plants and shrubs can be watered mainly in the height of summer when it is hot and dry for such long periods."

"That sounds very clever. And will you have tubes from the pump going to all the plants to water them?"

"Sorry. I don't know anything about that side of things, although I heard them discussing the need for a manifold in the pipework or something similar. I am sure the two of them will sort it out. Father Bernardo sounds very well informed."

"Oh, he is; he's a mine of information."

Alicia spoke about the occasional caller from the village asking for Rosa. Not everybody knew about her accident, which needed weeks of healing in a hospital and recovery at her daughter's home. A notable comment from Rosa was to be careful with any callers, especially late-night callers at the Finca.

"Why do you say that, Nana?"

"It's just that some of the locals can be a bit of a nuisance and take up a lot of your time if you're not careful. What you might call fussy bodies."

"Oh, I see. Yes, I hadn't thought about it like that, me being a nurse and all. A bit like yourself with medical knowledge."

"Exactly," was Rosa's retort. Although she wasn't telling an untruth, she certainly was not telling all she knew. In reality, more was happening locally than she was prepared to admit. There would be time enough to talk about the deeper, darker side of Caballo Verde when the time was right.

"Well, I must get going. I'm off to see Señora Ortega. She lost her husband just recently and needs a bit of assistance. So, I will see what I can do to help. Maybe nothing, but I always think it's nice to have some support and somebody to share your thoughts with over a cup of coffee."

"You haven't changed, Nana."

"And I never will, Alicia; it's in my blood. What you give out, you get back tenfold. Give my love to Carl and tell Father Bernardo I was asking about him."

FIFTEEN

On a rainy, windswept evening in early autumn, when the cold wind blew and drizzle frequented the dark mountainous expanse of Caballo Verde, Carl and Alicia settled in for the evening. As they drew the curtains, a sense of shutting out the world imbued their idyllic life with warmth and closeness. Tenderness and love for each other had blossomed even more since they moved to Murla. Rural isolation was blissful and introduced an element of life that they had never considered possible.

Both knew that, come evening, it was unlikely that anyone would call unannounced, so their private world became unique and special. They would prepare an evening meal together in an hour, open a bottle of Jalon Valley wine, chat, and reflect upon the day's events. Later, they would curl up on the sofa and watch television. Depending on work commitments, the following day, they usually retired at about eleven o'clock.

The log fire burnt brightly, and the evening seemed just like any other, except that this was Friday – Carl's favourite day. It signalled the start of the weekend. He did not work on Saturday or Sunday as a schoolteacher, which gave them precious time together when Alicia was off duty.

Alicia had found a job in a local hospital. It became apparent that she was a great asset to the medical unit. She brought vast knowledge and experience as a staff nurse, having worked in emergency medicine at a large hospital in Pamplona. As a newcomer, she was on probation; however, dismissal from her position was never an option. In no time, the staff approached and confided in her, asking for advice or help.

Peace and contentment prevailed in the Finca on that cold autumnal evening. Ralph, their grey-haired Schnauzer, lay on the rug, luxuriating in front of the fire. He stretched, got up, and turned around to toast the other side of his body. Alicia smiled at his love of warmth and comfort. He was part of the family, and it was good to have him around for companionship when Carl was absent, but more so for protection from strangers who would give their home a wide berth by hearing his bark. Carl commented on how wild the weather was that evening and was about to regale his wife with the odd British idiom, 'I wouldn't put a dog out on a night like this,' when a loud rapping at the front door pierced the silence, setting Ralph off. Carl and Alicia jumped with fright, startled and unhappy with a late caller. Ralph ran to the front door, barking, doing his job well as he guarded the home.

"Who could that be at this time of night?" said Alicia, feeling a prickle of disquiet.

"I don't know."

Carl was thankful he had fitted a security chain to the front door, which gave him a sense of safety when opening the door to an unknown caller. It also demonstrated that the owners were security-conscious. However, more than that, having a dog for protection was comforting. Fearless, Ralph would send anybody packing if they heard his vicious bark. It reassured both that their home was secure and protected.

"I'd better go and see," said Carl.

"Be careful," warned Alicia.

He switched on the outside light from the hallway, grabbed Ralph by the collar, quietened him, and opened the door three inches as far as the safety chain would allow. With his hackles raised, the dog snarled through the gap at the late-night caller. Once again, Carl quietened the dog. Outside on the windswept porch, rain drove in, drenching everything. An Arab-looking man stood in the howling wind. His head and face were wrapped in a Keffiyeh (headscarf) with a wide enough gap to peer through. Usually, it gave sufficient protection against the biting wind. However, keeping the individual dry on a bitterly cold evening was insufficient.

Ralph was not impressed. His protective instinct would be to leap and bite if let loose. Carl quietened the dog and looked at the stranger, who appeared somewhat like a desert Bedouin. His loose, brown cotton robe and outer garment, tied at the waist, seemed inappropriate for such a stormy night. Worryingly, attached to his corded belt, he displayed a highly decorated Jambiya (Arabic dagger). Wearing leather sandals on his feet seemed wholly inappropriate for the cold, wet evening. However, most noticeable was the apparent lack of a left arm. His left sleeve was tucked into his corded belt.

"Yes?" said Carl.

The Arab spoke in ancient Spanish. Although initially difficult to understand, Carl tuned into his dialect, getting approximately seven words out of every ten.

"You are Carlos, the brave," said the stranger.

"My name is Carlos, but people don't call me brave. They call me Carl."

"But I know you. You are Carlos, and you *are* brave. I owe my life to you. Don't you remember me?" His brief half-smile indicated he was not a threat, or maybe he was playacting.

Carl could not understand what the Arab was talking about. More to the point, why would he be at their front door late in the evening, trying to strike up a conversation over something that sounded utterly bizarre and out of context with the moment?

"Can we talk?" said the Arab, gazing over Carl's shoulder; he wanted to speak inside. Still, a more pressing concern would be the dagger tucked in his belt. That signified concern to Carl, and alarm bells rang. The Arab caught his gaze, removed the dagger, and laid it on the ground by the front door. "Now we are equal, my friend." He held his right arm up, demonstrating he was unarmed and posed no threat. "It is you I have come to see, Carlos."

The dog snarled again, unhappy with the Arab and his disruptive presence. In Ralph's eyes, the intruder *was* a threat and, as such, should be sent packing. Even though the visit seemed very weird, the man intrigued Carl. Usually, he would have been ultra-cautious in a common-sense way, made an excuse, and declined any further interaction or continuation of the conversation. Nevertheless, the strange meeting was unlike anything he had ever experienced before. In many ways, there was something reminiscent of his dad in the late-night caller. He had the same soulful brown eyes and polite social interaction. Carl's mind pushed him to say, 'Okay, come in,' but slight hesitation held him back. He looked at the Arab and saw the look of longing in his hypnotic eyes. Seconds passed. Then he relented. Carl took the dog by its collar, unhooked the chain, stepped to one side, and opened the door. The Arab pulled back the face covering. His wrinkled face revealed a life of hardship, yet he possessed an aura of integrity and strength. "You know who I am," said the Arab with conviction."

The puzzled look on Carl's face spoke volumes; he was at a loss for words.

"It has been such a long time, so I will introduce myself. I am Tariq-ibn-Wasim. Now, do you remember?"

Ralph began to growl. The dog's unease with the stranger did not abate. In an indistinct turn of phrase unknown to Carl, the Arab spoke a few words to Ralph; the dog responded by wagging his tail and sitting down by his master with no more growling or snarling – quite the opposite. Now, Ralph seemed happy in the Arab's company.

Tariq half-smiled and waited. However, he did not

enter Carl's home. He waited for something.

"Please, come in," said Carl. "You are most welcome."

This was what he had been waiting for. The Arab stooped in an act of reverence. "Alaykum (peace be upon you), Carlos the Brave."

Hearing the conversation, Alicia walked into the hallway to see the stranger.

"Alicia, this is Tariq-ibn-Wasim," said Carl. "He has called to see me."

"Alaykum, Señora Alicia." He bowed. "Please, I mean you no harm; I only want to talk with you, good people." He gave a reassuring look.

"Okay," said Alicia cautiously. "Can we offer you some refreshment?"

"Thank you, but I am good." Without the cloth wrapped around his head and face, he appeared to be in his late fifties or early sixties. His rugged, suntanned face bore a scar from his forehead across his eye to his left cheek. Even so, Tariq generated a feeling of kindness and serenity that shone through despite his formidable appearance, putting Alicia at ease. He was very gracious towards her.

"Well, please come in and warm yourself. "Carl held his hand out towards the living room in a gesture of – after you. Though there was no need to show him the direction, Tariq knew his way around Casa Azahar exceptionally well.

What became a noteworthy disruption of their evening, which lasted thirty minutes, ended in mystery. Carl and Alicia sat on the sofa, listening to Tariq's pleasing voice. He stood by the fire, drying out and warming his entire body.

"The fire reminds me of the many evenings we camped out in the country, Carlos, when we were cold and far from home. The summers were beautiful, but the winters were bitter and hostile." He stopped momentarily, thinking about what he had just said. "My friend, we had many long conversations. There were moments when we laughed and many when we cried. We discussed the war, wondering when it would end; we hoped to return to our homeland and reunite with our families.

Nevertheless, in truth, we knew it would never be possible. The Spanish King had made it very clear that even though we were born in this country and forced to convert to Christianity, we were outcasts in our own country – Spain." At that point, he stopped speaking for a moment of reflection. "I missed my family so much; it was the thought of returning home to them and normality that helped me through all the pain and carnage." At that point, he rubbed his tired eyes. Listening to Tariq's humanity, compassion, and kindness eased Carl and Alicia's concerns about him.

He spoke with authority about Valencia, the coastal regions down to Jalon, Murla and outlying districts. However, his account of Carl and himself fighting Spanish soldiers sounded bizarre. Defending the Moors fleeing to the hills, said to be kith and kin, seemed implausible. So much so that he found it hard to believe the story; yet Tariq's account was compelling. Carl had never considered or indulged in theorising about reincarnation or the afterlife. It was a world he knew nothing about, let alone thought about, but maybe he should give it his attention. Since living in Spain, many things had happened to him; so what difference would a little more intrigue and head-scratching matter? The conversation continued with a lot more detail.

"So, are you saying that we fought the soldiers to defend the escaping Moors who were being slaughtered and mutilated by the Spanish and that it all ended up here on Caballo Verde?"

"Yes, that is so, Carlos the Brave."

With such revelations, and additionally using psychometry – touching odd things such as rocks, the well housing, and drinking well water – all contributed to the obscene visions running like a film in his mind. "When and where did this take place exactly?" said Carl, testing his knowledge and trying to catch him out or pick holes in his statement of recall.

Tariq pointed out of the window toward the mountain, Caballo Verde. "Out there 1609."

Carl shook his head in disbelief. In apparent truth, he was saying some 400 years ago, they both stood side-by-side in a battle against the Spanish soldiers and that he had rescued Tariq on more than one occasion from injury or death. The conversation ran out of steam, becoming awkward and fragmented. Carl looked on, waiting for the story to continue, but nothing else happened.

"Are you sure you won't have something to eat or drink?" said Alicia, trying to normalise an extraordinary and bizarre moment. Yet, something was spellbinding in the way Tariq spoke. His exacting recall and knowledge of that specific period seemed inexhaustible and convincing.

"Thank you, Señora Alicia. I will have some bread and olive oil if I may." She headed for the kitchen to organise the very odd food request.

Her clever intellect kicked in as she thought about the conversation logically. If Tariq had been, as he said, a Muslim in 1609, then his diet would have been rudimentary, consisting of bread and olive oil. That seemed to make a lot of sense to her. Oddly enough, she had recently seen an old man in a tapas bar eating bread soaked in olive oil and washing it down with wine. How odd the whole thing was, she thought.

"Do you live far from here?" said Carl, trying to catch Tariq out.

"Oh, nearby," he said, not wanting to elucidate.

With a lull in the conversation, Carl excused himself and headed for the kitchen, leaving Tariq and Ralph warming their bodies.

Alicia had cut into a fresh loaf of bread as Carl searched the pantry for olive oil. Whispering, they exchanged thoughts about their visitor.

What else would he tell them? Would he continue with his absorbing conversation? Conversely, would he surprise them with something completely different?

Alicia carried the light snack, prepared on a tray, into the living room, followed by Carl. They looked around in disbelief. Their guest was nowhere to be seen.

They scoured their tiny Finca with no sight or sound of him. Meanwhile, Ralph was curled up fast asleep in front of the fire. Eerily, it appeared as if the enigmatic Tariq had never been present in their home. With a thought, Carl raced to the front door. It had been left ajar. The Jambiya placed on the porch earlier was gone.

The wind still prevailed, but the rain had stopped. Carl looked around the immediate area to see if he could locate their visitor. There was no movement, no sound, and no Tariq.

As Carl looked over towards Caballo Verde, he saw a small green light pulsating off in the distance. Then another, and then another. That was more than enough for him. He remembered the walk back from their friends when he witnessed pulsating light orbs that swooped down, bathing them in a strange luminosity. Carl quickly stepped inside the front door, slammed it shut, reconnected the security chain, and stood with his back against the door, searching his mind, trying to recall the conversation. There was a lot to digest, and it would take some time to make sense of it if indeed he could. The most puzzling recall was supposedly standing by Tariq's side in battle, fighting off Spanish troops. Carl's whole being was one of peace, love, and humanity, making the statement seem implausible.

A faint glow, three feet in height, resembling a half-human form, stood behind an outbuilding, observing the Finca and its residents. Then an eerie screech pierced the cold night air. Although both were indoors, they could hear the evil dissonance. It sent shivers down their spines. The unholy sound was unique in its ability to unsettle and disturb them both to the point where they stood near each other for comfort, reminiscent of the night they walked back from Jeff and Lynn's home. Yet, they chose to fool themselves into believing it to be a wolf attacking another animal high up in the mountain or an owl swooping down upon its prey, bringing about a cruel and painful death to some unsuspecting wild animal.

Ignorance was bliss, but in this case, ignorance was foolhardy.

SIXTEEN

Just outside Casa Azahar, a footpath ran at right angles from the main road, heading up to the lower slopes of Caballo Verde. Recently, Carl saw some hunters with shotguns making their way past his Finca, leading up the rocky footpath towards the mountain. Their double-barreled shotguns slung over their shoulders in a macho way troubled him. When living back in the UK, he recalled seeing a documentary about firearms in the UK that covered the restrictive carrying of shotguns in public, but always in a secure weapons slip, conforming to legal requirements. In Spain, carrying a gun over their shoulders, maybe even loaded, was far too cavalier for Carl. Later, he heard what he believed to be a gunshot and lead pellets raining down on their terracotta roof tiles. Of course, shooting in the air at birds meant that the lead shot had to fall to earth somewhere, but on his roof – that seemed too close for comfort and a tad unsettling. He did not tell Alicia about the locals with guns and dogs on their leisure pursuit for fear of alarming her. Although not an animal rights activist, she was very much against cruelty in any form, be it animal or human.

The incline up Caballo Verde Mountain was

initially easy-going on the rocky pathway; the shrub- and fir-covered slopes, with occasional sunlight glinting through the clouds, made for a pleasant early morning hike. Carl, Alicia, and Father Bernardo had chosen a lovely Saturday to explore the mountain and had come prepared for an extensive hike. Sensible footwear and clothing were the order of the day. They felt warm wearing zip-up jackets in the early stages of the walk. However, the father assured them that it would feel colder higher up the mountain. For the time being, Carl and Alicia tied the jackets around their waists and continued their trek. Although nowhere in sight, Carl remained vigilant, looking and listening out for the locals with their shotguns.

"Do you think the white light you originally saw the first night we met emanated anywhere near here, Carl?" The immediate area was a small, flat clearing in the trees, looking out across the Jalon Valley and beyond.

"I believe it was a bit higher up the mountain, in or near an open land area, Father. Although it is difficult to get a true perspective comparing nighttime to daytime." He looked around. "Yes, certainly higher up the mountain." Alicia nodded in agreement.

Initially, Father Bernardo was surprised by the account of the pulsating white lights. He had heard locals talking about such things, but he believed they were myths or perhaps scaremongering. However, as he came to know Carl and Alicia well, he realised they were honest people and not prone to exaggeration, so their account of the pulsating white lights bore credence.

Spending time on such a lovely autumnal day with two young people was a pleasure for the father and quite a change from his usual pastime. Much later in the day, upon their return to the Finca, they would sit down to a meal, talk about interesting highlights of the day, and maybe have a brandy or two.

Most of the father's parish covered villages in and around the Jalon Valley; they were home to people who led quiet, uneventful lives. Therefore, a chance to talk to and hear from engaging young people was very much to his liking.

"Let's take five minutes to get our breaths back," said Father Bernardo, pointing to large logs in a circle as seats on the leafy ground. There was ash, suggesting that someone had recently lit a campfire. A quiet moment ensued as they sat, looking at the lower mountain they had just traversed. Carl focused on the village of Murla with its main street, a few shops, and a bar. Leading out of Murla, the road passed the village cemetery, wound its way by their friend's home, and eventually continued past their home, heading towards the village of Campell.

Set inland from the coastal town of Denia, the Jalon Valley, according to the father, was a remarkable sight in spring. At that time of the year, the valley floor was transformed into a sea of pink and white almond tree blossoms, attracting many tourists with cameras, which was good for local trade. His two young friends pointed out various features near their Finca. An unusual cluster of buildings on a hillock nearby seemed oddly out of place. Extensive white buildings with terracotta roof tiles, arranged to form a large courtyard, was planted with palm trees and sat resplendent in the autumnal morning sun. Six-foot-tall white walls surrounded the buildings, giving the impression of isolation. Large gates to the hamlet afforded seclusion from the outside world.

"That is the Sanatorium of Fontilles for lepers," said the father. "It opened in 1909 and treated many poor souls with the condition of leprosy. The wall surrounding it extends for two and a half miles and encloses thirty-four buildings, springs, palms, and fruit trees. As you can see, it's surrounded by wooded mountains and isolated, just what the locals wanted. But despite that, most people objected to the Sanatorium being built at the outset." He smiled. "Strangely enough, there is a lovely story about local growers of Muscatel grapes that mature just in time for Christmas. The growers objected to the Sanatorium being built in the area for fear of the lepers tainting their grape crops." He looked to his friends with a smile, as if to say, 'Can you believe that?' Carl and Alicia shook their heads in disbelief; what more could be said?

The father pointed in Jalon's direction. "Can you see the blue dome on the church of Parroquia Nuestra Señora del Consuelo? A very distinctive and prominent feature for miles around. It has many visitors every year who contribute towards its maintenance and upkeep."

"Yes, and it was a Muslim mosque in 1609 before the expulsion of my people."

The surprise of hearing a voice join in with their conversation caused all three to turn their heads. Twenty feet away, Tariq stood in his brown robe and outer garment, wearing his Keffiyeh and the same insubstantial leather sandals.

"Hello, Tariq, how are you?" said Carl as he stood up to greet his friend.

"Carlos, the brave, it is good to see you again." He looked at Alicia and respectfully nodded, "Señora."

Carl was aware that the father had not met Tariq, so he made the introductions. "Father Bernardo, this is Tariq. He ... err. He called to see us the other night at our Finca and said, surprisingly, that he knew me in a past life."

"Oh," said the father, perplexed by the strange, otherworldly remark. He stood and turned to Tariq. "Hello, my friend. It's good to meet you. Please sit down with us if you have time."

"Thank you, but I will stand. I was out for a walk when I saw you." As the three sat, Tariq said something that floored the priest, "I knew your great, great grandfather, Archbishop of Valencia, for many years. Of course, we were of different religions, but that did not matter; we knew each other well, or so I thought. However, it seems he harboured deep sectarian views. Amongst all the bad feelings of Muslims in Spain, the Archbishop spoke to King Phillip, and fairly soon after, they pronounced all Moorish people to be heretics and traitors."

Father Bernardo sat open-mouthed. How could Tariq talk about events hundreds of years ago and still be alive today? The priest suspected him of fabricating the truth; however, as a man of the cloth, he could not, nor would he, accuse him of untruths, and certainly would not ridicule him for his comments, even if they seemed outlandish or far-fetched.

"Can we offer you something, Tariq?" Alicia reached for her backpack to hand out drinks and nibbles. She was always well-organised for such events, as Carl knew, and he left that to her.

"No, I am good, thank you, Señora Alicia," he said with a gracious look.

There was no mention of his disappearance from their Finca on that cold evening for fear of alienating him. Tariq appeared relaxed and engaging, yet distant in some way. To the father, he seemed to be of an ancient Spanish generation. His speech suggested that he was from a past life, yet how could that be, he thought? It seemed inconceivable that the person before them could be as old as he claimed.

Tariq pointed to a small rocky clearing nearby. Rocks of varying sizes stacked on each other in a cairn looked oddly out of place, yet untouched from when they were first put in place. More to the point, why were they in that location?

"Do you remember that area, Carlos the Brave? It was the resting place for your friend, Yusuf."

Carl felt a sudden wave of emotion, as if he had been transported back in time with his supposed friend. He experienced a momentary glimpse of a battle site, and then it was gone. Was it something spiritual that imbued that feeling, or had he just experienced a clever, unsubstantiated comment that struck a nerve? Carl was perplexed. Tariq seemed adept at surprising and causing bewilderment with his dialogue; it was as if he were a wise old sage, knowing more than he divulged and maintaining an air of mystery. Carl no longer knew what to believe. Since their initial meeting, he had questioned himself, thinking deeply and seeking answers, yet he was still perplexed about the whole affair. Even with Alicia's fine mind, they could not find a solution to his supposed connection with the past. None of it made any sense.

Carl began to question why he had gone along with the charade and listened to what seemed to be dubious recollections involving himself and the past, or more specifically, his past life. There was no substance to Tariq's story, only supposition. Carl had not challenged the validity of the stories in any shape or form. In some ways, he had encouraged Tariq's behaviour by going along with the anecdotal stories, failing to challenge them. The visit to Casa Azahar was most unusual, and his story sounded compelling. However, Tariq's declaration that they had met hundreds of years ago and that Carl was his next in command appeared preposterous. Yet, if that were the case, and he felt foolish for considering the thought, then it meant he had fought and killed Spanish people. Why would he kill his kind? Should he stop all the stupidity right now? The answer was affirmative. Yes, he would challenge Tariq this very minute and find out what he was about. Carl approached it diplomatically and asked Tariq if he could speak privately. They moved towards the footpath in clear sight of Alicia and the father, but far enough away for them to be out of earshot.

"Tariq, my friend, we have to talk."

"That is fine, Carlos the Brave. You always had to speak your mind and clear things up if it was not to your satisfaction. You haven't changed."

"I don't know how to say this, my friend, so I will just come straight out with it." He proceeded to put his hand on Tariq's shoulder to show his concern in a kindly manner. Yet, with unbelievable surprise and fright, his hand travelled through Tariq's shoulder. The shocked expressions on all their faces were of absolute disbelief. Carl froze as if amid a horrific nightmare, his colour ashen. Alicia looked to Father Bernardo, sitting motionless, wide-eyed, and open-mouthed. Despite Tariq appearing to be a fully formed human of the here and now, he was not. There was no substance to him. At that moment, his body quivered and lost colour and form. He disintegrated (as if on the Star Trek transporter, where a person had just dematerialised). What could have happened? Carl staggered back over to his wife and Father Bernardo, looking ghastly and in total shock. He took a hard, visible swallow and opened his mouth to speak, but it did not come. Carl turned and pointed to the spot where it had all happened. "Did you..." He was lost for words. The

Priest said nothing. He could not.

The only one to make a coherent comment was

Alicia. "I've never seen anything like that before in my life – Madre Mia."

Father Bernardo was still out of it altogether. His colour was appalling, his mind completely blank. His hand shook as he reached out for one of Alicia's drinks. It would take a while before they spoke or confirmed what they had just seen. Hereafter, the walk back down the mountain to Casa Azahar would be a strange and silent affair.

Following their incredible, energetic day, the evening meal of roast chicken, salad and fresh bread went down a treat. As they sat at the table eating, an enthusiastic conversation ensued, aided by a glass or two of wine. Theories, conjectures, and conflicting views abounded. However, considerable time was spent trying to understand the unusual and implausible occurrence on the mountain – Caballo Verde. Tariq's disappearance from the mountainside was out of this world, intriguing yet troubling them. They made a concerted effort to analyse Tariq's oddness and tried to explain his existence, with minimal effect. His revelation that Carl, presumably a soldier in the Moorish army fighting against the Spanish troops, seemed incredible and wholly unsubstantiated. Equally, the fact that he said he had known Father Bernardo's Great-great-grandfather, the Archbishop of Valencia, was, in many ways, sheer conjecture. The father knew his family's religious beliefs went back hundreds of years, and he confirmed that his spiritual family hailed from Valencia.

However, he did not know that the Archbishop was an Islamophobe and a bigot. That news came as a revelation, and he vowed to look into church records to clarify, and hopefully disprove, Tariq's sensational disclosure.

"Something troubles me," said Carl, putting his glass down to voice his question. "Tariq said I was by his side as his next in command back in 1609. If we accept his premise, for the time being, that means, quite obviously, I was a Moor, and my religion would have been Muslim. If that was the case, how and why would I be a Roman Catholic now?" He looked to both for an answer or at least a smattering of understanding.

"That's what he implied," said Alicia.

"No, that's what he said!" Carl felt mildly edgy about correcting Alicia. Maybe he was becoming upset with the suggestion of killing people in anger. It was troubling him, and he needed clear answers. However, no clear answers were forthcoming, nor would there be that night.

"I recall you told me the other night when we were talking that Muslims had been forcefully converted to Catholicism," said Alicia, trying to help by thinking aloud.

Carl smiled at Alicia as he tried to make amends for his terseness.

"Then maybe you were Muslim and converted to Catholicism."

"No, I can't see that," said Carl, even more perplexed. "Such an unholy shift, excuse the pun, would not make sense at all."

The evening was filled with speculation, allowing them to share their thoughts. In part, the strange discovery and shock of the day's events, spurred on by alcohol, encouraged them to verbalise theories and beliefs that maybe they otherwise would not have considered. Changing the subject but adding to the intrigue, Father Bernardo recalled something he had read in a newspaper years ago. In the wake of the 2011 Japanese earthquake and ensuing tsunami, he recalled a memorable story that caught his eye. The article was headed, 'Horrified cabbies pick up ghost passengers.'

"It would appear that the earthbound souls of dead people in Tohoku's devastated area of Japan would get into a taxi and ask for a locality that no longer existed due to the tsunami completely ripping the area away. With seemingly human passengers in their cabs, taxi drivers confirmed with their commuters if they were sure they wanted to go to their requested destination. The answer was always affirmative. Later in the journey, as they headed towards the requested destination, the taxi driver would realise that his traveller was no longer a passenger. They had disappeared from the back seat of the taxi." According to the father, this occurred so often that the taxi drivers spoke openly to normalise what was very abnormal.

"Are you serious, Father?" The spirit of a dead person would look and sound human enough to get into a taxi and tell the taxi driver to take them to an address and then disappear," said Alicia.

"Good grief," said Carl. "We were convinced that

Tariq was real when he called on us that night and again today when we met him on the mountain, until, of course, he vanished." Which made for a compelling, if not eerie, comparison.

"Exactly... I can't get over how real Tariq seemed. He acted just like you and me. And when he disintegrated before our eyes, well, I don't mind telling you I reached for my crucifix and asked for the Lord's protection," said Father Bernardo.

"But those people in Japan, and I don't doubt the story," said Alicia, "were wandering around like lost souls when the tsunami caused havoc, death, and destruction. I can somewhat understand that unusual story. So, if we accept that it could be possible for the spirits of dead people in Japan to roam around looking for their loved ones, then maybe we have to accept Tariq's assertion. So, being here 400 years after his death isn't so far-fetched," she said, thinking she had just summed it all up quite succinctly.

They sat quietly, thinking about her outline of the facts. In that brief moment, although she did not know it, the priest could see a trait of Rosa in her. She embodied her nana's articulation, movement, and presentation of her opinion with such uncanny similarity.

"Added to that, what are all the white lights on the mountain about?" she said, putting it out there, yet not expecting a conclusive answer.

"I'm not sure," said the father, still thinking about her last comment, but if the stories he had read were true, then they were souls of the dead trapped between worlds in the ether.

"Maybe Nana can tell us more about that," said Carl, searching for a satisfactory explanation for the unsettling affair yet looking to conclude the conversation. His mind was beginning to close down in places – a sure sign that tiredness was taking hold.

"All I can suggest is that we keep our eyes open for more sightings, information or gossip and meet again to pool our knowledge. In the meantime, I will talk to some of my parishioners and see if they know anything."

Weirdly, Father Bernardo was finding the day's proceedings quite exhilarating, and to his amazement, all of the events were happening in the sleepy little village of Murla. Even so, the circumstances surrounding spiritual belief, if that is what it was, raised questions about aspects of his religious teachings. Nevertheless, he was mature enough to understand that there were other things besides Heaven and Hell.

That night, he would pray for the Lord's guidance and strength to give him understanding and faith in performing his holy, blessed work. Nevertheless, before he left, he would have another glass of wine and maybe a brandy to see him on his way.

SEVENTEEN

Determination to find an answer to the appearing-and-disappearing Tariq became a need to know more than anything else. A dichotomy of thought surrounding the whole saga of their Arab friend persisted in Carl and Alicia's minds, demanding attention to the truth. They had to know.

Since their last visit to the mountain, unusual things had occurred in and around the Finca. One morning, before Alicia left for work, she found a basket of persimmon fruit on the doorstep. The locally grown reddish-orange sweet fruit became popular in Spain at Christmas. Even if she did not know where they came from, the fruit, a welcome gift, sat in the round wicker basket in the kitchen, waiting to please someone's taste buds. She suspected the present might be a gift from Tariq, a sort of apology for his abrupt departure.

Furthermore, the internet signal dropped out at any time, day or night, for no apparent reason. The interruption to Carl's online workload was frustrating as he tried to read and mark schoolwork. He aimed to update the pupils' classwork online and give advice. However, it suffered from frustrating disruptions. That aside, even the signal for the TV could die at a minute's notice. Carl suspected the problem was with their supplier, Telefonica, and contacted them. The system was thoroughly checked and found to be functioning correctly.

Days later, another problem occurred. When the television was on and functioning, it pixelated, causing any image on the TV to break up into small patches.

On one of those repetitive occasions, around dusk, the television pixelated. However, just before it happened, Carl thought he observed a light source outside the living room window out of the corner of his eye. He could not be entirely sure, as the curtains were drawn. If it happened again, he planned to leap out of his chair, make it to the window and open the curtains. The idea was set in his mind. For most of the evening, Carl watched TV but felt unsettled. Even Alicia knew he was not his usual relaxed self and asked him if he was okay. His unconvincing reply did nothing to ease her mind. She looked at him dubiously with raised eyebrows. After further questioning, he came clean.

"I wondered if somebody passing the living room window could have caused such a strange interference on the TV." He pointed. "Our satellite dish is mounted on the wall just by the window, so if somebody passed nearby..."

"Carl, you are frightening me by saying that."

He realised that his proposed solution to the pixelation mystery was too much for Alicia and tried to backpedal on his theory. "I'm sorry, Alicia," he said, wrapping his arms around her and pecking her on the cheek. "Maybe I should have used the word something instead of somebody, meaning it could have been an animal."

Alicia pulled back and looked into his eyes. "You think it a person?"

"I'm not sure, but if I think about it logically..." At that precise moment, a strange light passed by the window, and the TV pixelated. In mid-sentence, Carl ran to the window, pulled the curtains back, and saw a mysterious dark object outlined in a bright luminosity. It disappeared out of their driveway and up the lane. He had not realised that Alicia had been just as quick to follow him and had seen the same image fade into the distance. They stood spellbound, the sight sending shivers down their spines. Alicia took a big gulp. Carl stood motionless, staring toward the area of the image sighting, but by now, it was gone.

"What do you think it was, Carl?"

Recovering his composure sufficiently to turn and face her, Carl was flabbergasted. "I ... I have no idea... but we need help with this, Alicia. We need all the help we can get. I'm going to install a CCTV system around the Finca and see if we can determine what it is. Jeff has already installed cameras, so I'll ask him for help choosing a model to install around the home."

The remainder of the evening was spent in recollection and speculation. However, by late evening, neither were closer to understanding what had happened or why. The black image, edged in a strange luminosity, bedevilled their sleep. At one point, Alicia sat up in bed, covered in perspiration, shouting, 'Nooo.' Usually a deep sleeper, Carl came to with a fright, seeing Alicia in tears, her head in her hands.

Instantly, he turned on the light and comforted her. Eventually, she agreed to try to sleep, but only if she could nestle into Carl with his arm around her. Both slept sporadically that night and woke the following morning feeling trashed and unprepared for the day ahead.

Nevertheless, Alicia felt pleased to be working that day. Usually, there was so much going on in the hospital's busy accident and emergency department where she worked, and little time to think, let alone indulge in what had happened the night before. In addition, some nurses and doctors were a delight to work with, which made her shift go incredibly fast and even made it a tad enjoyable.

Although a much bigger mystery than the pixelating TV or the dark image presented itself to Carl at work that day, he received a text message in Arabic during an English class. He could not read Arabic, but later, one of his colleagues, who spoke and read fluent Arabic, was asked to look at the message on his mobile and explain its meaning. The fellow worker looked at the SMS – colour drained from his face. How very odd, thought Carl, notably as he refused to talk about the text. His colleague appeared frightened and upset and would not comment on the communication. With speed, he left the room, leaving Carl open-mouthed. The message had caused so much consternation and concern. Why should he become visibly upset and mentally blank out the message? But more than that, why should he show fear of reading a text?

Carl leafed through books on the Arabic language

in the school library during his break. By a lengthy process of elimination, putting letters together, and comparing the squiggled Arabic writing with other examples, he came up with a repetitive word – Jinn – Arabic for supernatural creatures and jinni for a singular supernatural entity. In his mind, this required more research and questioning.

When he spoke to Jeff and Lynn that evening about the CCTV, he raised the subject of the supernatural to gauge their views and see if they had heard any local gossip. They knew very little, except that when they were drinking in the local bar in Murla the other night, a local Spaniard who knew they spoke Valenciano asked them if they were happy where they lived. But more to the point, he asked if they were superstitious, having heard the local history about the mountain. It appeared they were being baited just for amusement. They looked around the bar and saw smiles on the locals' faces as they waited for their reply. Cleverly, their answer was positive and complimentary about the area, but it ended the conversation disappointingly.

EIGHTEEN

Rosa's circle of friends in Pamplona widened significantly. Her art class companions provided valuable advice on landscape composition (her chosen subject) and on working with perspective and shading, all of which added depth and feeling to her art. Even Elena had to confess that her paintings were beginning to look far more realistic and professional. Although more challenging and unlike her previous art ventures, her latest endeavour, poetry, progressed slowly. She was accepted into a close-knit writing group in Pamplona, which may have had something to do with her being the mother-in-law of the high-flying mayor. They met weekly and were required to read their submissions aloud and listen to constructive criticism from the group.

At first, Rosa felt bashful about reading, fearing ridicule or derision. However, once she had overcome her unjustified concerns about a lack of ability, it soon became apparent that the group was very supportive towards her, offering advice on writing sonnets, free verse, limericks, and haiku – all of which were new to her world, yet intriguing and challenging. Once settled and having made more friends and acquaintances, the poetic writing group appealed to Rosa all the more. Her newfound friends were sympathetic to the tragic death of her husband; they helped to normalise the loss by sympathetically discussing the sad parting.

Following further private discussions, it became apparent that although Rosa was doing her best to cope and put on a brave face, the pretence was not working. Sadness followed her in every aspect of life. Figuratively, Ernesto was there in everything she did or thought about. Although she continued on without her loved one, life was incomplete – without feeling. Rosa realised she was going through life without considering its subtleties or nuances. Her daily routine was like an automaton – she thought very little, just did. With this in mind, one of her close friends, Maria, sensitively encouraged her to write about her beloved Ernesto. After days of putting pen to paper, crossing out, and starting over, she decided to leave her attempt at writing a poem and spend time reading, walking, painting, and meeting friends.

Then, one day, sitting at Ernesto's desk, Rosa picked up a pen and looked longingly at a picture of him. His good-looking, mature image and distinctive greying hair were always on her mind. She stared around the small study, remembering their years of precious, enduring time together. The ornate brass plaque on the wall commemorating a golfing achievement – his celebratory retirement card from work, signed by all his colleagues and framed – a photograph of the two of them on holiday in France – all full of memories and life, and now nothing, just sadness.

At that point, she thought someone had passed the

window; for a brief moment, she genuinely believed Ernesto had just walked by, and she was about to call out, but she realised he was no longer with her. With tears in her eyes, she started writing as if someone was holding her hand, guiding the pen across the page. Sometime later, Rosa looked at the page of text and read the entirety of her automatic writing, surprised yet comforted by its sentiment.

A brave soul

I saw you pass the window,
but you were not there.
Our home stands alone, silent and bare.
Nobody knows where you are.
I do. You are in my heart.

I recall the days and precious ways
you cared for me so much.
Your charm and compassion enveloped me.
I smile, recalling your touch.

Sadly, our love is no more.
Still, we will meet again, of that I am sure.
Until we do, adieu, my love.
Watch over me, help me,
and heal my empty heart.

Given time, Rosa realised that her poem, entitled 'A Brave Soul', had been cathartic, helping her expose the deepest recesses of her mind, where Ernesto's soul lay. With time and help from friends and family, she felt more at ease with her loss and could mention her late husband's name without crying or feeling a lump in her throat. However, in a mildly emotional moment one afternoon, something unusual occurred as she contemplated the sorrow and loss of her loved one and life in their beautiful home in Murla. Rosa became aware of an uncanny feeling connected to Carl and Alicia's dog, Ralph. There was no particular reason for the thought. She had not seen the dog but had heard all about him and his doggy antics. The peculiarity of the thought puzzled her, but she paid minimal attention to the mind's peculiarity and moved past the man–dog thought that her psyche had raised.

Reassuringly, her general demeanour improved over the days and weeks, exhibiting a more confident and controlled Rosa.

One day, a conversation with one of her art friends took an unusual turn – one that she found truly astonishing. Her friend Marina looked at one of her woodland animal paintings. After studying it and asking several unusual questions about her lifestyle, she said, "You're a white witch, aren't you?" Amidst incredulity and disbelief at how anybody could come to such a conclusion, she had to agree. Of course, being a spiritual person, drawn to healing, understanding herbal medicine and treatments, and possessing a positive aura were strong signs. Even more incredible, her friend confessed to being a white witch herself. From then on, with a common bond, their friendship blossomed and provided help in the form of a confidante to fill the void that Ernesto's parting had left. The two became inseparable over the coming days and weeks. Rosa even spent the occasional night at her friend's house. They discussed witchcraft practices and helped each other by examining aspects of their pagan creed that they had not considered before, thereby reinforcing their practice values.

All in all, life became enjoyable and satisfying living in Pamplona. Marina never wanted to be part of a witch's coven, preferring to be an independent Wicca witch.

One evening, they prepared a meal, sat, ate, drank, and enjoyed discussing the art of witchcraft, especially since they were very close friends and felt relaxed enough in each other's company to open up completely.

"Have you ever practised magic other than white witch enchantments?" said Marina, glass in hand, looking on enquiringly. It was the sort of question that could only be asked because she knew Rosa well.

"No, never. I didn't want to delve into the darker aspects of the practice; it just isn't for me. So I kept away from that sort of thing," confirmed Rosa. She was enjoying the conversation and realised they had so much in common.

Marina went on to explain that she had never used anything other than white witchcraft practice methods. However, she had tried reading tarot cards and found them fascinating and an excellent aid for foretelling the future. Although not knowing much about tarot reading, Rosa was intrigued enough to ask some more. "So, what do you do, and how would you do it?"

"I can do a reading for you now if you like," said Marina, "then you can see how it works and if it connects with you and your personal life."

Happy to go ahead. Both finished their meals, cleared the table, and sat beside a coffee table prepared for fun.

"I am still learning, although I might say learning fast, so I will just put two cards in front of you and read them in connection with your story. Does that sound okay?"

"It sounds fine."

Marina randomly placed the Ace of Swords and a Six Sword card from the pack on the table.

"I see a hand holding a sword with a crown at the tip. Also, I see mountains, which usually indicate a challenge ahead."

"I used to live in a small village with mountains nearby, so that seems to chime with me, but I'm not sure about the sword unless it goes back in history to the fighting that took place on the mountainside near my home in Murla," said Rosa.

"The next card is the Six Swords, showing a woman and a child in a boat, moving along by a man punting. This could indicate a period of failure, poverty, or change, so the family is, in effect, moving on. It may be for a new way of life in a faraway land. Yet, this contrasts with the first card with the sword, which I believe has great meaning."

"The hills I can get, and even moving on to a different area, could be me moving away from Murla to live in Pamplona – very interesting... Hang on; it could also indicate my granddaughter and her husband. Now that does sound fascinating and maybe nearer the mark."

Marina agreed that card reading depended on individual practice, skill, and consistency in telling a story about an individual's tarot story.

"There are many styles of tarot cards, but these that I am using came recommended; they're a Rider-Waite Tarot deck, first produced in 1909," said Marina, impressing with her knowledge.

Although she did her best to describe Rosa's story using the cards, she unknowingly foreshadowed a real-life scenario yet to unfold. Given time, the first card showing a sword would be significant. Yet, the second card's description was more accurate and reflected Caballo Verde's history, life, and struggle against evil forces. Although just a bit of fun, the cards would become quite prophetic in the days to come and touch many people's lives.

NINETEEN

Following the first trek, partway up Caballo Verde Mountain, and again on a Saturday morning, Carl, Alicia and the father were determined to make better headway this time and travel farther, hopefully to the top of the mountain. Although it was an overcast, wet day, the weather conditions did not dampen their spirits. Their companionship was unique, the exercise refreshing, and the joy of discovering unseen mountain areas was exciting and fulfilling. Within fifty-five minutes, they had reached the site of logs arranged in a circle. However, the misty conditions limited the astounding views of the area. Despite that, they continued up the mountain. Ninety minutes later, Carl, Alicia, and the father came upon a sheer rocky escarpment surrounded by large rocks of varying sizes and shapes. Trees and shrubs obscured their onward journey. Their continued uphill progress seemed blocked at first glance, halting their ascent. Still, by carefully studying the terrain and pulling back the shrubs, a narrow walkway was created between what initially appeared to be an impassable rocky area. Overcoming the final difficulty would enable them to reach the very pinnacle of the mountain. Carl wondered if Father Bernado was up for the last leg of the journey and kept a close eye on him. Wearing appropriate clothing and footwear had prepared them for the mountainous climb, but now the only concern was their stamina. The final push was exhausting, and navigating the last leg proved challenging. Within a short time, the climb levelled out to a small pocket of land. They had made it to the top of the mountain, and the immense achievement showed in their happy, smiling faces.

Above eye level and to the right of the flat area, like a prehistoric monolith, stood a peculiar standing rock with a platform rock at right angles; it appeared purposefully slotted into place, yet served no useful purpose. None of the three had seen such an unusual structure on a mountain like this before. Maybe it was an artificial structure; nobody knew.

Later in the week, when talking to locals, they learned that the rocky structure was called the Devil's Chair. Reportedly, bright lights in the shape of orbs moved around the mountain at night, causing unease amongst villagers who dealt with their fears by closing shutters and blocking out the unmentionable dread. As a matter of course, locals avoided the area, and many did not even talk about the superstition for fear of provoking malevolent forces. Even macho locals with guns and dogs did not ascend to the chair's height on Caballo Verde.

With clearing conditions and a hint of blue sky in the distance, all three were thankful to take a break. As usual, Alicia came prepared and handed out bocadillos (baguettes) with tuna filling, which went down a treat. Small bottles of water quenched their thirst.

"Just look at that view," said Carl, gazing upon the unseen side of the mountain.

"It's magnificent," said Father Bernardo. It was a sight rarely seen locally.

For their dessert, Alicia had brought persimmon fruit for each of them. As she handed them around, the father's eyes lit up.

"Where did you get these from, Alicia?"

"If I say I don't know, that would be the exact truth, Father."

She explained that she had found the Persimmon fruits in a basket on the doorstep. How she came by them did not matter. The priest was salivating at the thought of such a tasty treat early in the season. He made immediate inroads into the juicy fruit without another moment's consideration. The look of sheer pleasure on his face was a treat to behold. Napkin in hand, Carl put his fruit down on a rock beside him as he took another thirst-quenching mouthful of water.

"Oh my word, that was so wonderful," said the father as he wiped his chin with the paper napkin. "Since I was a child, I've always loved persimmon fruit. They're synonymous with Christmas as a treat," he said, remembering his childhood.

Carl knew just what he meant. One of his childhood Christmas memories was eating navel oranges, which, coincidentally, grew in Spain; some were grown in the immediate area of Jalon. He put his hand down to the rock where he had placed his fruit on a napkin – it was gone. In disbelief, he looked to his fellow walkers, got up, and looked around the rocky, shrubby area next to him for his missing fruit. There was no sign of it anywhere. Despite that, Alicia gave him a bite of her fruit. Such a loving gesture of togetherness and sharing did not go unnoticed by the father. However, there was no answer to the disappearing fruit. It was yet another mystery connected with Caballo Verde.

"Well," said the priest. "Shall we briefly look around and consider our return journey before it gets too late? I don't want to miss the bus," he said hilariously, raising great laughter.

A large boulder, a short distance away, caught Carl's eye. Although there were many loose rocks and a few boulders, some scattered, some piled, others strewn. All were of varying shapes and sizes. Yet, nothing compared to the enormous boulder painstakingly chiselled to a rounded form, indicated by the marks on its surface. Father Bernardo estimated that the boulder weighed approximately four to five tons. It seemed out of place in the small setting, given the natural terrain of rocks and smaller boulders.

"That looks interesting," said Carl. "A rocky incline before us, yet it has a huge round boulder against its interface. It seems so out of place."

In reality, Carl would have liked to stay and explore some more. However, he could see the sense in setting off down the mountain to make it home before dark and to save the investigation of the large boulder and the surrounding area for another day. Only next time, they would set off earlier.

"I think it could have been rolled into place against the rocky interface," said Alicia, standing back from the scene, eyeing it up, and applying feminine logic. Both men looked at her askance as if she were talking drivel.

Nevertheless, there was no more time to pontificate upon its position or purpose. That would have to remain a mystery until next time. The sun was falling in the sky, and the light was fading fast. Although the area was worth further exploration, they preferred not to be on Caballo Verde fumbling around in the dark, where they might fall or injure themselves on rocks in poor light. Moreover, they did not want to encounter the white or green lights in Carl's case. Setting off, they traversed down the mountain, helping each other as they went – the father first in line, Alicia next, and following up the rear – Carl. As they left the immediate area, a dark, shadowy image watched them. Carl was unsure why he felt the need to glance back. Maybe it was nothing, or perhaps a gut feeling of being watched, that sixth sense feeling that nobody could explain; nevertheless, it alerted him. He was convinced as he turned around; he caught a momentary movement, maybe an image amongst the rocks. He rubbed his eyes and looked again – nothing. If his mind had not been playing tricks on him, he thought it might be similar to the thing he and Alicia had witnessed from their living room window disappearing up the lane. But he was unsure. Carl decided to keep the strange thoughts to himself; however, he had a weird notion that they were being followed – nothing visible, just a powerful feeling that continually alerted his senses.

TWENTY

The Year 1600.

The Wasim family lived and worked in Valencia, an entrepôt for luxury silk textiles, porcelain and spices from China and Central Asia. As the leading supplier of tiles, terracotta storage jars, and household goods from Africa, as well as enamelled glassware and tiles from Italy, the Wasim family business managed all enhancements to life and living. Well-known and respected for their business acumen, the Wasims, with notoriety, worked closely with local authorities and the community. Their presence was felt in every corner of society – in government departments, schools, businesses, and among traders and shop owners. They supported many workers and represented the broader community in all forms of governance. Their approach was genuinely revolutionary in a multi-ethnic, multicultural society. Many locals looked up to the Wasims for their kind, gentle and humane approach to life. Their philosophy was simple – peace, humanity, tranquillity and a belief in the Muslim faith.

Warehouses on the southeast side of the Valencian docks employed many local people and families.

Aali Wasim was born and raised in Valencia. He attended school and learned the trade of importation and sales from his father, Farouk Wasim, founder of the shipping business. He was well educated and always sought opportunities in commerce to generate a financial return. However, in addition to international trade, the family also learned horsemanship and maintained the tradition of training knights to a very high standard. The Wasims, due to their extensive trade, dominated the importation of overseas goods. The family always looked for obvious opportunities in business.

When a local business encountered financial difficulties within an already established shipping company in Valencia, Aali Wasim formulated plans to acquire and integrate the company into his organisation. Although the failing company was established, it was dated, inefficient and unreliable.

With extensive contacts in North Africa, Aali created and ran a thoroughly modern business, gaining notoriety for importing goods quickly and efficiently. Later, he acquired the older, failing company and merged it with his own. Additionally, most of the staff from the old business were retained, ensuring continuity and significant goodwill. With ingenuity, he had established a very professional shipping company.

Months later, by adding more quayside space to the port and expanding importation capabilities, he was able to serve a much wider community, including wealthy individuals on the Spanish peninsula. With hard work and expertise, the whole family's shipping and import/export business prospered.

How ironic it would seem that Aali Wasim would lose the entire business the family had worked so hard to build in Spain. Its benefactor was a wealthy, well-connected businessman who held no qualms about buying the company for a song from a local group of Spanish troops, thugs and opportunists. The Wasims' going concern was forcibly taken from them and sold to the wealthy Spanish national. Yet, this practice was not unique at a time of great upheaval in Spain. The transition of acquisitions from the Moors to the Spanish people was occurring throughout the Iberian Peninsula. Some workplaces were taken and occupied by the perpetrators. Others were stolen and sold for an agreeable price, enabling the thieves to become wealthy overnight.

Despite that, the Spanish people's imagined control and take-up of business failed miserably in the ensuing vacuum of war and loss of Moorish know-how. Foolishly, the country had ejected the people who had successfully run and controlled much of Spain's infrastructure. Within a short period, most Moors forcibly expelled from their trade, whether industrial, financial, social or agricultural, were gone, and the resulting trade within the country was left open to the vagaries of questionable decisions by dubious businessmen and would-be speculators.

In that time before the complete loss of his business, Aali's one and only child, Tariq ibn Wasim, following excellent schooling, had taken up the trade with his father and assumed a position within the Wasim business. Tariq learned horseback riding in his teens and joined an elite group of Arabian riders, gaining further knowledge and skills in horsemanship. He enjoyed the activity passionately and became exceptionally suited to that style of riding. Plainly, he was a natural and was later invited to train as a knight. Moorish troops in the Iberian Peninsula consistently maintained an army of combative knights and troops, yet preferred to handle disputes or quarrels through diplomacy. This practice was not unusual; it was merely the Moor's sense of fairness and respect for fellow man. Nevertheless, having invaded the Iberian Peninsula, the Moors ensured they were ready for any insurrection or minor fracas.

The Wasim family owned extensive properties and land on the outskirts of Valencia. They reared purebred Arabian horses on a stud – a throwback to the ancestral nomadic Bedouin people's love of horses. The breed and line of equines were unique to Spain and highly sought after. Always carrying a full order book for their stud, supplying royalty and the wealthy, their unique business flourished.

Unfortunately, it seemed the glory days were coming to a close for the Moors and their civilisation. Cataclysmic change would envelop the country, never to be the same again.

TWENTY-ONE

In the middle of housework, the phone rang. Alicia looked at the large pendulum, rhythm wall clock (a wedding present from her parents).

"Hi, Alicia. Mum here. I wanted to finalise our arrangements for the celebrations and our week together."

"Yes, it's fast approaching. My week was easy to organise, but Carl had a few problems getting someone to cover – anyway, all set now. We are so looking forward to seeing you all and catching up on the gossip."

"Me too. It seems like an eternity since you were last here. So, how are you?" inquired Elena.

"Fine. We are looking forward to the holiday with you, and the break will do Carl good. He has been swamped with exam papers for the pupils' end-of-term exams, so coming to stay will take him away from work and any pressures. How is everybody back in Pamplona?"

"Very well. Except the latest is that your dad isn't sure if he's doing the right thing by retiring – you know, a bit of self-doubt. We had discussed it many times without a firm decision, and then he spoke to his elder brother, who, as you know, is in finance. So, once again, your dad's sure he's doing the right thing, and retirement is back on the cards again. Now he's enthusiastic about it all. Good news there then, thank the Lord, but keep your fingers crossed just in case."

"Sure will."

Since their wedding, honeymoon, and move to Murla, neither Carl nor Alicia had returned to Pamplona for a holiday or even an overnight visit. All the same, Alicia felt guilty, having no great desire to return to her former home. Why would she? Her heart was now in Murla, just like Nana's, and she felt happy and content with everything in the small hamlet, despite the minor strangeness in the surrounding area. Alicia was enjoying her newfound independence, an experience she had never considered while living in Pamplona.

The week's holiday to Pamplona was to be part of her dad's retirement festivities and catch up with the family. A large celebration would be laid on to farewell Señor Romero as he stepped down as mayor of Pamplona. After many years of decisions, officiating in his legal capacity, controlling and balancing the budget, and taking care of the city's welfare, he was ready to retire from the pressures. Recent elections that gave the opposition party a slight majority would be challenging to manage. He felt that enough was enough at his age, prompting serious thoughts about retirement and encouraging conversations with whomever to ensure he had made the right decision. Retirement would enable him to spend more time with his family and pursue his love of fishing on the River Arga.

Celebrations and fireworks would bring a

magnificent ending to his tenure, and he wanted his family by his side to bid farewell to the job where he had worked methodically, dedicating himself to it with enthusiasm for so many years.

"We are so looking forward to seeing you and Carl. Your nana hasn't stopped talking about the visit."

"Bless her. How is she? Still well?"

"She's fine, still missing Murla, although she doesn't talk about it or the locals from Murla so much now. She has settled very well and made herself useful around the home. Nana has even taken up painting, attending night classes every week and thoroughly enjoying her newfound hobby."

"Wow, that is very different for her."

"Oh, I nearly forgot. She has even taken up writing poetry," Elena said dismissively. "Now then, tell me all about your travel arrangements."

Time ticked by quickly at work, and before long, Carl and Alicia were travelling northwards to Pamplona. They had planned a one-night stopover in Zaragoza, ready to drive the final leg to Pamplona the following day, feeling refreshed and prepared to meet up with the family.

Living in Murla was quieter and simpler, just as living closer to nature proved to be – no hustle or bustle, plans postponed for another day if necessary. As a bonus, locals were polite, pleasant, and engaging.

Meeting family and friends in Pamplona would be challenging, but they would do their utmost to enjoy it. Soon, they would be heading back to utopia, as Carl often called it.

Señor Romero was on his final day at work; the grand celebration would occur tomorrow.

Carl and Alicia entered the family home with warm welcomes full of hugs and kisses. They eyed each other up and down, looking for changes as if it had been years since they last saw each other.

"Just look at you, Alicia," said Mum, taking her hands and smiling at her lovely daughter. "I don't think I've ever seen you looking so healthy and happy. You are positively glowing. You're not pregnant, are you?"

"Mum, stop it?" said Alicia, feeling mildly embarrassed.

Elena looked over to Carl and smiled. "And how's the love of your life?"

"Very good, thank you," Carl responded.

"Alicia, my little one," said Rosa as she entered the room, arms outstretched. Her comment was funny because Rosa was smaller than her granddaughter, but everybody knew what she meant. They hugged like long-lost friends, swaying from side to side rhythmically – something they had always done to emphasise the meeting's happiness.

"Ooh, seeing you and Carl is so good." Rosa looked over at her grandson-in-law. "Come here, you gorgeous boy." They hugged. Carl kissed her on both cheeks.

"And it is so good to see you, Nana," said Carl, "And we really are in love with your beautiful Finca."

"No, *your* Finca," said Rosa emphatically.

"Okay. *Our* Finca is lovely and out of this world, and the people ... well, what can I say?" He agreed with Rosa that it was their Finca to keep the conversation polite and pleasant. That said, they paid a reduced-value rent every month via the Bank of Santander to satisfy their sense of paying their way in life.

"Yes, I know. Everything about the place is amazing. I only left because I had to." She glanced at Elena with a scornful look. "But it seems it was a good move for the best reasons."

Alicia joined in with the conversation. "Father Bernardo sends his regards and said that if you return to Murla for a visit, he would love to see you again."

She smiled. "Lovely Father, Bernardo. We met up on many occasions when I lived there. He used to call in for coffee some days. The poor love was so saddened when I left." She thought for a moment, and a tear appeared. "But, it was the right thing to do." She pushed the sadness away. "Getting old crept up on me, and I realised I wasn't as agile as I once used to be."

"I know. We were shocked to hear about your terrible fall." Alicia drew near to Nana and hugged her again. "But you're well now, aren't you? More than that, I think you're enjoying life here in Pamplona with the family... You know that the beautiful home in Murla is in good hands and loved just like you used to love it, don't you?"

"Of course... I must admit I enjoy having family and friends around me, and being near amenities is good. Did your mum tell you I've taken up painting and poetry?"

"Yes, she did. Maybe we can see some of your work later," said Alicia, surprised at her new interest.

"Of course, you can. So long as you promise not to laugh. You can criticise, but not laugh."

Introductions over – they all took seats in the living room except for Elena.

"Carl," said Elena. "I have a surprise for you."

"For me, what is it?"

"Not what is it – who is it?" She opened the door to the dining room, and Theo stepped out.

"Theo," shouted Carl, leaping from his seat. "What are you doing here, mate?"

"I'm here to see you and Alicia, my two terrific friends," he looked towards Elena, "and, of course, your family."

They hugged. Alicia joined in, making a group hug.

"Hello, Theo, it's so good to see you again. Are you well?" said Alicia.

"I am very well and so happy to see you both again. I must say, Alicia, your English sounds very... well, English."

She pointed to Carl. "It's all thanks to him. What a teacher."

The family, along with Theo, sat in comfort and chatted. They exchanged stories, old and new and caught up on gossip and plans for the future.

The morning gave way to a chilly but sunny day, typical for the time of year. Yet the weather had no effect on the group at the Romeros' home. Later in the day, the plan was to have a hearty meal with family, friends, and acquaintances held in the grand dining room of their Spanish Colonial home. As usual at such gatherings, the meal would often extend to excessive alcohol consumption, lasting well into the evening.

"So, how are things in Murla, particularly Caballo Verde?" asked Rosa. She had already heard a few stories from Alicia and Carl when they chatted on the phone or emailed, and the unusual tales had intrigued her to the point of wanting to know a lot more. She had heard more about the mysteries of Caballo Verde over the past few months than she had during her entire time living there. Yet there was careful, considered questioning about the mountain; it was more than just polite conversation.

"Well, Nana, if you want to know how things are? Murla and Caballo Verde are stunning, but things aren't quite what they seem. There are some odd happenings about the mountain." Alicia realised she had just made light of the situation back home. She was not quite sure why she had gone easy on her account of the Finca and Caballo Verde, given that, in truth, they had more than a few problems. Maybe this was Alicia's way of always making everything sound positive and good, but it was far from the truth.

"Really."

Carl knew what she was alluding to when she said 'odd happenings'; however, Theo was in the dark. As Alicia explained, he listened intently to the story of finding and meeting English friends living nearby, as well as the strange lights on the mountain they had seen while walking home late at night.

"And that was the first time you met Father, Bernardo, I believe?" said Rosa.

"It was, since then, we have become great friends," said Carl, "even meeting up in nearby Orba on occasions and walking up Caballo Verde on two separate occasions. During the day, of course."

"Did he struggle with the rigorous walk, climbing the mountain?" said Rosa, already knowing the answer.

"He did at first, but I suppose he did well for a man of the cloth who doesn't get much exercise."

"I told him many times he should be walking a lot more and driving his car less – and, of course, cut back on the drink," said Rosa, "but I suppose it goes with the job."

"Tell Nana about Tariq," said Carl.

Their first meeting with Tariq the Arab was filled with surprise, intrigue, and mystery. They explained the circumstances of his visit on that cold, wet night, his enthralling stories, and how he knew the Finca's layout so well. Yet, the most surprising revelation he imparted to them was the story of supposedly knowing Carl hundreds of years ago as his second in command, fighting by his side against the King's troops in Valencia and finally on the lower slopes of Caballo Verde, where both died.

"Yes, that will be correct," said Rosa.

"What will be correct?" said Carl.

"That he knew you hundreds of years ago," she said quite matter-of-fact.

Incredulity showed on his blank face; it was as if a

stun gun had just zapped him. Seconds passed without a word.

With his curious, logical mind, Theo looked at Carl and Alicia, then back at Rosa. "I'm not sure if I understand or want to understand what you are talking about," he said, never having heard someone speak with such conviction on an intensely controversial subject.

Alicia ignored Theo's interjection and pressed on for clarification. "What do you mean, Nana? That will be correct."

Rosa thought about the question, smiled, and threw out another sensation. "Do you believe in spiritual beings?"

"Well, I'm ... not sure," said Alicia. Her head was reeling with the challenging psychological onslaught. She was surprised and bewildered by Nana's unusual, out-of-character comments, but more so by her question about the supernatural world.

"What about shapeshifters then?" said Rosa.

If she was trying to shock and surprise everyone, she was doing an excellent job.

Spiritual beings may be perceived as a controversial subject, perhaps even unreal to some. Having said that, the mention of shapeshifters had them all holding their breath. They looked on in disbelief. If Theo could have verbalised his thoughts with his psychologist's hat on, he would probably have thought, 'Is this woman crazy or incredibly intelligent, cool and well-informed?'

Recovering her composure, Alicia fired a carefully worded question. "Okay, Nana, let's start again without any surprises. Please explain what you are talking about."

With great satisfaction, she smiled. Nana had bamboozled them all and set the scene for further revelations. She explained that while living in Murla, she had been a great believer in nature's ways and wholeheartedly embraced everything related to Mother Nature. But, more than that, she had concealed a deep secret for a long time. When her husband was alive, and later after he died, she had made friends with folks in the village. One of the friends had confided in Rosa, revealing that she was a white witch. At first, this had surprised and amazed Rosa. However, by acquiring greater knowledge on the subject through active conversation and demonstrations from her friend, she saw the potential for so much good in the world. Her friend was very knowledgeable about the pagan way of life and explained everything to Rosa in great depth. Being a white witch embraced all aspects of love and humanity in the natural world. Moreover, a white witch was somebody that she dearly wanted to become. Under her friend's tutelage, Rosa trained for a long time, honed her skills and eventually became proficient in witchcraft.

"Before you say any more," said Alicia, "Explain what you mean about being a white witch. Most people associate witches with flying on brooms, having a black cat, and having the ability to cast spells. "She smiled, knowing she was joking, and merely expressing the public's perception of witches.

"I admit that is most people's concept of witches;

however, being a white witch is very different," Rosa confirmed.

"How so?" said Carl.

"Well, we believe in natural remedies; I suppose you could say like believing in alternative medicines, herbs and the like."

"So, no eye of a toad and wing of a bat."

Rosa smiled, having heard it all before. "No, we believe in practical goodness and maintain belief in everything we do. We collectively observe the Wicca Rede."

"Sounds very mystical," said Alicia.

"No, it is just a standard that we uphold. It goes – *And shall it harm no one, do what ye will.*"

Theo sat, taking it all in, not asking any questions, but happy to hear it all in its entirety, as if sitting in on a hospital consultation.

All, except Elena, were enthralled, listening to something that sounded like the teachings from a clandestine inner circle.

"And what about spells?" said Alicia, smiling, not taking Nana's enlightening thoughts too seriously.

"Yes, we do spells. However, not the way you think. We have close ties to all realms of nature and spirit. If we cast a spell, the magic is used to protect from black magic or to reverse black curses. So, you could say white magic spells were positive spells born out of love and a healthy mindset intent on helping humanity."

Sitting around listening to Nana, the white witch, was very illuminating. She surprised everybody, including Theo, whose light-hearted comment was,

"The only witches I knew before meeting you, Rosa, were in Shakespeare's Macbeth."

However, Alicia was mildly troubled by Rosa's declaration that she was a witch. She felt troubled that she was only now hearing about something in Nana's life that she thought she should have known sooner, maybe even when it first came to light.

Carl took up the conversation. "You mentioned, Tariq. How did you get to know him, and when?"

"Well, I met Tariq years ago. I saw him walking near the mountain one day, where we had a brief conversation. After that, we saw each other occasionally in passing, and much later, after Ernesto's death, we began to see more of each other for companionship than anything else. He never accepted my offer of food or coffee the entire time I knew him, which made me somewhat curious about who I was dealing with or what he was. No one can exist without food or drink, and to my knowledge, he never took any sustenance, certainly not in all the time I knew him. But, of course, it isn't something you can ask a person outright, especially given that he is a very private person."

"You said, 'he is a private person.' Do you mean he is wholeheartedly with us in the here and now?" said Carl.

"Yes," came the reply.

"So, he's not a ghost or spirit of the past or something else we don't know about."

Rather annoyingly, Nana shrugged, which did not help Carl or the others listening to the conversation.

"You have to remember that at first, we met infrequently. As I got to know Tariq, a very kind and special friend emerged. Each time we met, I seemed to enjoy his company more and more. On one of those occasions, Tariq said how sorry he was that my husband was ill. I was astonished as he did not know Ernesto and, to my knowledge, had never seen him. At that time, Ernesto did not go out. His lung cancer had worsened, and it was very debilitating and painful for him. Day after day, I saw a dramatic change in his condition." Rosa stopped for a moment to control her emotions. A pained expression registered on her face. She let out a deep sigh and closed her eyes. Seconds passed, and then a slow return to normality. Eyes opened, she looked at those present and smiled reassuringly.

"Anyway, following the conversation about Ernesto, every time we met, Tariq always asked after him and talked about his condition, suggesting ways to manage his illness to make him more comfortable. I must admit it amazed me how caring and compassionate he was. When the cancer was at its worst, one day, Tariq gave me a bag of what seemed to be herbs ground into small particles, none of which I had ever seen before. Surprisingly, at his suggestion, whatever the herb was, it eased his pain considerably. Having been given the distressing diagnosis, all that Ernesto ever wanted to do was to remain at home and die in the surroundings that he loved and cherished. He did not want to be in a hospital with all that medical stuff. All he wanted was to die in peace at home with me by his side. Weeks turned to months, and Ernesto slowly faded away and died." At that point, Rosa stopped talking, took a lace handkerchief from her pocket and dabbed her eyes.

Alicia sat beside her for comfort and reassurance. "Do you want to leave it there, Nana? I think it's becoming too much for you to talk about, Grandad."

"No, I'm alright, thank you, Alicia. Besides, it is good to talk about it after all this time. It doesn't go away, you know, but the pain becomes less if I can share my feelings." She took a sip of her drink, drew a deep breath, steadied herself and prepared to continue. Carl wanted to ask Rosa more questions about Tariq's so-called former life in Valencia, but he held off for the moment out of concern for her distress.

Rosa picked up the conversation and returned to her original reply. "Yes, we knew each other for a long time. Long enough to get to know each other very well."

"How do you think he knew about grandad?" intoned Alicia, feeling her pain and wanting to help her through the sadness. She covered Nana's hand with hers and gave a reassuring smile of comfort.

"I can't answer that. I don't know. A lot of mystery surrounded Tariq in those early days. His whole demeanour appeared secretive and somewhat distant. If I ever asked questions, he would answer in an obtuse manner, or should I say, in an unhelpful way. I quickly learned not to be too direct with him and avoided asking for explanations of things he had spoken about. I could see he was weighing me up, and I believe he began to understand my nature, personality, and who I was. Tariq would often throw out a tidbit of knowledge or history here and there to satisfy my curiosity. On one of those special occasions, he talked about being a descendant of a Moorish knight. He talked about his family, trade, and life in Valencia, which he declared went back for him to the late 1500s."

"Did you question that?" said Carl, eager to know the answer to such an astounding statement.

"I tried to; however, Tariq never bared his soul or gave a complete explanation about that or other things we spoke about. He only provided clear, concise answers when he wanted to or when he felt it was truly necessary. It reminded me of Kwai Chang Caine. Do you remember the television series Kung Fu, in which the Shaolin monk referred to David Carradine as Grasshopper?"

"Yes, I remember."

"The monk treated him like a child, which is how Tariq handled my questions and me. I learned to stop being my usual questioning self and instead became a good friend who listened. When I adopted that way of being, our get-togethers changed, and I learned more by not asking than by asking, if you see what I mean. On one of those occasions, he spoke about you, Carl." Rosa looked intently and smiled. "It seems he knew your distant grandparents – merchants in Valencia. Do you know if your father originated from there?"

"Yes, he and his family have always lived there. Unfortunately, I haven't researched our family tree, which is something I keep meaning to do. There again, now I am living in Spain and aware of Tariq's comments about my family. I must take it up, start enquiring, and see if I can unearth anything."

"That all ties in then," said Rosa. It appears that your family has a long history in Valencia, and everything Tariq said was indeed true. Well, I never."

"Did you ever see Tariq with other people, or did he have friends?" said Alicia.

"I don't believe so. I think he is quite picky and certainly doesn't tolerate fools easily. For example, one day, when we were outside the Finca chatting and enjoying the sun, I saw one of my friends walking up the lane. I waved to her. When I turned to say something to Tariq, he was gone."

"Wow. That sounds just like our experience," said Carl, pleased that someone else had witnessed the same weird disappearing act.

"I realised that Tariq did not like meeting people, so I asked him about that at a later time. His short reply was that some people were good and some were not so good." She smiled to herself. "That's a phrase I like to use... He said nothing else about the subject from that day on, and I understood that he was a very unusual character. However, I was still curious about the enigmatic Arab, so I watched and listened. Over the coming weeks, I came to believe he was not of this earth and concluded he was a wise old sage. And this is the one you will find hard to understand: that he was a four-hundred-year-old, wise sage."

"But...?" said Alicia, even more confused and searching for clarity on the subject.

"I know," said Rosa, looking at Carl and Alicia, sympathising with the lack of clarity, not knowing or not having a complete answer to Tariq's presence.

From a young age, Alicia had always asked many questions, sometimes frustrating her parents. However, at present, she was utterly exasperated with Nana's answers and felt thwarted to the point of feeling mildly disgruntled. The desire to know ran through her entire DNA and could not be switched off. Although it was true to say she had tried hard in the past to temper her compulsion to know. Perhaps her questioning mind had made her the clever and intelligent person everyone knew and loved. But she found it so frustrating when the answers fell short of her high standards.

"Well, then," she said, moving on from the imagined brick wall she had just encountered. "Do you have an explanation for Tariq's disappearance from time to time? I mean, what is that all about?"

"Well, I don't know about you," said Elena, speaking openly, "but I need a coffee and a chance to think about what we've all just heard. If that fits in with everybody else here." Her utterance at such a prominent stage in the proceedings was said in such a direct manner that it was not meant to be challenged. The intervention was an attempt to bring the conversation to a close and move on to more convivial topics – topics she understood and preferred, and not mumbo jumbo.

In practice, Theo had seen many such interventions used in group situations before, usually to disrupt proceedings or, as in this case, to bring a conversation to a halt.

In many ways, discussing witches and the supernatural had unsettled Elena, and it showed in her awkward attempt to wrap up the discussion.

No more was said about the numinous Tariq except that they agreed to meet after the retirement celebration and talk some more about spooks, witches, and things that went bump in the night. That was if Elena did not spoil the intended cosy chat.

TWENTY-TWO

A grand ceremony, marked by a mix of joy and sadness, celebrated the retirement of Señor Romero. For the following days and weeks, he found it most strange not to get up early in the morning and prepare for work, which was not helped by inadvertently setting the alarm for six o'clock on many thoughtless evenings. Then, one day, it all fell into place. He told himself he was retired for good. Overcoming the strangeness of not having to work, he diverted his attention to meaningful pursuits and listed jobs that needed to be done around the home and in the extensive garden. However, he received daily calls from his former secretary and deputy mayor seeking advice or clarification on specific issues. Señor Romero did not mind; it made him feel important and needed in many ways. Even so, his wife gave him a look of disapproval each time he received a call; usually, he smiled at her and continued with what he believed to be the right course of action – helping his former staff. He knew it would eventually tail off, and it did.

Meanwhile, Elena's dissatisfaction with her mum, who declared herself to be a white witch, was discussed in private with her husband. Surprisingly, he was pretty matter-of-fact about the revelation and encouraged his wife to accept her declaration and move on. His final words were that she was still her mother, no matter what was said in discussions, good or bad.

The day after the retirement celebrations, Carl, Alicia, Theo, and Rosa met mid-morning in the living room's comfortable surroundings in the grand home. Elena was absent for obvious reasons, leaving the way clear for an unfettered conversation, which carried on where they had left off, discussing things that go bump in the night. In the meantime, since he knew very little about the subject, Theo had searched the web for more information about modern-day witchcraft. He had interesting information to share with Carl and Alicia, adding more intrigue to Rosa and the whole discussion of pagan witchcraft throughout the ages.

"Have you recovered from drinking too much alcohol last night, Nana?" said Alicia, trying to gauge how she seemed and wondering if she felt up to chatting and resuming their discussion from two days prior.

"I'm feeling fine, Alicia. Thank you for asking. However, to be safe, I took some of my herbs last night to give me a good night's sleep."

Rosa smiled an all-knowing smile. "Shall we continue with our chat, then?"

"Yes, please," said Carl, keen to learn more about Caballo Verde's mysteries but also wanting to ask many probing questions. However, Alicia was slightly reticent, obviously concerned about something.

"We've talked much about the Finca, Caballo Verde, and Murla. I wonder if you've ever experienced any odd happenings in and around the Finca? But also, do you know why these strange things should be happening at all?"

"I will try to answer your questions by giving you my experiences living in Murla. No, I have never been aware of any strange things happening to me, possibly because Tariq and I were friends, and he was a strong force, or should I say a strong power, in the locality. That in itself would have kept any intended odd happenings under control. I'm beginning to believe we may have kept evil at bay because of what we did and how we were; that is a force to be reckoned with."

"Evil, what do you mean by evil?" said Alicia.

"Well, it's a difficult one to quantify, but first of all, before we proceed any further, you must understand that had I believed strange things would start happening to you when you moved into the lovely Finca, I would never have put you in such a difficult position. Nevertheless, it seems that when I moved here to Pamplona, malevolence became active on Caballo Verde, maybe even in Murla and the surrounding area."

"Malevolence?" said Alicia enquiringly.

Rosa explained the appalling savagery that took place hundreds of years ago with the mass killing of Muslims trying to escape the Spanish army's persecution. Over the years, Rosa became aware of the occasional white orbs on the mountain at night, believing they were merely the spirits of the dead. However, she did not find them threatening in any way, quite the opposite. Having spoken to Tariq, he confirmed just that. Although not asking him, Rosa felt sure he was in contact with or could relate to the orbs. In the following weeks, and at Tariq's request, they met on warm evenings outside and used their unique powers and life experiences to guide souls onto another realm. In essence, Rosa was discussing the concept of the afterlife in Christianity. Equally, in the Muslim faith, there was an acknowledgement of life after death (Akhirah).

"Hold on. Are you saying you did spiritual work to help earthbound souls move on?" said Alicia, quite agog and incredibly surprised.

"Yes, with the help of Tariq, I watched, listened, and learned. Together, we helped many souls seeking a connection with the afterlife. In a sense, they were trapped on the mountain, like lost souls searching in vain but unable to fulfil their ultimate goal of joining their loved ones. What we did was very satisfying, working in such a unique, yet practical way of helping them find eternal peace instead of wandering around aimlessly for an eternity."

Theo was curious and posed a question. "Can I ask you about these earthbound spirits, Rosa?"

"Of course."

"Are they the white orb types that I've seen on psychic programmes, usually floating around graveyards and maybe, occasionally, an orb or two in someone's house or cellar?"

"Yes, virtually that. Except they are normally white, but they can also be silver, depending on circumstances. But that is only part of the story. What I have to tell you next is the big showstopper." She looked around and could see she had their attention. "I just mentioned evil and malevolence promoted by the jinn, which is plural for the evil spirits. In this situation, the jinni is just one spirit that can be a formidable presence, capable of assuming human or animal form, according to Tariq. I believe this jinni is responsible for all the problems on and around Caballo Verde."

"I'm troubled, Nana," said Alicia, rubbing the back of her neck and glancing at others to see their reactions.

"Why is that?" said Rosa, surprised and uncertain by her statement.

"I wanted to question this last time when you said you were a white witch. But I held back because you were upset, and then Mum brought our meeting to a close in her unique way. In truth, I thought I knew you; now it appears I only knew part of you, and the rest was a big secret."

Rosa answered in a calm, unruffled manner as only she could. "I understand what you are saying, Alicia, but in all honesty, you've never lived with me or got to know me in depth. You holidayed with me and occasionally saw me in this beautiful house. You lived your life here in Pamplona, and this is where your world has been for most of your life."

As a psychologist, Theo was very attuned to what Rosa was saying. "She's right, Alicia. In my work, I have seen married couples who have lived together for many years, perhaps even all their lives, and still do not completely know each other's ways and temperament. We live in our inner worlds at work, at play and with our families. In my opinion, you need to live with that person or persons – get to know them and their habits thoroughly, and ask many questions to become well-acquainted. Even then, you will only know what someone is willing to tell you. So, Rosa is correct in what she says. How could you have known everything about her when you only knew her, shall we say, in small doses?"

Rosa smiled with satisfaction at Theo's explanation.

However, there was something that she had kept very much to herself and would forever stay secret, taking it to the grave. Speaking with Tariq before she ever knew Carl, she recalled agreeing to cast a spell of attraction to bring Carl and Alicia together. Although the young couple never knew that she had intervened in their lives, the magic had enabled Alicia to find her soulmate, Carlos the Brave.

For hundreds of years, Tariq knew that his very good friend would one day return to the mountain, where they could be together again in one form or another.

From their first meeting in the bar in Pamplona, Carl and Alicia were besotted with each other. The spell of attraction was Rosa's joyous masterpiece and plan for their carefully coordinated destiny. Eventually, Carl would discover the answer to his conundrum – why had he fought alongside Tariq? If he were then, as now, a Catholic, why would he be on the side of Tariq, fighting his Spanish Catholic brethren?

TWENTY-THREE

On their journey back to Murla, Carl and Alicia had many opportunities to discuss their stay in Pamplona. The revelations that Rosa spoke about were mind-blowing and, to some extent, seemingly implausible. Yet, they knew Nana was sincere, trustworthy and never prone to exaggeration. She was a bona fide white witch with powers beyond their imagination or comprehension, and spoke with great authority on the subject of witchcraft, spells and magic. As a medium, Rosa helped earthbound souls trapped between worlds move on, find their loved ones, and ultimately find a place of rest.

Despite the explanation that she regretfully did not know or understand Nana completely, Alicia regretted questioning Rosa's sincerity, suggesting that she was secretive about her white witch credentials.

During her childhood, Alicia spent holidays at her grandparents' home. She had perceived them as ordinary folk living a plain and simple life. In her mind, there was nothing to suggest otherwise. What troubled Alicia was her long-held misconception about Nana, which had persisted for many years. The quiet, insignificant old lady was a modern-day, trendy, accomplished, yet fairly complicated person, unbeknown to Alicia. However, given time, she would come to understand and forgive. If indeed forgiveness was required.

As they turned off the coast road driving towards Jalon, their excitement and fondness for the area came to the fore. They wound their windows down and smelled the air; even *that* was special. Looking at each other, they smiled and said aloud in a sing-song voice, "We're ho–oome."

Carl likened their homecoming to being away for a long time, looking forward to returning home and knowing all was well within their happy, protective bubble. However, there was just a tinge of uncertainty, maybe even foreboding, in his mind, enough to warrant a comment: "I wonder what we'll find when we arrive home?"

"Yes, I wonder."

Like Alicia, he was grateful to have two good friends – Tariq and Father Bernardo, and to have kindly neighbours living nearby. They had found a unique and outstanding part of Spain and were thankful to be living in Murla.

Driving through Jalon re-ignited their joy for the valley and its unique locality. It was their newly discovered homeland, and they felt a sense of pleasure and glee wash over them. The atmosphere was intoxicating.

After unpacking, Carl rang their close friends to arrange for the collection of Ralph, who had been in their care. However, the news was not good. Last night, they had let Ralph out, as usual, to answer the call of nature without his return. After searching the countryside for an hour in the darkness, whistling, calling his name and shining their torches around. Ralph did not appear. They were consumed with worry, feeling terrible about having to deliver the bad news to Carl and Alicia. Although Ralph had never run away before, Carl and Alicia felt hopeful for his return.

Nevertheless, with the passage of a few days and no news of the dog, although not saying so, both began to fear the worst. Either Ralph had been taken, which seemed unlikely given that he disappeared late at night, or he had had an accident and was lying somewhere unconscious and unable to move, which was even more troubling. What they had not considered was that wolves might have attacked Ralph. The uncertainty of it all disturbed their sleep and daily life. Jeff and Lynn did their best to reassure their friends. But, of course, they felt terrible knowing Ralph had gone missing whilst in their care. They had offered to buy another puppy, which was rejected outright.

The following day, while walking, Carl and Alicia came upon Tariq near the mountain. They stopped and spoke about their trip to Pamplona and the loss of their dog. That said, Tariq already knew about the missing dog when he heard their friends calling for Ralph the night he disappeared. There was no news of Ralph's whereabouts, but Tariq assured them he would keep his eyes and ears open. Of course, Tariq knew all that happened in and around the locality as he frequented both familiar and unfamiliar areas around the mountain. He was a very special, all-seeing, all-hearing presence with vast knowledge. If anybody could help them, it was Tariq.

That night, the white orbs seemed particularly active and in greater numbers than usual. The view from the Finca exhibited orbs hovering at a distance, moving about the mountain and, at times, gathering in clusters. It was akin to a light show silhouetted against the backdrop of Caballo Verde. Fascinating and wondrous in many ways, yet ominous, as if heralding something was about to happen, the orbs continued to circulate of their own free will. They recalled that Nana had spoken of them as the souls of people who had departed this world, and, as such, souls bound for the light. She sounded optimistic about the orbs in many ways, even discussing how Tariq and she had helped the spirits move on to another dimension. In itself, Alicia found the act of assisting the energies to crossover completely mind-blowing and unimaginable. Yet, her Nana Rosa had assured everybody at the get-together in Pamplona that this was what she and Tariq regularly accomplished.

The display of orbs moving and flowing was so spectacular that Carl suggested they both walk out onto the driveway, take in the evening air, and look more clearly at the mountain's wondrous sights. Although slightly hesitant, Alicia agreed after choosing a jacket to protect her from the evening chill. They locked the front door behind them for safety and strolled onto the front porch. Hand-in-hand, they took in the delights of the clear night sky unpolluted by neon lighting. The wondrous starry sky glittered like twinkling Christmas lights.

"Let's walk to the lane and see if we can see any orbs close-up," suggested Carl. He kissed Alicia as a gesture of love and reassurance that all was well. Walking to the property's entrance, which opened onto the lane, they stood hand in hand, breathing in the clear, intoxicating evening air.

"You make me so happy, Carl; I can't believe we are here together. When I was a little girl on holiday, staying with my grandparents, I never imagined I would one day live here with the love of my life. Even now, I find it so incredible." She kissed and hugged him and looked heavenward. A shooting star zipped across the night sky like a rocket firework.

"You are out late," came a familiar voice nearby. Tariq appeared from behind some shrubs in the lane. "This is my favourite time of the day," he said. "It seems you enjoy it also."

"Hello, Tariq. Yes, we were taking in the beautiful evening air." He smiled and looked at his friend, feeling a strong attraction as if he were his long-lost brother.

"We used to do this many years ago," said his good friend.

Although unseen, Carl's brow furrowed.

"We would walk away from the campfires and the Muslim troops, find a quiet spot, sit and talk for hours. Such was the joy and peace of the country and our great friendship. We would look at the glittering stars and constellations on the beautiful, warm summer evenings, such as Ursa Major, Cygnus, and others. All around us, we heard the cicadas and wolves howling in the distance. It was magical and yet challenging to believe that the enemy was camped just outside Gandia on the coast north of Denia, some twenty miles away. I recall many nights in that mortal world, yet the night before, the great battle was most significant. We accepted that we would have to fight the Spanish troops the following day, yet we showed little concern. We didn't know then, but that was our last night together all those many years ago.

"You mean what you're saying, don't you, Tariq?" said Carl, detecting sincerity and recall in his emotional voice.

"Yes, of course," he said, surprised at Carl's statement. "But, if I had to spend my last night on Earth with someone, then I would want to spend it with you, my friend." Carl felt incredibly emotional. He had just heard words so fervent that they tugged at his heartstrings – his emotions were on edge.

"As we sat, you talked about your parents, Carlos and the fact that they had suffered at the hands of the Spanish and how the family home was ransacked just because you worked for my father, Aali Wasim. Life was so unfair and so brutal then."

Alicia asked a question. "What do you mean, your last night, Tariq?"

He studiously ignored her question, caught up in profound feelings, and did not want to divulge the sickening truth of their final days. Yet he greatly respected Alicia and did not want to ignore her.

"Maybe I can tell you again sometime, señora." He nodded with reverence.

"We sat and chatted, drank wine, and ate bread. You looked at the stars and pointed out the constellation of Pegasus, a winged horse. It all seemed so long ago, and yet it seemed like yesterday. At that time, we looked at life and enjoyed the..."

Tariq stopped suddenly and put his hand up, halting the conversation. Like a cat, he moved his head from side to side, listening, and sensed something out there. He put a finger to his lips for silence. Worryingly, he slid his knife out of its sheath and gestured, pointing towards the Finca. Both followed him closely. Glancing back, Tariq could see his friends were close behind. Within seconds, they arrived at the front door. He gestured to them inside the home and whispered.

"Lock your doors and windows." He slipped off into the night full of mystery and secrecy.

Carl checked the doors and windows and made a mental note to discuss the bizarre goings-on with their friends tomorrow. Given the strange events of the previous night and Ralph's absence, it seemed prudent to be able to view and record on CCTV the exterior of their home twenty-four hours a day. It was an expense that would bring peace of mind and a positive way to record anything unusual or out of the ordinary.

A final glance through the living room window before retiring to bed showed nothing unusual. It was doubtful if either would sleep well that night. Still, they were safe and secure in their home and were grateful to Tariq for his protection and caring nature, which kept them safe from harm.

It was an awareness of the jinni that had alerted him – he instinctively knew of its presence in the darkness as he talked to his friends. What they had not seen was Tariq pursuing his nemesis further up the mountain. Although unable to confront the conniving, dangerous spirit, Tariq employed the best tactic in his mindful arsenal – to be proactive and chase the menacing spirit, not allowing it to settle or become comfortable in its surroundings. This policy worked; nevertheless, he was clever enough to know that one day the spirit capable of appearing in animal or human form would be emboldened enough to attempt something more audacious, cunning, and downright evil. Such was the nature of the jinni.

TWENTY-FOUR

Christmas was just weeks away, diverting attention away from the loss of Ralph and giving the loving couple something positive to focus on – the Yuletide season. Despite an invitation from her parents to stay in Pamplona for the festive season and New Year, Carl and Alicia declined the offer. They decided to spend Christmas together in their own home, which was no surprise to her parents. They would have done the same thing if the situation were reversed. Besides, Alicia still had to work in the local accident and emergency department, although she hoped to have Christmas Day off to celebrate with Carl and their good friends.

Although full of mystery and intrigue, their brief meeting with Tariq the other night was, in fact, a non-event. Carl and Alicia met up with their friend on a subsequent evening walk, enquiring about the threatening situation, when Tariq quickly moved them back to their Finca for safety. When asked about the problem, he replied that the evil had been nearby, but it was nothing to worry about; he had chased it away. His deliberation was brief but did nothing to reassure or dismiss their concerns, which was typical of Tariq: very little feedback or comment on the question.

Jeff and Carl chose a Sunday to fit the four CCTV cameras around the home while Alicia and Lynn baked pastries. It was a collaborative effort, with ideas pooled. Lynn showed Alicia how to bake scones and shortbreads whilst Alicia made traditional empanadillas – pastries with various fillings. The concept of different fillings gave Lynn an idea. She considered making them and selling them fresh at their weekly market stall. On a cold winter's morning, attracting customers to make money was difficult. But then again, who wouldn't want a hot drink and an empanadilla with a tuna and tomato filling, or even sweet fillings such as Raisin and Apple or Banana?

Fitting the cameras outside was a simple affair. They decided to position them to capture busy areas around the home, such as the driveway, the back of the home, and the side aspects of the Finca – then wire them back to Carl's study.

"Why did *you* install cameras around your home in the first place?" said Carl, chatting with his friend. He hoped his idea wasn't too out of the ordinary, involving the installation of cameras on a village home, knowing it would generate a lot of talk amongst the locals.

"Oh, nothing sinister. I just wanted to be seen as having cameras and displaying stickers on our windows, roadside, saying '**CCTV Cameras Fitted**'. It just lets any would-be thief know that we are watching. We thought it was a necessary evil because we are out most of the day. I suppose you could say it was using a bit of psychology. It also pleases the insurance company."

"Talking like that, you would get on well with my friend, Theo. He's a psychologist working in the UK and a good guy. I sometimes wonder what I would do without him; he's an absolute rock." Carl smiled at the thought of his close friend. "I'd love you to meet him one day."

Jeff continued clipping cables to the wooden section under the roof tiles, standing on a stepladder as he talked. "Yeah, next time he's here, I'd be happy for us to meet up . . . When I've clipped the cable to the fascia board and down the wall, do you want to connect the end to the camera, Carl?"

He was no electrician, but easily read the instructions in Spanish and found it very simple to complete.

Two hours later, the cameras were in place and connected to the digital video recorder. Jeff showed Carl how to operate the cameras and recorder, and how to record unique or unusual events onto a memory stick, pointing out further aspects of interest.

"So, what are you hoping to record, Carl?" He wondered if the cameras were purely to protect against criminal activity or maybe to capture something spiritual.

"Difficult to say, Jeff, but a good example was one night when I thought I saw a moving light outside the living room window."

"What a torchlight?"

"No, not a torchlight." He took a moment to

compose his response. "I know this is going to sound weird, but I want to capture light orbs, the sort we've seen floating around, sometimes near the Finca." He made light of his response to installing the security system for fear of sounding paranoid or worse – an absolute nutter.

"I see. So you want to determine what is floating around your pad and confirm you aren't going mad?" Jeff gave a wry smile and patted his good friend on the back. "Don't worry, mate; I know you're not going mad; at least, that's what Lynn told me to tell you." His big, cheesy grin brought a sense of fun to the moment, breaking Carl's serious mood and mild obsession with the odd and intrusive phenomenon about his home. Moreover, the intended fun helped him ease back to his more light-hearted way of being.

Carl had been aware for a while that he had lost the fun-loving aspect of his character and hoped it did not affect their close relationship. His inner caution made him determined to stop obsessing about orbs, the mountain, and his phantasmagorical visions of past events. Theo, his friend, thought he was letting the strange events on the mountain dominate his mind too much. He believed Carl should focus more on the realities of life, on what he and Alicia had together, and not let pessimism control his thoughts. Of course, Theo was right; Carl was paying too much attention and too much time focusing on the dark side of strange local events, but it was difficult to dismiss when that little thing inside his mind kept switching on, shouting 'alert, alert.'

He recalled one of Theo's accounts of a female patient who became obsessed with everything in life, exhibiting many strange thoughts and creating embarrassing situations. Her hyperactivity impinged on many aspects of their personal life, including an extravagance on frivolous purchases and forming friendships with strangers. Her husband and close friends began to back off after initially showing great care, patience, and fortitude, which lasted many weeks during the course of her illness. In reality, the whole saga was becoming too much for them to handle in the long term. Her husband, who loved his wife dearly, was finding it increasingly challenging to be his usual patient and loving self with the person he had lived with for twenty-four years. Consequently, the relationship soured, and they eventually separated and divorced.

Recalling the story Theo had described to him was a timely reminder. Although the phrase, 'Love hath no bounds,' was correct in general, it certainly was not in that case.

Carl began to fear that Alicia might find his general demeanour odd and start to look at him differently. If anything, he was intensely preoccupied with losing her, which seemed strange for someone who was normally confident and in control. He began to see that his assessment of their relationship was a little skewed. Losing that spark in their life was unthinkable... God, how he loved her.

Sleepless nights occurred due to his ruminative mind, leaving him feeling tired and irritable. He could not, and would not, ignore what could potentially damage their unique, loving relationship. Although he believed their marriage was secure and that they loved each other dearly, Carl did not want to risk endangering the relationship by worrying excessively and influencing the status quo. He knew it was all too easy to take things for granted, take his eye off the ball, then wake up one day to realise there were problems. A compulsion to act and prioritise, love, fun and consideration in their relationship was fundamental and would happen as far as he was concerned.

His friend's advice made sense, prompting him to reconsider his life. Carl had a beautiful wife, a lovely home, good friends and excellent health. What more could he want?

TWENTY-FIVE

D
ue to work commitments, the priest was unable to attend the planned walk with Carl and Alicia. However, they promised to meet later, after the walk, to have coffee and discuss their trek up the mountain (Caballo Verde).

As soon as breakfast was over and Alicia had washed the dishes and tidied around, they both prepared for the morning's hike, mindful of the cold morning. The plan was to leave as soon as possible and make the most of the ten hours of daylight on a typical November day. The morning proved mildly inclement, with low-lying mist as they set off. It seemed strange not to have Father Bernardo's company; he was always so jolly and such good fun. Inwardly, they believed the father was eager to become fitter and inevitably lose weight, which was why he accompanied them, but they never discussed personal issues. Carl took photos or videos of anything unusual or interesting on his mobile phone for later discussion and to share their adventure.

When they arrived at the circle of logs, slightly quicker than they had traversed the mountain previously, everything seemed as they remembered it in the rest area. The surrounding hillside was cloaked in mist, temporarily reducing their view of villages in the area. Trees appeared cut off just below the branches, like skeletons reaching upwards out of the white vapour. The air was chilly as the mist swirled around, prompting them to zip up their jackets and pull their beanies down over their ears. However, nature's serenity was a treasure to behold, even in such wintry conditions.

Given the mildly unpleasant conditions, they decided to keep moving to get to the location of the devil's chair, hopefully by mid-morning, giving them plenty of opportunity to explore the area.

By the time they had reached the small clearing not far from the giant boulder, they were pleased to sit down, rest, relax, and have a snack to keep their energy levels up. The morning sun peeked out from the clouds, burning away the mist in the lower valley and on the hillsides, creating a clearer outlook and a slightly warmer atmosphere. Alicia produced some Turron (traditional Spanish dessert) and coffee from a small flask. The snack went down a treat and enlivened them after the challenging climb to the Devil's Chair. Carl took out his mobile and videoed the scene around him, not forgetting Alicia's smile from under her beanie. They chatted and recalled their first visit to the area when Carl misplaced his persimmon fruit – or had it been taken? There was no explanation for the disappearance, so Carl and Alicia put it down to the mountain's strangeness, forgot all about it, and moved on. Finishing their snacks and about to get up and investigate their surroundings, they heard movement from behind some shrubs and rocks. Their friend Tariq stepped forward, his face welcoming. It wasn't a smile; Tariq rarely smiled, but a look of appreciation at being in the company of two lovely people.

"Hello, Tariq." They stood, returning the look of surprise and happiness at being in his company. "We haven't seen you for a while. Are you well?"

"I am." He looked around. "The priest, not with you today?"

"Unfortunately, not; he is too busy with work for the church. We wanted to explore more of the mountain and look at this fascinating area." he looked around, his eyes fixed on the giant boulder. "We haven't stopped talking about it since our last visit." He pointed upwards to the location of the Devil's Chair. "I would have to say, though, listening to people locally, they have some pretty strange perceptions about the mountain, particularly the chair. It is steeped in so much mystery."

"It is, and if you have time, I would like to explain how it all came about," said Tariq.

They looked on in surprise, given that he was about to disclose some history from hundreds of years ago, yet to Tariq it all seemed like yesterday. They sat and waited for his moment of enlightenment, which was slow to come. Even on a chilly November morning, he seemed unfazed by the cold conditions. He paced about in his usual attire, stopped, and stood looking pensive as if troubled by something.

"Can I offer you a drink or something to eat, Tariq?" said Alicia, asking more to break the strange moment, yet not expecting him to accept any sustenance.

"Thank you, but I am good, señora ... So you think this area is mysterious."

"Yes – maybe there is a better word than mysterious, but it is the best I can come up with right now. Of course, I don't want to belittle what happened here all those years ago. It was a serious time that only you know about and can recall. Apart from having an incredible view of the surrounding valleys, we found the area memorable but strangely troubling. Alicia thought that the boulder over there, for some reason, had been rolled into place to block something off."

"She is correct. The Spanish troops moved the boulder into place four hundred and eleven years ago, and you are correct to say the area is troubled."

"Just give me a moment, Tariq." Walking over to the boulder, Carl placed his fingertips lightly on its surface and concentrated. It did not take too long for him to sense the boulder's deeply disturbing past and why it was rolled into place. Although not speaking Arabic, he uttered something in the tongue as if remonstrating or commenting on something sinister.

Nevertheless, Tariq understood what he was saying. Tears streamed down Carl's face. He trembled violently, shouting out in Arabic. Letting go of the rock, he buried his head in his hands. Alicia ran over to put an arm around him.

"You are seeing it, aren't you?" observed Tariq. "The cruel, evil behaviour by the soldiers on the innocent – my people."

Carl looked at him with concern. Left unsaid, they both knew they were privy to the horrors of ethnic cleansing and wanton cruelty on a grand scale.

"Come and sit, and I will tell you what I witnessed hundreds of years ago; it will help you understand the enormity of such inhumanity."

With a heavy heart, Tariq revealed that when the people had escaped the marauding troops, lower down the blood-soaked hillside, civilians fled for their lives whilst the Spanish troops were kept busy defending themselves from the initial thrust of the Moorish forces on foot and horseback. With love and self-sacrifice, the soldiers were giving up their lives for the sake of their Muslim kinfolk. The civilians were desperate, wanting to distance themselves from the Spanish or die atrociously. Their only hope of escape was to climb high up the mountain as quickly as possible, thus giving security and protection for the remaining eighty-five men, women, and children. Some of the escaping Moors were injured, some near death, yet all severely traumatised. However, the King's troops swore to finish the job – to eradicate the remaining Moors in one final massacre.

Tariq pointed to the area where they stood. "This is where the final horror played out. Over eighty men, women, and children, dying, injured, hungry, and thirsty – all wanting to end the nightmare, but the troops were right behind them and ready to take their lives without a second thought."

Carl picked up a small rock from the ground and held it with his fingertips. It did not take long before the sensations registered in his mind. He sensed an individual's terror – their desperation and fear. In his mind's eye, he witnessed women and children screaming, crying, hysterical with fear. Some were injured, but mostly, everyone desperately feared for their lives. They were traumatised – about to be slain in cold blood, and no amount of comfort helped to dissipate their fear. Men who had tried to protect their escaping families had sustained slashes to their bodies, open wounds from stabbings, and even broken bones, ending any hope of escape from the fray.

Envisioning their final demise as marauding soldiers with blood on their faces and hands and wearing blood-soaked tunics and weapons, the panic-stricken clambered the final leg of the mountain. Spanish troops would be upon their luckless foe in ten to fifteen minutes, ready to kill.

Yet, having reached the mountain's uppermost part, the large group of homeless Moors came to a dead end. They were within a large, flattened, rocky scrub area with nowhere else to go. Very soon, they would be found and slain. However, some of the desperate civilians had not entirely given up hope. Men frantically searched for a solution, knowing they had little time left. A cave entrance, partially obscured by rocks and shrubs, stood on one side of the flattened rocky area. Inside was a rough, uneven area the size of an average room with an irregular, jagged roof. As quickly as they could, the two men approached some of the elders and explained what they believed to be their only hope for salvation.

They suggested hiding in the cave, out of sight of the soldiers. Despite their desperate plea, no one seemed to be listening amid the pandemonium; sheer panic had taken hold. Aided by those who had found the shelter, the elders held children's hands and led some of the terrified towards the cavern's entrance. Witnessing a few making their way to the concealed area, others followed. There was just enough light to see inside, but not enough to light their way through and beyond into the dark unknown. However, to be slaughtered by the soldiers or make their way into the dark cave with other possible dangers needed no consideration. Mustafa, one of the elders, took charge of organising the group. He was sure, listening to the sounds of the troops nearby yelling, banging swords and axes on their shields, creating terror in the minds of the Moors, that they only had minutes before being overrun by the manic troops. The group assembled just inside the cave entrance, which gave no protection from their adversaries. Mustafa, intent on finding a way forward, pushed through the people milling around. He could not see the interior, particularly well in the fading light; all he could do was feel around the craggy rock face inside the cave. More help was needed. He organised men to stand side-by-side and run their hands over the rocky wall – finally, a breakthrough. Although not apparent, one of the men followed his hands around a column-like shape and realised he could no longer see the fading light from the cave entrance. He called for some of the families to walk towards his voice. As they arrived, he urged them to touch the wall and move to the right, taking them around to the hidden space. More families entered the cavern and felt their way past the helpers to the back of the cave. Overcoming fear of the unknown became fundamental in moving many people into the cave. However, the inability to see ahead in the dark created significant difficulties and anxiety. It required understanding and gentle persuasion to aid terrified families and their loved ones as they ventured into the unknown. In what seemed an eternity to Mustafa, mere minutes passed; families made their way into the cave and beyond.

Worryingly, the troops' nearby noise continued to cause panic. Sounds of crying and calls of desperation thronged the air. The cave's entrance seemed to be acting as an amplifier, magnifying the sound of the Moorish people.

The sanctuary in the cave appeared to be a clever move; still, the sounds of the troops nearby and the knowledge of their cruel ferocity from earlier on the battlefield created a grand-scale hysteria. They could not escape. They were trapped and at the mercy of the devil and his cohorts. The soldiers would show no mercy, and desperate families knew that to be the case. Shaking, feeling sick, crying, and retching with fear became prevalent among the remaining civilians in the darkened cave. An elderly lady collapsed to the ground, causing further panic as people tripped over her.

Trying to overcome the dread, Mustafa sounded hopeful. "We think the cave is like a J-shape," he said as quietly as possible but loud enough to make himself heard. "And I believe we are on the curve of the J. Some men have walked further around the curve and found more space. Please walk on and keep your hands in front of and above your head to avoid injury. If we can move further, we can escape the troops. They won't want to follow us here; they are too cowardly." His words of encouragement had just offered hope; his words of derision called out the soldiers to be what they were – cowards. Distancing themselves from the soldiers would encourage optimism, maybe even relief and assurance, but that would take time.

"If we can move into the cave, it will protect us from the troops. Be courageous, my people; remain calm and move forward. I know it is dark, damp, and smelly, but this is our only hope to save ourselves. Think of your loved ones who have died so that you may live and survive."

Although not apparent at the time, the sound of water dripping somewhere in the dark distance was a good sign. At least the families would not go thirsty.

He asked for quiet again, but people began talking among themselves, increasing the risk of being overheard by the soldiers.

"We must be silent," he said again in a slightly elevated whisper. "I know you are worried and frightened, but if you need to say anything, talk in a whisper into people's ears, not aloud. When the troops arrive, they might not know we are here if we remain silent."

His positive message of hope was ill-founded. Having been pulled, broken and twisted – shrubs at the cave entrance indicated recent rough treatment. Disturbed ground and evidence of blood from wounds suggested to the troops that their quarry was inside the chamber.

"Meanwhile," said Mustafa, repeating his positive message of hope. "We'll see if we can continue further into the cave. Nobody knows how it will go, but we must try; Allah will guide and keep us safe."

At that point, shouting, banging, and a general hubbub occurred at the cave entrance. The soldiers had arrived. Mustafa peeped at the entrance to the cave from behind the J section that he had indicated to the civilians. The troops entered the cave swinging their swords, shouting profanities and assurances of death to the Moors.

A sense of foreboding filled the blackness for them all. Behind were the Spanish troops, and ahead of them, the unknown. Fear, panic, and dread rose again at the sound of the soldiers. The smell from bat droppings was atrocious, attracting insects and vermin that scurried around underfoot. The plea for silence was challenging, to say the least, particularly for children already traumatised, unable to understand why anybody would want to kill them, their parents or anybody. However, the troops could hear the panic and revelled in their cruel, fear-mongering, rabid behaviour.

For those inside the cave who had progressed further down passages, touching the cave wall or rocks around them instilled trepidation, yet it had to be done. It was highly probable they would place their hands in bat guano, but it did not matter; they were alive and kept putting distance between themselves and the troops.

Sometimes, small, cavernous areas with little headroom proved hazardous, requiring caution; other times, ample headroom was available. Yet, all gave way to more irregular passageways, right, left or deeper into the morass. Millions of years of rainfall had carved channels into the mountain.

Although he did not share his feelings, Mustafa feared that humans or animals in the past might have entered the underground chambers, just as they had. Unable to find their way out, they may have died of starvation, leaving their skeletons behind. Such gruesome remains would have a devastating effect on morale.

Another apparent fear for Mustafa was that wolves could inhabit the caves. Equally concerning was the sound of dripping water, which raised the possibility of underground lakes or water-filled potholes that could be very hazardous in the dark cave. Fumbling around, it felt like a death trap–a threat to life and limb, but there was no other choice. A more significant potential problem was the fear of the unknown.

Eventually, a feeling of having gone far enough prevailed. Stopping to sit it out was the only option for the Moors caught up in the horrendous nightmare of existence.

"It was pitch black, damp and fetid," said Tariq. His head hung in torment, heart aching, reliving the desperate plight of his dead and dying people in the cave. Of course, at that point, he was already dead and in spirit form when his compatriots were traversing the cave's passageways. He remembered being speared to death by the pike of a Spanish soldier.

Nevertheless, he observed the carnage first-hand as he floated around. Hundreds of dead souls had done precisely the same as Tariq. Yet, as souls of the afterlife, they could not understand what had happened to them and so lingered, unsure of what to do next.

However, Tariq's soul was different. He established in his mind exactly what had happened to his fellow people and tried his utmost to help rebuild their sorry existence.

TWENTY-SIX

The Year 1609.

Following the Moorish Knight's daring confrontation and subsequent battle, coupled with exhaustion of the Spanish troops who had travelled hundreds of miles and fought for the past year, it was decided by General Arroyo that the main body of soldiers would camp at the base of Caballo Verde.

The opening near the cave entrance was filled with soldiers ready to kill on sight; such was their bloodlust. However, the killing did not play out as was thought. Following a quick inspection of the area and understanding that the Moors could not have gone anywhere else but inside the cave, it was evident that this was where they were. They had made their way into the cave's depths to hide away.

Under instructions from the highest-ranking soldier present, ten Spanish troops would remain to guard the cave entrance overnight and be in readiness to repel any Moors trying to escape the deadly tomb. The rest of the soldiers descended the mountain back to the encampment. In the fading light, they reported to the general that the remaining Moors had sought escape in a cave at the top of the mountain and that a guard had been left to ensure no one could escape. Food and items for those guarding the cave would be sent back up the mountain to the soldiers.

Flickering campfires lit up the surrounding hillside, providing warmth and a focal point for gathering. Supportive of the troops, locals visited the encampment carrying bread, meat, fruit, and wine. The food and drink, although insufficient, pleased the general and the upper echelon of soldiers. The generosity of the pleasures of homelife was heartwarming, and there was more to come once the final phase had been achieved, killing all the Moors.

In amongst the camp, the remainder of the foot troops received only bread after the lion's share of food had been eaten; they were expected to scavenge for scraps, drink water from wells, and do their best. Such was the way of life in the Spanish army in 1609, when the supply chain was stretched, and hunger, illness, and disease were rife amongst fighting troops. Still, they were paid for their discomfort and pain in battle, which was good compared with some Spaniards, who could be starving to death with little or no prospect of change in their immediate circumstances. Life was cheap, and the soldiers knew it.

Travelling back to their respective homes in the coming days, albeit taking weeks to do so, they would find more food en route, with many well-intentioned Spaniards greeting the troops with food and wine. The grape crop had been good that year, and wine was plentiful.

The following morning brought a damp, cold day. The army general and his troops were eager to proceed and bring the demise of the remaining Moors to a conclusion. With a sinister plan, the general sent twenty men with tools, heavy-duty ropes, and long wooden props back up the mountain to complete the job. Then the army could return to their homelands once the Moors had been left for dead.

Meanwhile, the camp was dismantled; tents and paraphernalia were packed away on carts, horses were taken care of in final preparation, and an ultimate meeting over wine with his officers would conclude the plans for the campaign, culminating in the successful rout of all those remaining in the cave at the peak of Caballo Verde. As soon as the last handful of men had rejoined the troops, they would travel back up the coast, taking many days to return to their homes in and around Valencia. Overall, it had been an excellent success for the general and, ultimately, King Phillip III.

With lengths of sturdy wood acting as pivots, with brute force and ropes to pull, the chiselled boulder was rolled into place wholly and securely, blocking the cave entrance. Job done, the troops congratulated themselves and eagerly left the area, their minds focused on the war's completion and the prospect of life back home. They were thankful to have survived the severe conditions and hand-to-hand combat so many times, particularly on Caballo Verde's lower-level slope, where their metal was severely put to the test. Most of all, they were proud to have served the King and driven the Moors from Iberia, cleansing their land forever.

Without food but with plenty of water, the families

inside the cave managed to cope as best they could. Following twenty-four hours with no sound of activity from soldiers at the cave entrance, two men ventured back up the craggy passageway in complete darkness to the internal cave entrance to investigate. Chinks of sunlight glinted around the edge of the cavern's entrance. A huge boulder had been placed to block the only entry and exit.

Mustapha, the assumed leader, was worried when hearing about their inhumane plight. They had been interred. The reality was that they had to deal with it and look for a positive solution to free themselves from incarceration. Mustafa had the unenviable job of informing the rest of the families of their plight. However, the most important thing of all was to find food quickly. But how was that possible? Moving the sick and injured back up to the relatively flat area inside the cave's entrance, where it was dry, was well-received by the families. At least there, people could see daylight, albeit meagre, shining through around the edges of the massive boulder; they would be able to keep track of time, which would help their body clocks. However, finding a way out of their confinement was even more critical; otherwise, all feared a horrendous outcome. Time passed with no solution to their impending demise. The sick and injured became weak without food. A sense of hopelessness permeated the families, loved ones, and lone individuals alike. One male with horrific injuries died a terrible death due to infection of his wounds. Living in the countryside, they could have used their natural ability to use herbs in traditional methods of curing ailments to save the man from his fatal condition. However, that was not to be. Two more injured men and a pregnant female were desperately ill and needed sustenance and medical care. In desperation and feeling low, they began to question their faith. Surely Allah would come to their aid.

Mustapha was beginning to feel despondent; there was little hope of escape, although he kept his counsel on the matter. He cursed the troops and their evilness. Even so, his mind was preoccupied with taking care of the male who had tragically died from infection. So as not to cause distress to the others, his body was kept in another chamber. How could he prepare the body for a Muslim burial? Moreover, how could he avoid further deaths?

Without any family, one brave boy, Dekel, who lost his parents in Valencia, explored the cave's passageways. He continued searching even as others had given up all hope and accepted their demise. With no light around him, he memorised his surroundings, shape, and size by feeling as best he could. Perhaps his memory skill was tied to his father's banking business in Valencia, where memory was crucial for financial transactions and calculations. His positivity and motivation to find a way out stemmed from his desire to return to his homeland, where he was certain he would find his grandparents waiting for him. Even so, seeing his parents slaughtered at the hands of the Spanish troops in front of him was still profoundly troubling for him. He dealt with the mental anguish by pushing the horrific images to the back of his mind as if they had never happened.

Nevertheless, one day, he would have to deal with the trauma. He saw the present plight in the cave as temporary and would not give up until he returned home to his grandparents. If it were possible to find a way out of the cave, then he would. This was Dekel's way of giving back to the families that had been so kind and protective of him over the weeks he had been orphaned.

More probing, feeling his way around, and exploring new areas urged him on, compelling him to do even more probing. He had a fine mind, which proved beneficial whenever he noticed a difference in the cave's surface or shape; psychologically, it registered as a diagram in his mind. In a tactile sense, he mapped the inner space where families were imprisoned.

On one such quest, searching the darkness by some rocks stacked to the side of a passageway, he sensed a chilly breeze rushing past his face. At first, he did not think too much about it. He continued to move around, and yet again, for a second time, the same thing happened. The chill hit his face. Curiosity got the better of him. He turned his head from side to side and could feel the cold around him. One of the young adults listening to his movements had become interested in his strange behaviour.

"Dekel, what are you doing?"

"I'm looking for a way out of this wretched place, and I'm not giving up until I find one."

"From the sound of your voice, it seems you are

above me." He said, unable to see Dekel in the cave's darkness.

"I am. I found some rocks that I could easily climb. I'm just searching for a way out of this prison."

"There is no way out, Dekel. We are imprisoned – left to rot just as the Spanish intended it to be." He cursed the troops for their barbarity, which was unusual for him and his faith – a sign that desperation was foremost in his mind.

"You can lie down, die and rot if you want, but I'm not going to accept what they did to us. If I have to, I will die trying. There has to be a solution to our problem; I know it."

His courage and drive impressed another adult, Hassan, who chose to listen some more. As Dekel described his find, he felt the breeze again. Moving his hands around, he felt a void above his head. His hands moved upwards until he felt a flattened base. It seemed strange amongst all the rough cragginess of the internal rockwork to find a smooth, flattened rock above his head. Dekel exerted pressure here and there on the flat surface above him; without warning, the rocky plinth above moved ever so slightly.

Nevertheless, it was too heavy for him to deal with. Dekel came down from the rocky steps and explained what he had discovered. With care, Hassan enthusiastically climbed up the six-foot-high rocks and found the flat rock above his head, as described by Dekel. With much greater strength, he pushed the flat rock upwards and outwards. As he did so, light streamed down, bathing the cave below as if a switch had been flipped. Those present looked around in amazement, temporarily shielding their eyes. They could see the inner walls and floor of the passageway where they sat. Unknowingly, Dekel and Hassan had found an answer to their grave situation. There was a way out, and their lives had been saved.

Hassan had just moved the flat seat of the rock formation known locally as the Devil's Chair. Now, there was hope. Praise be to Allah, they intoned, feeling encouraged by the light and promise of a way out of their terrible dilemma.

TWENTY-SEVEN

Carl explained to Alicia, as best he could, what he had experienced when he touched the boulder. Along with Tariq's account, she began to understand the trauma and enormity of the historical Caballo Verde battle that had occurred hundreds of years ago in the area where they now lived.

"What I still don't understand is what happened to the Moors. And how and why was the boulder rolled into place?" she asked.

Tariq took up the conversation and explained that instead of pursuing the remaining Moors into the cave, the soldiers were troubled by the problem – a potential life-threatening attack awaiting them in the cave's darkness. For quickness, it was decided to use a nearby large boulder, chisel off its sharp edges, and roll it to the cave entrance to block any attempt by the Moors to escape. It was meant to be the cruel death knell of the poor unfortunates confined within. Their demise would be slow and agonising, or so the general believed. However, ingenuity and belief proved to be the saviour for the remaining persecuted Moors, who were presumed to be left for dead.

With trepidation, Hassan's head cautiously emerged from his confinement. If circumstances were not so severe, it would have been funny seeing his head emerge from the seat of the Devil's Chair. Although not sunny, the cave below was blanched in an agreeable light. For the first time, cave residents could see around the confines of rocky pathways, craggy walls, and undulating roof areas, with some small but prominent stalagmites and stalactites. Although by no means bright, Hassan shielded his eyes. Having lived the past days in complete darkness, the light took some getting used to. He estimated it to be mid-afternoon and noted the direction of the hazy sun. His tentative look around and careful listening confirmed that the soldiers had gone and the Moorish families were alone. However, that would need to be verified.

With careful planning undertaken by Mustafa and the elders, Dekel climbed up the rocky steps and peered out of the opening for a second time. The plan was to forage and find essential foods – anything that would make life more manageable for the families inside the cave. Because of the size constraint of the outlet forming the seat of the devil's chair, the gap, although not tiny, would only permit the shape of a small to a medium-sized person to squeeze through the aperture, and they had to be fit to contort around and through the only opening to the outer world. There were eight youths capable of squeezing through the seat's aperture. However, on the first occasion, it was decided to scour the land, so four youths were sent out in the relative safety of the fading light. The brief was to bring back any food they could find to help the families on the verge of starvation; secondly, anything to help them live more comfortably in their enforced incarceration would be welcomed.

Descending the hill, the youths, led by Dekel, searched outbuildings and orchards for food in the form of fruit, nuts, and vegetables. One particularly opportune find was locating a herd of goats. Having purloined containers from various outbuildings, the goats were milked, but only a small amount was collected. The milk would be watered down to give everyone meagre sustenance. Dekel was clever enough to ensure that the theft was spread widely throughout the herd, so as not to draw attention to a sudden loss of milk quota from the goats. The goat shepherds probably would not notice a discernible difference in the milk yield. If they did, it would be attributed to the goats being old, the time of year, or simply an off day. A small amount of fruit and vegetables taken from the cold store in an outhouse added to the prize.

Armed with their booty, the lads returned feeling elated and thankful for their evening's work foraging the land. The fruit, goat's milk, nuts, and a few vegetables they found were an excellent start to feeding those in need. The following night, the lads would have to spread their search wider to avoid drawing undue attention to the diminishing food supplies in the immediate locality. However, the provisions had to be rationed: Mustapha and other folks put together ideas for a more comfortable internment in the cave. For example, a fire could be lit at the base of the Devil's Chair inside the cave with kindling and thin branches.

With the plinth pulled back, it acted as a flue for the fire. Light streamed in when the rocky chair base was left open, adding to a general feeling of positivity. Fortuitously, nobody ventured high up Caballo Verde's mountain because of morbid belief and primitive superstitions, not to mention the deaths of eighty-plus Moors (they thought) entombed, dead, dying, and rotting in their catacomb.

Consequently, the Moors were free within reason to live life in the cave without discovery. Still, only dry wood could be burnt. If smoke were seen by locals emerging from the Devil's Chair, it would alert the community to their presence. To avoid any risks, one or two youths were assigned to keep a lookout as they backed up their plan to maintain secrecy.

Over the coming days, more items were collected from the land and brought back to the grateful families. Waiting for the boys to return was exciting, wondering what they would find on their nightly expeditions. One night, the collection included thin straight tree branches. Bound in six-foot-by-two-foot rectangular shapes, lashed with vines and propped up on rocks at each corner, the addition of short crosspieces fastened in place completed the structures as makeshift beds, elevating them off the cave's rocky, damp floor. Slowly, with innovative ideas, life became more tolerable. Yet, life remained hard in the cave they called home.

Mustapha was mindful of the dead man and made plans to bury him according to the Muslim religion. They moved the body out of the cave through the

Devil's Chair opening.

With a slim build and now even thinner due to a lack of food, Mustapha squeezed through the opening with incredible effort and determination, but not without some discomfort. He scraped his shoulders on the rocky opening. Yet, to him, this was a price worth paying for the satisfactory outcome of the burial. With the body wrapped around and tied, the rope supporting him around his body and under his arms was passed through the portal. The deceased was slowly pulled up, through, and out of the Devil's Chair opening.

With help from the younger lads, they found an area of bracken and soil amongst some rocks. They dug with their bare hands and pieces of a branch to create a burial site for the brave man who died defending families escaping from the violence. Unfortunately, he was seriously injured in the melee by Spanish troops and never recovered.

They buried him a hero in the clothes he died in, according to the Muslim religion. The shallow grave, nestled among rocks, seemed an ideal resting place for one of their departed heroes who had fought valiantly in the face of cruelty. With dignity, he was placed in the grave on his right-hand side, facing Mecca. Following the soil infill, they carefully placed rocks on the burial site to avoid drawing any unwanted attention to the area should anyone ever venture near the plateau within sight of the blocked cave entrance. A scattering of leaves and branches added to the gravesite ensured the land showed no sign of disturbance. The youngsters gathered around as Mustapha prayed. Graciously bowing their heads out of respect for one of their own. They left the area a little saddened but thankful for the honourable burial of the brave soul.

However, poor Mustapha dearly paid for his sense of responsibility and kindness. Moving back down the secret cave entrance was the reverse of getting out. However, this time, he took more care protecting his shoulders from the rocky protrusions as he re-entered the cave.

Thanks to the lad's nightly searches and the collection of herbs, roots, and certain medicinal plants, Mustapha's shoulders were treated with a balm made up by one of the elder ladies who knew a great deal about the healing properties of nature's medicine.

People within the cave moved around with makeshift flaming torches that burned for approximately an hour. Short branches of pinewood split four ways at the top were wrapped with old fabric strips. Thin shavings of bark were pressed into the slits. As the torch burned, it wicked the sap of the short branch, burning dimly but sufficiently for the residents of the cave. Accordingly, the cavern and passageways became more familiar as they were explored using makeshift torches. However, they still had to practice caution as it could be slippery underfoot.

With the benefit of light, a remarkable discovery was made deep underground – a tiny lake that provided clean drinking water for the cave community.

Additionally, water was taken to wash and clean clothes and utensils in another part of the cave complex. Throughout, hygiene was crucial to living together safely and harmoniously.

There was even a programme for cleaning the passages of bat guano. Spanish troops had blocked the cave with a huge, rounded boulder in the morning, trapping the Moors but also the bats in the dark passageways. Eventually, the bats died off because they could no longer fly or forage for food. It was a horrible experience to clear the dead flying mammals, Chiroptera, from the cave. Slowly but surely, the cave and passageways became the domain of the Moorish people.

In the coming days, weeks, and months, everyone assumed a job to contribute to the routine of their extraordinary home. The horror of confinement in the cave turned out to be a haven compared to what their cruel oppressors had intended.

TWENTY-EIGHT

A mixture of revulsion and disbelief occupied their troubled minds. Tariq's enlightenment about that period in history (a subject rarely spoken about) hit home hard for Carl and Alicia.

"I didn't realise that such extreme barbarity took place all those hundreds of years ago and on such an appalling scale," said Carl. "Of course, I've heard of the Spanish Inquisition, but..." his voice faltered. He shook his head in disbelief. The look in his eyes spoke volumes. Alicia welled up with sadness for the oppressed and the terrible cruelty shown to poor, defenceless people. She felt distressed. Her lips moved, but words refused to come. "I ... I believe people would have preferred that particular period in history to go away and to forget all about the Moors and the extreme cruelty committed by the troops," she said, finding her voice. "It makes me wonder what would have happened if the Moorish people hadn't been banished as a civilisation and we had lived together in harmony. Maybe we would have become a great nation."

Sadness still lingered in Carl's eyes. "I know what you're saying. I did some research on this before we spent the week with your parents in Pamplona. The Muslims built an advanced civilisation with a great understanding and tolerance of other cultures and religions. Muslims, Christians, Jews, and the like lived together in harmony. Books of great knowledge were written and stored in differing languages in libraries, towns, and cities. They were world-class books on engineering, building, farming, religion, and many more subjects, incredibly advanced, and all for what? It takes some understanding to try and work out why it would all be halted, and the people that changed the nation for the better would be ejected, *en masse*, in such a cruel way."

Tariq intervened. "Well, I was there and saw it for myself."

His comment astounded Carl and Alicia. From his claim that he was around then, it was evident he had accurately recalled it. Once again, it reinforced the notion that he had been around for hundreds of years, but in reality, they knew that most people only lived till their 70s or 80s if they were lucky.

Surprisingly, he was a kind, sincere, faultless companion, and they had never regretted getting to know him. Yet the question of living for hundreds of years still raised uncertainties in their logical minds. It was difficult to handle, and they did not know how to make sense of the claims or historical facts he conveyed with apparent ease and accuracy.

"Tariq, I have a question for you, and I would like a complete answer if you don't mind."

"Carlos, the Brave; I know and love you and have done so for many years. I will try to answer your question as best I can."

Once again, with the statement of having known him for many years, Carl was already at a disadvantage in formulating a question. In reality, he felt convinced that he had only met Tariq for the first time when he entered their home and stood by the fire to warm himself, not back in the 17th century, as he had been led to believe. So he decided to sidestep any outlandish notions of an association with someone from the past and continue searching for answers, hoping to find constructive and complete information to challenge the presumed special relationship.

"Okay," said Carl, taking a deep breath. "If you were mortally wounded and died in 1609..."

"I was," he affirmed.

His utterance of just two words, said with conviction, amazed Carl. "How and why are you still here with us? How is that possible? And, if you are a spirit, how can a dead spirit live on *ad infinitum*?"

Carl knew his questions were probing; however, he needed to understand how and why it had all transpired. He was informed he was at Tariq's side in battle and thought long and hard about it. However, he was still unable to provide an answer to the assumption. The nearest he felt to understanding what Tariq had said came from a remark by the priest when he spoke of the Japanese tsunami that killed 20,000 people. Even so, the revelation of spirits living on and getting taxis sounded quite illusory. Besides, Carl believed the Japanese story was relatively recent, and that the spirits, if that was what they really were, did not persist for any significant length of time. Yet, Tariq was talking about four hundred years or more.

"Carlos the Brave, at present, you are a human being and, as such, view the world from your mortal perspective. Unlike you here in your present form, I died and yet did not go to Jannah (Paradise) as a Muslim. For what seemed like an eternity, I roamed this area of Murla and Jalon; I saw the dead bodies without burial left on Caballo Verde perish and decay. The wolves ate some of the bodies, and the crows and other birds feasted on the flesh. I saw their bodies decompose, leaving bones that eventually broke down and fragmented in the sun, rain and cold. Then I saw green grass and shrubs growing in their place, and many spirits in the mortal world floating about in the ether, unable to pass over to Jannah. It disturbed me greatly, so I tried to help the earthbound spirits. At first, I was unsuccessful. Nevertheless, with time, patience, and observation, I came to understand that they were looking for their loved ones. They experienced fear of the unknown in that in-between world; maybe they felt aggrieved with the killing of their people, and possibly wanted to right a wrong. In some cases, their anger stopped them from moving on. Whatever was at play stopped them from continuing their spiritual journey. On one such day, I made contact with a religious leader who had died and was in the alternative world. He knew many people in that in-between existence. We met regularly and made slow progress in helping spirits move on to Jannah. I think you call it passing over; spirits became more amenable to change and moved on at the mention of their loved ones. Slowly, we were able to help reduce the number of spirits roaming Caballo Verde, and some good began to shine through."

"Now, I'm beginning to understand," said Carl. "I remember Rosa told us she helped you move souls on so they would be at peace. So what happened to the religious leader who helped you initially?"

"That is easy. One day, when I tried to contact him, he did not answer. I can only assume that with our work together and with insight, he had moved on to a much nicer place to be with his family."

"Okay, so when Nana met you, what happened?" said Alicia.

"I saw her as a kindred spirit. Very wise, very compassionate, and very understanding. I knew she would work well with me to help the lost souls still looking for their loved ones."

"And these lost souls, are they what we have seen as orbs on the mountain?" said Alicia.

"The very same. However, some of the lost souls were the spirits of Spanish troops who died in battle. Although they were the aggressors and wrong to do what they did, they were still God's children. So we helped them move on without prejudice."

Carl and Alicia sat spellbound, reeling from the revelations. But, for all that, Carl still had a challenging question that needed to be answered. However, with burgeoning reticence, Tariq's patience seemed to be wearing a bit thin.

"Okay, Tariq. I can go along with what you said, but I need to understand why, if I were a Muslim and stood at your side fighting and supporting you, why am I a Roman Catholic now and not a Muslim? It lacks consistency, but more to the point, it doesn't make any sense. I need to know how and why."

"Carlos, the brave, so many questions, so much you need to know. You have heard enough for one day. I want you to search your heart and mind for the answer. Meditate, but let your mind step outside your mortal body, as I have told you. Contemplation will help you raise your vibrational frequency and provide you with the answers that you seek. Next time we meet, let's see what you have determined yourself."

His answer left Carl feeling dissatisfied and mildly frustrated; there was so much more he needed to know. However, when Tariq said that was the end of the conversation, it truly was, and no one, friend or foe, could change that.

TWENTY-NINE

Days elapsed. Carl and Alicia got on with their lives. Christmas neared, and Ralph had not returned. Carl made good use of the outdoor cameras, which showed the occasional orb floating in and out of view around the Finca. Both accepted the moving, circulating orbs as part of life; although strange and mysterious, they were gentle and serene, just like their counterparts. A week passed before something of genuine interest appeared on the monitor. If Carl had not seen it for himself, he would not have believed it. A camera on the side of their home captured views of their driveway, the lane, and the surrounding area. As the light faded, the CCTV switched to black-and-white night video mode. In the corner of the screen, a wispy, dark shape about twenty-four inches tall, surrounded by a strange luminescence, coalesced. The peculiar form passed behind a wild shrub next to their driveway gatepost. As it emerged on the opposing side of the post, the glowing wisp had transformed into the shape of an adult fox. It sauntered across their driveway and approached the front door.

Carl switched his view to another camera and saw the fox up close. In many ways, the fox looked too good to be true. The bushy tail and coat looked unusually well-groomed, and its face bore no scars or imperfections, unlike those he had witnessed on wildlife programmes, where he had observed close-up shots of fauna in the natural world. They frequently clashed with other foxes and regularly sustained scratches and lacerations to the face. He was perplexed about the transmutation. How on earth could that happen? As he tried to work out what was happening, the fox in front of the camera transformed into Tariq's shape and form. Carl rubbed his eyes, shook his head, and looked back at the monitor. Sure enough, there was Tariq with just one inconsistency about him that he could tell. He felt sure his friend had a short stump where his arm had been amputated.

In contrast, this Tariq had no apparent stump to be seen at all. He knew there was a lot of mystery to Tariq, and perhaps this was him in a slightly different form. Maybe he could change his shape into whatever he wanted, whenever he liked. When he thought about it, Carl did not know Tariq's movements, where he came from, or where he resided. Perhaps this really was him, and this was his way of appearing whenever or wherever. Carl ran out of the study to find Alicia as quickly as possible, then told her to follow him. She sensed the urgency in his voice and followed without question. He pointed to the monitor.

"Look!"

"It's Tariq," said Alicia, staring. Even though it was now dusk, his image was readily distinguishable.

As she spoke, they both saw him knocking on the Finca's front door. Seconds elapsed.

"Well, shall we let him in?" said Alicia, surprised at

Carl's hesitation.

"I don't know."

"Carl, you're acting weird. Is there a problem?"

"I don't know. I'm not certain that is Tariq."

"Well, it looks very much like him to me," she said, staring back at the monitor and then at her husband's moment of uncertainty. "Maybe we should let him in, and then you can be certain it's Tariq."

"I'm not sure . . ."

Alicia turned on her heel and headed to the front door. Carl followed, still reeling from the transmogrification he had witnessed on the monitor, if that was what it was. Right now, he did not want to make a fool of himself by being wrong about something as basic as recognising Tariq, his very good friend.

"Tariq, it's lovely to see you again," said Alicia as she stepped back from the door. He entered, yet said nothing, and now *she* was unsure. Tariq was usually most courteous and polite, with a reassuring presence.

Carl quickly stood alongside his wife, ready for any oddity or strangeness that might kick off. However, he sincerely hoped he was wrong. Nevertheless, instincts were essential in life, and Carl could not ignore his gut instinct telling him to be careful. Something was wrong.

"Is this a social visit, Tariq?" said Alicia as Carl focused on the lack of protrusion where there should be a left shoulder stump. Maybe he was overreacting, but Tariq's belt and dagger were different. Perhaps he had more than one dagger and belt. A more ornate

Jambiya hung from a leather belt, not a corded one.

With great surprise, the Tariq look-alike, if that's what he was, held his hand out to Carl, which seemed strange given that Tariq never shook hands – he could not because there was no physical substance to him. This, in Carl's mind, would be the decisive test. He, in turn, offered his hand and caught hold of a firm, solid grip. At that moment, Carl was thrown headlong into an unknown abyss of darkness, agony, despair, and suffering. He was paralysed – at the mercy of an evil force assaulting his mind and soul. Instead of it being a polite welcome with a friend, his handshake was akin to a highway to Hell. So far, since acquiring his unique gift of being able to touch an object and read its history, Carl had always been in control. Now, with seemingly no way out of the desperate plight, his life faded quickly. All his love, light and happiness were ebbing away, replaced by darkness and evil without compassion, kindness or regard for humanity.

"Are you alright, Carl?" Alicia exclaimed, knowing something was amiss, yet uncertain of what she could do. The two men stood holding hands, motionless. Carl took on a strange, dark aura. Alicia was scared; she shook uncontrollably, trying to think but unable to. Her mind was clouded. Carl was at the point of no return. Just like a battery sapped of its charge, his light would soon go out. He would be driven mad by the devilish, unholy shapeshifter draining all his energy. Finally, and with enormous will, Alicia took action to frustrate the being who was conducting a numbing assault on her loved one. She took a firm hold of Carl's sleeve and tugged violently, causing the hands to disconnect abruptly. The lookalike Tariq instantly shot her a withering look. He had been thwarted and knew it. Her bravery was unexpected; even she was surprised by the remarkable outcome.

Alicia raised her voice. "Carl! Carl! Come with me!" She pulled hard on his sleeve and dragged him away from the nemesis. Having taken lifesaving action, she did not stop there. Her courage and daring in the face of evil were exemplary, and the courageous action lifted her.

"You will have to go now." She pointed to the front door. "Go now! Right now!"

Carl was recovering quickly and adopting a confrontational mode. He saw the situation for what it was – and stepped in front of Alicia. "Go now, you son of a bitch! Begone, and don't come back!" Carl raised his fist. However, the evilness was not done. Within a second, his body disintegrated into a black wisp and flew into the front room.

With surprise, and now another dimension to the unfolding saga, there was another knock at the front door. Alicia looked to Carl; he motioned her towards the front door as he ran into the front room. Alicia opened the door; Tariq, their very good friend, surprisingly pushed past her as he shouted.

"Quick, there is no time; we must rid your home of this evil right now!"

He ran into the front room, drawing his dagger as he quickly scanned the room. Carl stood with a dining room chair gripped in his hands, raised and ready for action. Adrenaline was pumping. Within a flash, he would swing at what he thought to be the evil imposter. Tariq knew what was about to happen. The chair was seconds away from flying through the air in his direction.

"Nooo, Carlos the Brave! It is I, your friend."

In an instant, Carl countered his aggressive action. He managed a half-smile. "That bastard was pretending to be you."

Although Tariq heard his comment, he did not react. There were more pressing issues at hand that required attention. Both stood pensive like coiled springs, ready to pounce. Then, out of the corner of his eye, Tariq saw it. High up, in the corner of the room, between the beam and the ceiling, barely noticeable, a black haze, mere inches in size, had squeezed itself tightly into the corner. Tariq approached, throwing his dagger, hoping to pin it to the beam. Yet, he missed his mark. With speed, he picked the blade up. They focused on the corner of the room where the evilness tried to conceal itself. However, in desperation, knowing the odds were against it, the wisp flew across the room, past Alicia, and out of the front door. The evil imposter had been driven from their home.

"There is something I must tell you so that this never happens again," said Tariq, concerned for his friends. "What you saw tonight was the evilness of the shape-shifting jinni."

"Jinni?" said Alicia, in shock.

"Yes, jinni. It describes the spirit that can appear in

human and animal form and other strange guises and is to be treated with contempt."

"I saw it change from the wisp into a fox, and then your look-alike," said Carl, knowing that something felt wrong when the clever imposter called at the finca. His instinct told him something was amiss, and he was right. He would never make the same mistake again.

"That was so it could enter your home and do its worst. It certainly wouldn't have attempted it when your nana lived here. However, it is becoming bold now, and I fear working on a bigger plan. The jinni is equivalent to a demon in your religion and is feared just the same by my religion. Muslims are scared of the spirit, and most won't even mention its name. So, just like any evilness in your religion, take it seriously, my good friends.

"But you have no fear of it, Tariq," said Carl, intrigued. "Why is that?"

"I have power on my side, but that is another story for another time."

"When I leave here, keep your doors and windows locked and bolted. Don't answer the door to anybody else tonight.

The sinister, eventful evening ended with Tariq's commitment to keeping a close eye on the situation and for Carl and Alicia to be aware of the jinni's underhanded and conniving nature. It was easy for them to be duped, but Tariq was sure they would never repeat the same mistake. Before heading into the darkness, his final thought was to make sure Alicia told her nana precisely what had happened.

"Carlos the Brave – Alicia, I bid you farewell. Remember what I said, and all will be well. Just shout my name aloud into the night if you need me urgently, and I will be here for you. You have what I believe you call cameras around the Finca to see outside, just like your friends. Use them wisely. Keep safe. Assalam Alaikum: (Peace be upon you). He disappeared into the night as he came, full of conviction, surprise, and incredible supremacy.

Over an evening drink, Carl and Alicia spoke at length about the unforgettable visits, how they coped with the evil intruder, and how brave Alicia was in saving Carl from imminent danger. Although on the tip of their tongues, neither mentioned the words 'imminent death.' It was something they could not even begin to think about, let alone envisage. His gratitude was endless in his praise for such a lovely wife. In particular, they spoke about their amazing bond. Their unity would help them through anything, and believing in the power of love was something the jinni could never understand or take away. Moreover, their strong bond had foiled the plan to take Carl's soul. Both were prepared to lay down their lives for each other, a testament to their total and sincere commitment of love.

The final conversation of the night centred on what Alicia would say to Nana. Again, the discussion about the jinni would be off the scale in terms of surprise, and Nana would be astonished beyond belief.

Sleep came slowly to Carl and Alicia; however, at 2:30 am, Alicia awoke to find the bedclothes on Carl's side pulled back, but Carl was gone. As she looked around the bedroom, Alicia became aware of a bright light from the hallway. Slipping her dressing gown on and sliding her feet into mules, she moved cautiously to the bedroom door, looking down the corridor that led to the front room.

In a subdued, nervous voice, she called out. "Carl, where are you?"

"Here in the study," came the reply. The light in the corridor seemed even brighter as she approached. Entering the study, she found white light shining through the window, illuminating the whole room as if it were day. Equally, the monitor shone brightly.

Earlier, Carl woke to find the bedroom bathed in light like early morning; yet, it was nighttime, and he had got up to investigate. The CCTV camera was picking up light from a source at the farthest part of the driveway. As usual, with his colour blindness, Carl sensed it as a green light, making the spectacle look even weirder.

"What is it, Carl?"

"I don't know, but I'm sure it has something to do with the devilish visit tonight."

"Maybe it is trying to psych us out," said Alicia, half-serious, half-joking. Nevertheless, she was troubled by the unusual emanation from the lane lighting their home. They watched the glowing light for a minute without any change or flicker in its intensity. Then Carl had a thought.

"I remember at school using a tactic to thwart any idiot bully who wanted to make my life Hell."

Alicia looked at him oddly.

"Don't worry; there's more to come," he said. "In the crazy situation I just described, I learned to be obtuse."

"What is obtuse?"

"Well, if somebody is trying to make you do something, you do the opposite, and then it fools them. That is being obtuse. So, here we are in a possible situation where the jinni is trying to scare us. Let's show whatever it is, we aren't bothered, and in fact, we are ignoring its attempt to psych us out. Let's do something completely the opposite."

"Okay," said Alicia, starting to get his drift. "Shall I make us a drink?"

"Yes, that sounds like a great idea. I'll have cocoa. And we can stand here in full sight of the light thing and pretend we're cool with it, taking in the light show, drinking our cocoa, and maybe even giving a wave. How annoying that would be for Mr Jinni," said Carl humourlessly.

"Good idea," said Alicia, looking for and pleased to do normal in a very abnormal situation.

There was no need to turn on the kitchen light. The room was bathed in bright, white light from floor to ceiling.

Drinks made – she strolled back into the study with two mugs.

"Alicia, look!" bellowed Carl.

Her heart raced as she stared at the monitor.

"Look." Carl pointed to the lane. The light shone from what appeared to be a lustrous figure. However, all that could be seen was a faint impression of a face on a small, radiant body. For all the world, Carl thought the figure looked remarkably like Casper the Ghost. Instead of being troubled by the sight, they thought it was adorable, the opposite of what the spirit hoped to engender. The light began pulsating. Then, a reduction: visual brightness dimmed to nothing; it was all over. The being had gone.

The phone rang. It was Lynn, their good friend who lived nearby, who called.

"Alicia, thank God you answered. Is everything alright?"

THIRTY

Lynn and Jeff invited their friends to dinner the subsequent evening. Mainly to keep in touch, but primarily to talk about the white light that lit up the night sky in the early morning hours. It must have seemed unbelievable to be woken by such an immense white light, which made the whole area appear as if it were daylight. Jeff's theory at the time was that it could be a UFO. He had heard and read about such things happening in far-flung places, and living on the outskirts of Murla was indeed remote. Although most people would have shied away from such conversations, they knew Carl and Alicia would be open and outspoken about the crazy experience.

Having followed the usual courtesies of welcoming and seating Carl and Alicia, Lynn could no longer contain herself. She asked directly what the light thing was all about. The problem was explaining something so odd and out of this world, and making the account sound credible. Fortunately, their friends were open-minded and always game for discussing something new or far-fetched. For clarity, to bring the whole story together, and to make it sound believable, Carl discussed the strange occurrences around the home and the incredible revelations about the supernatural world. As well-adjusted people, the weird conversation about orbs, shape-shifting, Tariq, and Carl's unique Psychometry gift seemed to go down well. They needed some clarification here and there on aspects of the unearthly, frightening experiences, but generally, all were accepted without a second's thought. However, it soon became apparent that talking to their two good friends about the incidents was helping Carl and Alicia come to terms with the unholy saga. It was like speaking to a therapist; they both bared their souls to all the strangeness – well, nearly all of it. The whole experience became so beneficial that they wondered why they had not spoken more openly about it sooner. Lynn, in particular, sounded upbeat during their account. This was mainly because her mother, back in the UK, was a practising spiritualist. Lynn often heard about unusual or odd incidents when living at home. Her mum spoke on one occasion about being possessed by the spirit of a deceased person. In that instance, she spoke in a different voice and acted utterly alien to her usual self; such was the extent of the so-called possession and of her immersion in the spirit world.

"That's amazing, hearing you talk about your mum like that, Lynn. It makes me feel somewhat normal when I speak about the Tariq impostor in our home, and the way he changed into a wisp was all so incredible," said Carl. Alicia added her thoughts on the matter and spoke about the incredible light in the early hours of the morning, hoping that their finca was far enough away from Murla so as not to have drawn any attention. Although it was likely that some poor sleepers might have observed the unusual light, they kept quiet about the occurrence out of fear of ridicule and the potential for awkwardness among their friends.

Then, with the benefit of more wine, the conversation took an amusing turn when Alicia referred to the wisp as a wasp. There was so much laughter because of her mispronunciation; she vowed she would never make the same mistake again. Even so, she took it all in good fun and added a few more intentional *faux pas* for good measure. A refill of her wine glass had enabled the stories to flow freely and louder.

"Well, what you saw and heard was just a little bit weirder than some of the things mum used to talk about so often back home. Likewise, as for your nana being a white witch, good on her, that's all I can say. Next time you speak to her, tell Rosa she has two fans here, and if we ever need a spell or two, we'll contact her."

The fact that Jeff and Lynn were recreational pot smokers gave way to more open-minded, off-the-wall conversations. Carl had mentioned in private to his wife that he thought they might have tried hard drugs as well. Nevertheless, this was not a problem within the foursome. Jeff and Lynn kept their lifestyle very much to themselves. As such, it was their business and their decision what they did in the confines of their own home. Still, Carl and Alicia thought that if pot were ever offered to them, they would decline the offer politely. Respect for each other made for a warm, friendly, and enduring relationship that they all treasured.

"So, what about that incredible white light in the early hours of the morning?" said Jeff. "Lynn and I thought we were under attack from an alien force of Klingons," he smiled at his joke.

"Well, we aren't sure what it was all about," said Carl, looking at his wife. She shrugged her shoulders in agreement. "However, I feel it must have been the incredible power of the jinni I was telling you about. Perhaps his anger or frustration stemmed from being thwarted by Tariq. Or maybe his display of power, lighting the night sky, was meant to frighten us; I don't know."

"It did frighten us," said Alicia. "It really did, I can say it was the powerful unnatural force I ever experience in my life. But, one thing is certain: it was not a bonfire, the world's biggest Roman candle, or a weather balloon ...."

Just like Theo, Lynn complimented Alicia, surprised at her improving English.

"My God, Alicia. What you just said sounded amazingly fluent, and together, had I closed my eyes and listened, you could have passed for an English lady."

Complimented on her command of the language, she had to ask what 'fluent' meant, which gave way to more laughter, requiring an explanation. However, in keeping with the person she was, there were times when she played along with the situation for amusement. First, she would ask for an explanation of a word. Then, finally, when it had been explained to her in depth, she would say. "Oh, yes, I already knew that," smiling sweetly. This was the fun-loving side of her personality.

Not to be overshadowed by it all, Alicia had one final comment. "The other crazy thing I must tell is that Carl sees anything white at night-time, such as the white orbs floating around the night sky, as green. He has colour blindness, or so he tells me."

"Really," said Lynn. "That sounds really psychedelic. Some people would pay a fortune for that, you know. How crazy."

"Hey, stop referring to me as crazy," said Carl with a smile.

They all laughed and enjoyed the light-hearted moment, realising what great friends they had in each other.

Next up was a game of Scrabble, one of Alicia's favourite games. Her enthusiasm was plain for all to see, especially when she had a glass of wine.

However, despite their fun and laughter, they did not know that trouble with the jinni over the coming days would become far worse. Their mettle would be severely tested, and life would never be the same again.

THIRTY-ONE

The Year 1609.

People from villages, hamlets, and lowly hovels cheered the Spanish troops as they paraded along country roads heading for the village of Murla. Despite tiredness, marching for days, and sometimes stopping to exert their dominance over the occasional isolated feud involving Spanish and Muslim people. The troops were buoyed up in the knowledge that they would be heading home very soon.

Ceremonial flags, festive banners, loud drumming, and flute playing created a carnival atmosphere as the troops marched along winding streets and lanes of the Spanish countryside. Inhabitants, never having seen such a show of supremacy, cheered with approval as the King's troop paraded through villages on their final mission to eliminate the remaining Moors (200 plus men, women and children) headed for the nearby hills.

Public sentiment towards the Moors had changed dramatically since the King's decree; most Spaniards remained steadfast in their ill-conceived judgment of the Moors and were willing to help expel their former friends, acquaintances, and even employers – now they were the enemy and despised in most quarters of Spanish life. Some communities became fanatical, showing a willingness to indulge in extreme brutality against the Moors.

The troops' ultimate goal was to march in hot pursuit of the fleeing horde of Moors headed to Caballo Verde on the outskirts of Murla. Nevertheless, the soldiers had plenty of time to gorge on bread, chorizo, poultry, fruit, water and wine, which locals handed out to the weary soldiers.

José, a resident landowner and wine producer in the valley, had heard that the King's troop were nearby and would pass through the village pursuing the rabble of Moors, as he described them. He moved two kegs of wine to the roadside in the town's square in readiness. As the troops marched through, wine was distributed in substantial quantities. After a brief respite, they moved onwards, hot on the trail of the ill-fated families making a run for it.

Earlier, villagers shouted abuse, spat, and threw rocks and excrement at the fleeing Moors travelling through the village. The king and his followers had undeniably created an air of hatred towards the Moorish people. It would appear that no behaviour towards them was excessive or aggressive. An air of daring arose amongst the crowd. Spaniards, fired up with aggression, took it upon themselves to do their worst. In some cases, their actions led to injury or inhumane acts of genocide. Such was the hatred and contempt for the Moors.

THIRTY-TWO

General Miguel Cabrera Arroyo sat astride his Spanish thoroughbred horse, scrutinising acres of rocky terrain covered with shrubs, small trees, and intermittent patches of open land. He had fought in many battles and skirmishes in his distinguished career, and each one was unique. They all required control, imagination and fortitude to achieve a satisfactory outcome.

Rocky outcrops of varying sizes and small trees afforded little if any protection for the men, women and children hiding in fear for their lives from the Spanish army. Men and youths grouped together, not wanting to fight but knowing they had to if they wanted to protect their vulnerable families, friends, and loved ones. Although there were only a mere one hundred and ninety-three in number by now (some dying *en route*), they were ready to lay down their lives to protect their own. With few weapons, they had to fight against the might of the Spanish army. A few swords, daggers, and farming implements, such as rakes and pitchforks, along with lengths of wood, had to suffice. Moreover, behind them, they had come to a dead end, Caballo Verde's rock face, whose irregular, towering configuration made it virtually impossible to ascend the treacherous terrain except for those desperate enough to risk their lives. The Moors were trapped with seemingly no way out, and the general knew it.

Viewing the adversary in the distance, the general saw the final battle and how it would play out before him.

In his youth, Miguel Cabrera Arroyo joined the army. He climbed the ranks to become a very successful general in the Spanish army of Valencia through dedication, guile, and hard work. His shrewd, uncompromising, and aggressive personality ensured that any job he undertook was always completed to perfection. If butchery was needed on a grand scale, he stood head and shoulders above the rest of his ilk to complete the task.

The general's mount trotted along the assembled lines of two hundred and fifty troops. Snorting and nodding, the trustworthy horse, Fiel (faithful), seemed to enjoy the occasion as if inspecting the troops. General Cabrera Arroyo milked the moment, feeling the power of his status, watching the men's faces of adoration and respect. He knew they revered him, which gave a feeling of gratification, maybe even vanity. Sitting bolt upright in the saddle, he scanned the men for readiness. A slight pull of the reins brought his Spanish thoroughbred horse to a halt. Glancing at the hapless Moors, the general sneered and turned back to face his troops.

"Men, you see before you the dogs, who would invade Iberia, seize our land, belongings, and lives." He pointed to the Moors with his sword. "This will never happen again." He observed his troop of Pikemen in colourful uniforms, metal breastplates, and helmets glinting in the sun. Foot soldiers carrying Arquebus muskets, feared amongst the fleeing Moors or anyone in opposition, were menacing and the ultimate in killing from a distance. Cavalry, positioned towards the rear, completed the fighting force.

The general determined that a volley of musket fire directed at the unfortunate Moors hidden in the scrub would kill, maim, and ultimately demoralise the poor unfortunates. Next, he would send in his pikemen amid panic and confusion. Long Pikes against people who were trapped meant instant death with little if any injury to Spanish troops. Thrusting with the mighty barbed pikes, savagely killed and maimed the unfortunate foe. Should it be necessary, fast-moving cavalry could take up the fight with the power of speed and unquestionable force. They would be the ultimate killing machine on horseback, slashing right and left with their Toledo steel swords, cutting a path as they went.

"This, my men, is the last battle. When the campaign ends, we can go home to our families, homes, and loved ones."

The cheering troops could be heard a mile and a half away in Murla.

"We can all be proud of our achievement, and you have all earned a rest. We have driven the scum from our land, never to be seen again in Iberia.

The troops cheered again.

"Long live King Phillip, yelled the general to his men, holding his sword skywards.

The troops cheered even louder at the mention of their King. Fear rose all the more within the pockets of Moors, hiding from the Spanish, uncertain of what to do next. With the impending attack, troops stood psyching themselves up for the final onslaught. Minutes elapsed. Finally, the general gave his next-in-command a signal, calling for the soldiers' silence and attention.

"Musketeers, make ready...!" Their call to arms was immediate.

"Prime and load...!" They quickly complied, preparing their muskets to fire as they had done many times before. All the firearms were immaculate. Their training had instilled in them the importance of maintaining, cleaning, and inspecting their weapons to ensure they were always ready for battle.

The Moors, seeing the preparation of muskets amongst the Spanish, passed a message around to anyone exposed to conceal themselves behind rocks, trees, or anything that would give cover. However, they were exposed to the might of the Spanish army. As the musket shot became imminent, some Moors without cover lay flat on the ground, hoping to escape the volley of shots.

"Make ready!" They mounted their muskets on metal rests and took aim.

"Present!"

Seconds elapsed. "Fire!"

A line of smoke rose from the Musketeers as the

lethal Musket balls flew through the air at one thousand feet per second, seeking out their human targets. However, at three hundred yards distance from the Moors, the accuracy of the Arquebus muskets would lack precision. Nevertheless, damage was inflicted. Some musket balls found their targets, causing injury, but overall, there were only four deaths. One man's deltoid arm bone was shattered. Blood splattered his wife and child, who were crouched nearby. Large fragments of wood splintered away from small tree trunks. Some shrubs were shot ragged by the volley of fire.

Although mildly frustrated by the Musketeer's lack of killing, the general satisfied himself that fear would circulate amongst the Moorish families. His second in command ordered the pikemen to step forward between the Musketeers' line. A drumroll reverberated in the afternoon air, indicating attention and readiness. Soldiers stood in line with eighteen-foot Pikes erect and threatening. Sharp, barbed pikes stood on high, evil and menacing, ready to dispatch those who stood before them. Finally, the order to advance was given. The line proceeded forward in unison as drummers set a pace for the pikemen to advance. They lowered their Pikes horizontally at one hundred yards, observing the nearest signs of life before them. Their targets were in disarray, except for a few brave men and youths who stood before their families, defending and waiting for the onslaught.

The cavalry trotted behind the Pike men, giving support, prepared to deal with anyone who broke through the Pike men's line.

The general's tactic was unconventional, but it appeared he was playing with the poor unfortunates or using them to try out new warfare strategies. Such was his appalling evil.

Moors, prepared to defend their loved ones, held the line in a show of extreme bravery. The clash ensued. A few Moors at the front held homemade wooden shields to parry the pikes whilst trying to chop the metal spikes off or pull the pikes away from the musketeer's grip.

The battle raged on the lower slopes of the mountain. Inhumane, infernal sounds could be heard in Murla. Moors trying to protect themselves and their loved ones from the Spanish soldiers' aggression only succeeded in losing their lives. The sickening slash and thrust of swords, daggers stabbing, and pikes thrusting continued unabated. Wild, hellish, brutal atrocities continued as if they were entertainment for Rome's Colosseum with indulgent gladiatorial slaughter. Mothers saw their husbands and sons slain as they stood, trying to protect them. Blood-splattered soldiers wiped their faces and cleared their vision, only to continue with the sickening, repulsive bloodshed. Their actions were dishonourable, inhumane, and evil, yet they continued their savage slaughter.

Fathers fell by the bodies of their children. Young, elderly, infirm, and females stood to the rear of the brave men for protection, holding onto their children and babies, screaming for safety from the frenzied attack as they saw their loved ones die, never to be seen, loved or cherished again. But, standing at the back, they could see that there was little hope of salvation. Soon, it would be their turn to experience a torturous death.

Then, out of nowhere, a force of Moorish knights ahead of running foot soldiers rode straight into the fray, slashing, stabbing and trampling Spanish soldiers. It was unexpected, and the surprise attack of accomplished Moorish knights and foot soldiers caught the general completely off guard. What should have been a simple incursion turned into a desperate fight for the Spanish army. Toe-to-toe fighting saw the balance of power shift backwards and forwards in the melee.

A drum roll pierced the air, committing the Spanish cavalry. Yet, chaos and confusion engulfed the scene. Both sides killed and injured each other in the best way they could. Now, it was a battle of numbers – a killing zone. Although not joining in with the fight, General Cabrero Arroyo was heard shouting as loudly as he could over the struggle. "Kill them! Kill them, you pathetic clowns. Kill them!"

Determining that the Moors were outnumbered and starting to lose the fight, the remaining Moorish families, along with the injured, moved backwards, away from the appalling scene, climbing over steep rocks and negotiating an overgrowth of wild shrubs and trees; their only thought was to get away from the horror of inevitability. They climbed the rugged, craggy rocks as best they could. With bloodied hands, knees, and shins, their desperate overriding thoughts were to escape or be slaughtered. Others, too weary, tired or injured, gave up. The climb to freedom for them seemed impossible, yet the inevitability of the worsening scene for others heightened the need to react. Screams and shouts of agony from behind those fleeing quickened the pace of those desperate to find a route up the rugged, treacherous mountain. Some unfortunate souls were caught and butchered. Others fell, becoming victims of the cold-hearted troops. However, many miraculously escaped up a perilous mountain goat track to temporary safety.

Just two soldiers remained on the side of the Moorish troops amid the battle scene. One Moor – one a Spaniard, fighting side-by-side like wildcats. They slashed, stabbed, and dodged swords and dagger thrusts. Spanish troops, witnessing their apparent superhuman strength, backed off somewhat. However, the occasional brave Spaniard pushed forward to challenge, only to be cut down. The longer the impasse continued, the more the remaining two fighters' superhuman actions strengthened. With bodies heaped around them, they changed positions to defend themselves more efficiently. Surprisingly, the Moorish knight fought like a gladiator, albeit with a missing left arm. On more than one occasion, his Spanish compadre deflected thrusts to the Moor's left side, knowing that this was his weak flank. How long could the stand-off continue? Eventually, the end came in the form of a pike thrust forward, burying itself in the chest of the Moorish knight. A second's distraction, looking out for his comrade, was the final act. Both fell to the ground in a heap, bloodied and lifeless.

As in battles everywhere, horrific tales were told by the Spanish troops to anyone willing to listen to such vile carnage. Yet, none more incredible than the story of the final two brave soldiers opposing the Spanish forces. As the two fell in combat, a mysterious and frightening vision caused troops nearby to hysterically leave the battle scene, screaming, 'It's the Devil's work.' Out of the body of the Moorish knight rose a semi-transparent replica of the Moor, minus its left arm, staring at the troops, understanding how pointless the whole tragedy of fighting had been. The act of annihilation served no purpose; instead, it created hatred, suffering, and shame. As he stood looking around at the opposing forces, there was no sound. No bird noises, no men talking, shouting, or screaming in agony, merely complete and utter silence. The Knight looked down upon his fallen comrade with love, compassion, and respect. Stooping towards Carlos with his right hand outstretched, imploringly, he urged the spirit to rise out of the body and join him. Any stragglers on the battlefield, feeling brave or pretending to be so, once they witnessed the otherworldly scene, screamed with fear.

The killing had reached its finality. The bodies of fallen soldiers and horses lay on the rocky ground, some clinging to life amongst the dead. With little care, compassion, or help in their dying moments, they slowly expired and passed on into the afterlife. A concentration of spirits in the form of white orbs floated around the battlefield, drifting – wafting like dandelion clock seeds caught on the breeze, looking for a place to settle.

However, like a harbinger of doom, the jinni, in the form of a nebulous haze, moved around the combat zone, glorifying the needless death and destruction of humanity's children. The entity flew at an accumulation of orbs, scattering them here and there. As if losing their lives in such an ignominious, horrific fashion was not enough, the evil spirit delighted in hounding the lost souls. Its self-appointed mission was to terrorise the unfortunate spirits of the dead, whose one remaining wish was to look for peace and tranquillity in the hereafter. Yet, the evil jinni had other ideas for them. In its cruel and twisted way, they would be persecuted forever.

The battlefield held a gratifying attraction for the dark spirit, where it could do its damnedest. Cruelty and suffering were the appalling attractions. Further disturbing encounters with the spirit continued; white orbs drifted higher up the mountain in search of solace. A few white orbs floated down the mountain, attracted by human lifeforms in the semblance of Spanish soldiers. Unseen, the orbs drifted in and around the camp in the fading light, observing men as they erected tents, lit fires, and sat around nursing their wounds or being attended to by personnel with the most basic skills in binding dreadful injuries and open gashes.

In some cases, cauterising wounds with a hot iron straight from the fire took place with unbearable pain, but bear it, they must.

Broken ribs, arms and leg bones were merely dealt with in the most rudimentary way. Having bound broken arms or leg bones using short, thin branches cut to length, some soldiers travelled on canvas stretchers, or in a wagon, unable to walk. Others would have basic, sometimes filthy material slings holding their broken arms in an immobilised position.

Many troops would succumb to horrific wound infections and suffer prolonged, painful deaths running high temperatures, experiencing delirium, and, in some cases, hallucinating, fearing the devil had occupied their bodies. Such was the general superstition of the time.

Many would live with nasty deformities for the rest of their lives, all thanks to King Phillip and the Royal decree of 1609.

THIRTY-THREE

ather, Bernardo arrived at Casa Azahar, enthusiastic for the long-awaited reunion with Rosa. Earlier in the day, Carl and Alicia met Nana at Alicante airport. The one-and-a-half-hour drive from the airport terminal along the coastal road to Jalon passed by quickly as they talked nonstop, catching up on all the latest news, gossip, and, of course, the goings-on in and around Murla. The latest gossip about what was happening on Caballo Verde featured extensively.

The car left the coast road and headed inland towards the Jalon Valley. At that point, Rosa became visibly excited. Her eyes darted from side to side, searching for any perceptible changes made in the short space of time that she had left the region. The marble-cutting factory on the left was still there, as was the Bodega belonging to her friend Diego. It was as if they were stuck in a time warp; hardly anything had changed, moved on, or been upgraded. Maybe passing by that way in fifty years, the buildings would still be standing in the same place, plying their same trade.

Jalon's market was in full swing in the town centre as it was a Saturday. Passing the market, Jeff and Lynn's vegetable stall was very noticeable with a huge papier mâché tomato, painted in a vivid red, and standing high on a pole over their stall. Further down the display pole, a one-foot model of a Tuna and Tomato empanadilla, painted in authentic colours, advertised some of their wares. The produce was selling quickly, particularly given that all their vegetables were grown organically and the empanadillas were homemade. Alicia wound down the window, shouted, and waved to the couple. They responded with enthusiastic waves and cheers, causing people to look around. From the town of Jalon, they drove through the pleasant countryside through Alcalali, Parcent and on to Murla.

"Rosa, how truly lovely to see you again," said Father Bernardo as he entered the living room door, closely followed by Carl. He stooped to kiss her on each cheek and held her hands. They looked at each other, enjoying the precious moment. Seven months had elapsed since their last meeting at the Finca, and it felt so good to be in each other's company again. They caught up on the latest news and changes to properties in the locality, as well as general gossip on various topics. However, he did not divulge any church business. He was a great believer in confidentiality, and that would never change.

"I thought about you so much, Father Bernardo, and the Finca and my friends in the village. Only then did the impact of how much she had missed her home, the father, and their platonic relationship become apparent. Rosa dabbed an emotional tear and gave a nervous smile to hide her sadness. Their friendship was born of mutual respect and admiration. The days when they met up for a coffee or to discuss church matters led to an extra-special friendship that only they could appreciate and understand. In humorous moments, when Rosa called him "father," he sometimes replied by calling her "mother." Father Bernardo was like that. His kindly, quick-witted humour made him a hit in the parish, young and old alike. Companionship helped to soften the blow of the sad loss of her husband, for which she was eternally grateful. Rosa could never forget the father's kind and caring support when she was at her lowest ebb following the bereavement. It all became too much for her to organise the funeral and the funeral wake in the ensuing days. However, he was always at hand to help with any proceedings, small or large.

One such day, Rosa phoned the father, cancelling some of her intended help for the church. She felt low and dispirited, as evidenced by her voice. As soon as he could, the father arrived at the Finca and virtually took over. He made a cup of coffee and sandwiches for them, sat down, and talked through her worries and concerns. His mobile rang twice while they were talking, and she heard him tactfully rearrange appointments so he could spend more time with Rosa, which she wholeheartedly appreciated. His dedication and genuine interest in her well-being were instrumental in a slow but sustained recovery. Yet, she could never fully overcome her loss of Ernesto; in time, she learned to cope and carry on. However, she admitted to feeling unhappy with the constant use of the phrase 'Time heals' used with the best of intentions by well-meaning friends and family. In her better moments, she knew that they were trying to help. It was just the repetition that rankled. Rosa prayed daily and often strolled around the garden where she felt Ernesto's presence.

"Would you like coffee, Father Bernardo?" said Alicia as they sat in the Finca's living room.

He looked at his watch. Alicia knew instinctively what that meant, and her response was perfect.

"And maybe a brandy."

"That sounds very nice, Alicia, thank you."

Drinks sorted, and everyone seated. Rosa spoke about her last-minute stopover, keeping her feelings a secret until now. Under worsening circumstances, she felt compelled to visit Murla after Alicia's worrying phone call about the jinni that had gained access to their home and nearly brought about Carl's demise. Rosa knew she had to do her utmost to calm the deteriorating situation and make things safe again. If necessary, she would commit herself to a confrontation with the evil being, but first, she must see Tariq alone.

"I'm sure the weird goings-on came as quite a surprise to you," said Rosa. "However, I must admit that I am astonished that such bizarre happenings could have occurred here in the lovely community of Murla, and I wonder if it came about because I left. I most certainly heard tales and rumours whilst living here, but I thought it was just that – tales and rumours. So, I must say I'm very sorry that you two have had problems with the evilness." In reality, she felt upset to have handed them problems of such magnitude when she passed the Finca on as a lovely dwelling and supposedly ideal in her eyes for a young couple. Although for many weeks, Rosa had been following Caballo Verde's situation closely. With the benefit of emails, texts and phone calls from her friends and, of course, Alicia, she had concluded that the infernal jinni's malicious behaviour in and around the mountain had become worse and needed to be stopped before it became too emboldened. Rosa feared that her granddaughter and grandson-in-law could be caught up in something that endangered their lives, and she could never allow that. The other night proved her concern to be well-founded when the jinni had stealthily entered the Finca. Now, she needed to pit her skills as a white witch and her lifelong experiences against an evil that seemed to be growing in strength, confidence, and courage. Unchallenged, it would continue with impunity to demoralise and wreak havoc in the small community of Murla, possibly even the whole of the Jalon Valley and beyond.

Rosa excused herself, left the Finca, and paced out into the lane that ran up to the mountain. She met with Tariq. A long time had passed since they last met. However, this wasn't altogether a social occasion; within minutes, she spoke urgently. Ideas and thoughts bounced backwards and forwards. After twenty minutes, Rosa rejoined the others, full of smiles. No one could tell if it was a smile of joy at meeting Tariq once again or a smile of confidence in tackling the jinni with all its deceptive terror. Yet, in reality, her smile was intended to evoke a sense of calm within the room.

As they sat discussing the latest weird events in the living room, Carl happened to gaze out of the window. "What on earth ...?" He leapt up from his chair and quickly reached the living room window, which caught everyone's attention. Promptly, they moved outside under Carl's instruction and stared upwards. Birds flew from the mountain in the fading light, not in formation like geese or a murmuration of starlings, but at random in varying directions, but always away from the mountain. A hysterical mass exodus by the bird population away from Caballo Verde was underway, and they appeared to be fleeing for their lives. Then Alicia noticed movement in the lane. Rats, mice, hedgehogs, and squirrels could also be seen scurrying in the opposite direction from the mountain. All three, except Rosa, looked on in disbelief at the wildlife's extreme and bizarre behaviour. However, Rosa knew precisely why the mass exodus of wildlife was occurring. She knew instinctively that it was an ominous sign of things to come. The night was closing in rapidly. Looking around, Rosa sensed the atmosphere. "The jinni is close. We must prepare right away." She hurriedly headed indoors, followed by the rest of the group; they looked on, somewhat mystified, maybe even frightened.

"What does that mean exactly?" said Alicia in a worried tone. "The jinni is close?"

THIRTY-FOUR

Carl, Alicia and the father talked nervously, trying to understand the seriousness of the night. Rosa appeared from the spare bedroom with a rustic box, which she placed on the coffee table and sat nearby.

"Now then, here is what we have to do. Please listen carefully. We only get one chance and must ensure there are no errors."

She went on to explain that the evilness had no scruples and knew no bounds. It could appear in any form, whether animal or human. It was incredibly cunning as a shapeshifter and capable of doing anything to kill or take possession of anybody he so wished. Such was his twisted desire. Nothing was sacred, and nothing scared him. He was mindless, nasty, and an evil, hostile force – worst of all, a trickster. Many people had been taken in by his persuasive, conniving manner at their peril. She looked at Carl and Alicia, knowing her remarks had special meaning when Tariq's imposter gained access to their home.

"So, here is what we must do to confront it. We will go outside, stand together in unity, and I will create an impenetrable circle of safety."

"Impenetrable circle?" asked Alicia.

"Not now," said Rosa. "We are in imminent

danger, with much to do; we need to act quickly and decisively. Just listen to me and do as I say. Tonight is a full moon, greatly boosting my magical power as a white witch. Outside, we will stand in a circle and face the fiend who would bring death, destruction, and terror to the community and all of us here." She stopped for a second to look at the worried faces.

"But why do *we* have to do this, Nana?" asked Alicia, unsure why the responsibility should fall upon their shoulders and theirs alone.

"Because we are the only ones here right now, Alicia, and the time is nigh, my dear." She focused her attention on the priest. "Father, have you brought your vestment, altar crucifix and other items?"

"I have, although I must say, Rosa, your email sounded very strange, particularly when you spoke of driving out an evil spirit. You know I can't do an exorcism without permission from the Vatican in Rome, don't you?" He crossed himself and uttered a few words under his breath.

She did not answer his question, probably because it would have required a lengthy explanation that would have exposed her innermost thoughts, and likely troubled Alicia and Carl, causing significant concern. Sometimes, things were better left unsaid.

"All I want, Father, is for you to represent the might of the church and, on full view, for the jinni to see. He cannot be allowed to go unchallenged. We are going to need all the help we can get."

Even so, Rosa realised she had just said a bit too much, which caused Alicia greater consternation and apprehension.

At that point, Carl got up from his chair to switch on the lights in the growing shades of night. Just then, a strange thud emanated from the living room window. Blood and gore had been thrown at the windowpane, now sliding down the glass. A rat, mercilessly torn apart and thrown at the Finca window in the act of bloody aggression, caused great trepidation amongst the group, but not Rosa. She knew the action was a challenge to the occupants but, in particular, a provocative display of supremacy, or so the jinni thought. Alicia squealed. Her face blanched with terror. Despite her blood and gore experiences as a nurse, the surprise of a cruel, horrendous act shocked and frightened her. Carl immediately put his arm around her to comfort and reassure.

"Father Bernardo, please bless the Finca as quickly as you can!" said Rosa.

Without further prompting, he opened his leather bag, took out his stole, kissed it, and placed it around his neck. Next, he placed a silver altar cross centrally on the coffee table, on top of Rosa's wooden box. He then took a thurible (Incense burner) out of his bag and lit it. All those present stood, made a sign of the cross, and listened intently to the blessing. Finally, he wandered around the Finca to complete the blessing of the home with holy water from an Aspergillum. Baying hounds could be heard outside on the driveway, striking fear into their minds. Rosa looked to the father and asked for a few lines of a psalm. He readily chose Psalm 23:4: "The Lord is my Shepherd." As they uttered the evocative lines in unison, the words sounded wholly appropriate and comforting. The stirring words gave each a sense of strength, buoying up their determination. Even so, they would have to act decisively and very soon. Rosa put her arms around Carl and Alicia and spoke words of comfort.

"It will be fine. They are just trying to provoke and intimidate us – to get under our skin, so to speak. Well, there is something the fiend hasn't thought about. It can never win because we are from the light. God will protect us and keep us safe; I promise you. All you have to do is be courageous and believe in the power of the Almighty. Now, let's go out there and flatten the son of a bitch."

They smiled, hearing Nana's out-of-character phraseology, but it made them feel good and brought a sense of reality, yet humour to the proceedings. There she was, an elderly lady ready to battle an evil shapeshifting jinni. What could go wrong?

"Carl, please light that candle in the lantern and carry it outside for me. Alicia, can you get a small bowl of water from the kitchen and carry it outside?" said Rosa. "As quickly as you can."

They viewed her instructions with uncertainty but followed them without question.

"Father, are you ready to face the evil – the unholy fiend, in the name of God and bring the Lord's will to prevail this night?"

"I am, Rosa."

Although he appeared confident, the look in his eyes told a different story. He was very uncertain what would happen next. Maybe it was just as well under the circumstances; naivety would protect him from the fiend's onslaught.

Minutes later, the group stood outside, preparing to face evil. Yet they did not fully understand the implications of confronting the jinni and of being subjected to his masterful scheming.

Nobody knew what to expect – what would happen or how it would all end. However, one thing was certain: no one had ever clashed with the evil entity before, and no one knew whether the encounter would bring an end to the evilness or embolden it further.

Nevertheless, as people opposed to the forces of malevolence, they did not consider that things might not go according to plan and that they may die in opposing the evil entity.

THIRTY-FIVE

Rosa carried her wooden box and placed it outside on a small flat rock on the driveway, not too far from the Finca but far enough to be adequate for her needs. A full moon in the cloudless night sky shone brightly like a giant pearl, lighting the whole area.

"Now," she said. "I want you to stand behind me. Watch what I do and be ready to do as I say." Her exacting words had a slight edge to them. She removed items from the box and closed the lid. A black-and-white Pentagon cloth on the box turned it into a makeshift altar. Carl and Alicia looked at each other, a mixture of mystification and confusion on their faces. Next, she placed a blackthorn wand on the fabric, plus shells, potions, herbs, and other interesting pagan items. Rosa closed her eyes, uttered a few indistinguishable words and then placed a feather held by a small rock on the driveway. She instructed Carl to set the lantern in a particular position and Alicia to put the water bowl in a specific position on the driveway. She looked at the plant pot outside the Finca – everything was set.

Rosa stood, wand in hand, and pointed it to the easterly compass point where she had placed a feather. She bowed her head for a moment and intoned. "I call upon the Guardian of the East and the element of air to watch over this sacred circle." In her mind's eye, she saw a hooded guardian before her and bowed in reverence. After a few seconds, she swung clockwise to the South, pointed her wand at a candlelit lantern that Carl had placed, and uttered, "I call upon the Guardian of the South and element of fire to watch over this sacred circle. Once again, she bowed her head for a moment in reverence. The two remaining compass points were dealt with in much the same way – West for water and North for earth in a terracotta pot. The twenty-foot-wide imaginary circle in her mind was complete. Father Bernardo looked at Alicia and Carl, uncertain about what would happen next or whether he should even be present at a pagan practice of sorts, even though Rosa was a Catholic.

As if by magic, and it was, a pale white shimmering circle appeared on the driveway encompassing the four points of air, fire, water and earth. But incredibly, more was about to happen. If the circle's appearance seemed otherworldly to the three observers, then the next bit of magic would blow their minds. Feeling confident her skills had not deserted her, Rosa stood near the makeshift altar in the centre of the circle, raised her wand over her head, and pointed it skywards. "I call upon the spirit of the universe to watch over the circle, fill it with love, peace, divinity, and strength. Nothing happened. Seconds ticked away. Then, out of nowhere, a narrow beam of light emanating from the atmosphere travelled straight down through Rosa's wand, then her body, and entered the ground. The spectacle took all three by surprise, leaving them aghast.

Never in their lives had they seen such a fantastic manifestation of occult power. Even more surprising was the thought that Rosa, the elderly lady everyone knew and loved, could possess such extraordinary authority and power as a white witch.

The circle transformed into a clear, protective dome that surrounded and shielded them completely.

Now everything was set in Rosa's mind, just in the nick of time. In the lane outside the Finca's driveway, they saw movement. To their surprise, Ralph, their dog who had been absent for many days and was thought to be lost, stolen, or even worse, trotted down the driveway towards them.

"Ralph!" shouted Alicia and Carl, so happy to see him again.

"No, don't," said Rosa, raising her hand to stop any movement forward towards the dog. "He isn't real. The jinni is trying to trick us."

The look on their faces spoke volumes. Ralph sidled up to the dome's edge, sat, and pawed the ground as he often did when he wanted something.

"Ralph. Good boy. You came back to us," said Carl, vocally making a fuss of their precious dog but with the dome's wall between them. At the same time, he tried to assimilate Rosa's warning, which made no sense at all. As far as he was concerned, this was their dog, Ralph.

Alicia seemed intent on overruling Nana's warning regarding making a fuss with the dog.

"No, Alicia! Stay in the circle!"

"But it's Ralph."

Rosa raised her voice, asserting her authority. "No, it isn't! Trust me, he isn't for real...! Would I lie to you?"

Rosa placed a hand on Alicia's arm to hold her, stopping the advance. Now, she spoke more calmly, trying to sound convincing. "Believe me, it is all pretence by the jinni to deceive us."

"Deceive?" said Alicia, not wanting to but disbelieving what she had been told.

The psychological stand-off continued for a few more seconds, and then Ralph turned and walked away. Alicia had given way to the strength of Nana's compelling argument, but she did not like it. At any rate, she believed if it were Ralph, then he was alive and well, and as soon as the process of whatever they were doing was over, she could call the dog, and he would come running.

Rosa spoke aloud, "We will be tested this night, but we must remain strong and united! This will be the jinni's charade, looking for weaknesses in our defence. We will be safe if we keep calm and stay together in this dome. Trust me." No sooner had she finished her stirring words than there was further movement in the lane. A sudden change in atmospheric pressure allowed air to waft in from the East, obscuring the moon in clouds.

"The evilness has just shrouded the moon," she said in a predictable tone.

Dark, nefarious images moved around in the lane. Alicia's lips and chin trembled in fear; Carl became aware that his muscles had tightened, rooting him to the spot. Sinking in the pit of their stomachs troubled them. A sense of dread overwhelmed any positivity they had mustered.

"Quickly hold hands and create a circle around the altar. Let's face the evil with our combined strength," said Rosa.

In holding hands, forming a circle, and looking outwards, Rosa ensured Alicia faced the Finca, holding hands with the father and Carl. The intentional positioning protected her from the impending visual terror. She would be able to hear but not see the wickedness unfolding. Carl and Rosa faced the lane, watching the evil manifest. They stood in silence, waiting, but it was hugely unnerving. In response, Father Bernardo addressed all as if he were preaching to the congregation. His words had stirring, inspirational conviction and positivity.

"I believe in God, the Almighty Creator of Heaven and Earth. I believe in Jesus Christ, his only son, our Lord." Everyone joined in with the Apostles' Creed. The stirring credo became one of those extra-special, hallowed moments; all perceived a connection to a higher being, confirming in their minds that the Almighty was present and watching over them. Yet, the jinni's strength was cunningly powerful and not to be dismissed as insignificant or weak.

Human-like black, faceless shadows in the distance advanced like zombies, moving forward in a mindless trance. Alarmingly, two appeared on the driveway, holding a female in front of them.

Carl stared, believing he knew the female. As they

neared the dome, the poor unfortunate's head was pulled backwards by the hair; Carl was shocked to see it was his mum.

"Carl, help me," she implored. In his mind, this was his Mum, Isabel, for definite.

"I travelled here to see you, my love. They are holding me. Please, help me. Take me in your arms and protect me. I love you so much." Although it sounded like Isabel's, the speech was mildly odd and disjointed.

Alicia, facing away from the scene, recognised the voice. "Carl, is that your mother? What is she doing here?"

Rosa shrieked loudly. "Everyone, close your eyes – don't look. Fear not; this is the evilness reading our minds, trying to shatter our resolve. Be strong; stay together, and refuse to believe what you hear and see."

"Carl, save me? Please save me?" said the figure in the form of his mother. More black shadows began to fill the driveway. The image of Isabel was dragged about and pawed by the shadow people, disturbing Carl all the more. He broke the circle, intent on saving Mum. Yet, Rosa held his hand tightly and grabbed his arm with her other hand. She fought to hold onto him. The father and Alicia joined in at that moment, holding onto Carl.

"No, Carl, remember Tariq's clone who gained entry to our Finca. This is the same all over again."

The black shadow figures moved around the driveway, swaying and rolling as they neared the dome. They were at the very edge of the protective dome, looking menacing and confrontational. Alicia now believed, like Nana, that the black bodies were feeding off their collective fear. As a child, she had often watched the undead films from behind a cushion, continually screaming with fright. Yet, now, her fear was absolute; her eyes bulged, and her nostrils flared as she hyperventilated, trying to cope with the grotesque black beings on the driveway. It seemed that the shadow people – the first wave of the assault – were doing a good job of disturbing and challenging the four souls in the bubble.

Meanwhile, Carl had calmed down, seeing the logic in Rosa's reasoning. The image of the female could not be his mum; he was now sure.

Rosa speedily took items from the wooden box; she lit a large, red candle, poured water into a pewter bowl, and began speaking in an elevated, disquieting, strange tone.

"Rain that brings and lands rebirth. Time to weep upon this earth."

She stirred the water with a wooden spoon, then dipped a sprig of broom into it.

"Winds shall follow, you shall see, blowing wildly through the tree."

At that point, the trees along the lane began swaying in a breeze, which quickly intensified into a strong wind. Items blew about the driveway. A branch on one of the nearby fruit trees snapped and fell to the ground. Yet, inside the dome, all was quiet and still. Rosa dripped hot red candle wax into the water.

"Lightning quick, lightning long. Make it last; make it strong."

She added salt to the water, stirred it, and threw the contents of the pewter bowl out of the dome towards the advancing figures, quickly withdrawing her hand back into the dome. Lightning struck a tree in the lane, reducing it to fiery ash. All the evilness on the driveway lost momentum and moved backwards, forced to retreat by the dominant white witch's incredible power. As they looked on, the false image of Isabel on the driveway dissipated into a black wisp. They looked at each other, dumbfounded, emitting an audible sigh. Regardless, they were in shock, uncertain what would happen next, if anything at all. Finally, the storm abated, the trees stopped swaying, and the moon shone brightly.

Rosa had expected an onslaught by devilish souls and had countered a powerful attack, but fighting back had required considerable power and resilience. She calmly approached her altar box and checked its contents. Carl, Alicia, and the priest were left speechless, having never encountered such offensive and vile apparitions before. Modern films and TV portrayed evil – satanic beings, apparitions, or possession, adding to the public's belief that such things could occur. However, the events in the sleepy little village of Murla were far from reality.

"See," Rosa said, closing the lid on her box and its contents. "They tried to tempt and draw us out of the circle, but failed. Even so, it isn't over; they'll be back. So we must be ready."

Hearts sank, feelings were stunned. In the stillness, a moment of reflection ensued.

"Can anybody tell me what we just witnessed?" said Father Bernardo, finding his voice, and it would seem speaking for everybody.

"It sounds hard to believe," said Rosa. "This is the wickedness of the jinni, but he found it tough to exert his will over our combined goodness and resolve. We are peaceful, loving people in God's realm, so we will overcome evil. Good always prevails. I think you could say round one to us." With fun, she licked her right index finger, held it up in the air, and struck one.

Rosa had been surprised at the ferocity and cunning demonstrated. However, she knew that all three had no concept of the jinni, its evilness, or its depraved, calculating manner. In general, the fiend was a close comparison to the devil in Christianity. According to Tariq, it had been frightening and harassing spirits wherever it went for centuries and would continue to do so in Murla unless stopped. Knowing the way of the evil one, Tariq had prepared Rosa for what had just occurred. But could they continue to thwart the immense power of the wicked being?

Following the impressive spell that Nana had cast, the full moon shone brightly. On reflection, it seemed as if the evil had tried to snuff out the moonshine and cast darkness upon the land to aid its dark, devilish strategy.

"Do you think they will be back?" said Alicia, reeling from what she had just witnessed. Of those present, Alicia seemed to have the weakest will, needing constant reassurance. Although it didn't alleviate her concern, a massive hug from Rosa helped bring her wandering mind back and put her at ease. However, it was imperative to watch her closely.

Carl was unusually quiet. When questioned, he admitted that seeing the form of his mum being manhandled had shocked him. Of course, he loved her dearly, and the troubling illusion had shocked him significantly, even if it was all trickery and make-believe.

"I know how you feel, Carl, but as I said, he is looking into your mind, trying to find something that is dear and precious to you so that he can use it to peddle his evilness," said Rosa. "But please try to understand and believe what I say. I know it was a shock for you to experience what he did. However, it is rare and very unusual for the jinni to reveal itself as it did tonight. Normally, it keeps out of the mainstream of life and does its diabolical work surreptitiously. Nonetheless, it can change its form and feelings to become whatever it wants, hence the term shapeshifter. We have seen tonight what the evilness is capable of; remember that, be courageous, and we will overcome all that is thrown at us. We are all good souls and have a superior power behind us – the Lord. Believe me when I say the jinni is formidable, yet our love and conviction are even more powerful. Goodness prevails over all; you can be certain of that. Now... we need to prepare for what I feel will be the final confrontation."

"Tell us what we have to do, Nana, and we will do it," Carl said, feeling positive hearing her inspirational words. He liked calling Rosa Nana; it made him feel like he fitted into the kind, loving, all-encompassing

Romero family. A sense of belonging felt so crucial at the moment.

"Our dome of love, peace, and divinity has held up well, but I don't know how long it will continue. It has endured many hostile forces tonight.

"Oh," said Alicia. "Does that mean we could be in trouble?"

Immediately, Rosa realised her *faux pas*, "No, not at all." She quickly dismissed her negative comment and tried to engender a feeling of positivity and hope.

"We will be fine. Just be prepared to follow me and remain positive; that's all you need to do. Now let's prepare."

Carl spoke to Alicia. He hugged her and spoke words of comfort and reassurance. Father Bernardo and Rosa looked at each other and gave one of their all-knowing, albeit nervous smiles. Despite the depraved assault by evil forces, Carl and Alicia's loving embrace showed the real power.

"How did we do, Rosa?" said the priest, finding a minute to question his thoughts. Oddly enough, he felt out of place with his religious beliefs and Rosa's pagan beliefs. She saw things slightly differently from most people, but that was okay. She was one of God's children, first and foremost.

"We did well. I wasn't completely sure what to expect myself. However, positivity and strength of feeling got us through."

"I could feel the warmth and love of the Lord around us," said the father, "but I was astonished when you summoned that storm to drive the evil back. How is that possible, Rosa?" he said inquiringly.

Before she had time to reply, Carl called out. "They're here again."

Out in the lane, the dark shadow spirits gathered. However, they seemed organised this time – regimented as a muster of shadow figures. Standing side-by-side, they waited just like a vast wall of black shadows. In itself, their presence was terrifying enough, but to be organised and display a controlled, menacing united front was deeply troubling. For Rosa, the collection of spirits waiting, watching, and calculating was akin to a mighty battle where two opposing armies faced off just before the command to attack. Although concerned, she hid her feelings.

"Father Bernardo, please light the incense and pray for us," she nearly said in our time of need, but corrected her thought just in time.

Out in the lane, the shadow spirits parted. A huge, formidable soldier stepped forward. The form was over six feet tall and broad – very broad. Rosa guessed that he was some twenty stone and the jinni in one of his many terrifying guises, maybe a duplicate of one of the Spanish soldiers from 1609. His enormous size was terrifying. Glancing at the dome, he sneered and spat on the ground. His bulky figure, clad in leather with a metal breastplate, looked intimidating. His morion cabasset – Spanish helmet and large sword completed the revenant. A further look disturbed them even more.

Along with blood and gore on his hands and face, a fox's head hung from his leather waist belt. They stared in disbelief, disgust, and fear. Carl gulped; Alicia stepped back, looking towards the Finca for safety and sanctuary. Father Bernardo's eyes widened at the imminent danger. Yet, to everyone's surprise, Nana stepped to the front of the dome with purpose and pointed her wand at the enormous soldier in a sign of bravado and defiance.

"See if we care, you malevolent, disgusting, badass brute."

It seemed so out of place for Rosa to use such language, yet it displayed her strength of feeling and boldness. Carl wanted to stop Nana from voicing defiance that would enrage the brute all the more; however, his mouth was dry with fear. No words passed his lips.

In no time, the soldier pointed his sword at the dome, and the black shadow spirits advanced. As they entered the driveway, the soldier stood his ground, watching intensely like a general waiting for his troops to do battle. Bit by bit, the black, humanlike shadows advanced.

All four stood watching and waiting within the dome, unsure of what to do next.

"Okay," said Rosa, with inspiration coming to the fore, "everybody, join hands just like before."

They did as Rosa asked and linked, forming a circular, solid bond of resistance.

"Now, it is important for your minds to be strong. Think of a time when you overcame something bad or used great positivity to overcome misfortune. Then, feel that strength in your mind."

Carl instantly thought about being set upon by the raging bull and how he had overcome death twice. Since that ferocious day in Pamplona, this was the first time he had actively viewed the trauma with a positive perspective.

Alicia thought about the same scenario and how, with determination and phenomenal positivity, she had watched over Carl, cared for him, and turned the tide to help him recover to complete health. It was a wonderful feeling that she often ran through her mind when she sat and looked at Carl.

Father Bernardo recalled assisting in an exorcism many years ago. The person in question was a young man possessed by the devil. The monsignor and father cast out the devil and returned a possessed human being to normality, effectively cleansing him, thwarting the devil's evil work. He viewed that time with enthusiasm, success, and a desire to make a difference in the world and help humanity.

Nana's *joie de vivre* was endearing. With many joyful years on earth, every day was heavenly. She lived her life with appreciation, a fundamental belief in the goodness of life, and an undying faith in the inevitable reunion with Ernesto, her beloved husband.

THIRTY-SIX

Shadow spirits nearing the dome would soon test the structure's integrity. The first spirits to arrive came upon an unseen defence. They pushed against the clear dome to no avail. Then, out of stupidity, or was it clever planning? The spirits behind them climbed over the original spirits, standing on their shoulders to make a wall of human-like black shadows. Inside the dome, the evil spirits could be seen up close. Their bodies had heads, yet no faces; however, the shadow spirits could relate to one another and connect well. Fleetingly, Carl compared them with tiny human-like toy figures he had as a boy in the UK many years ago. Surprisingly, they joined together just like the black figures before him. Rosa feared the dome might collapse or pop like a soap bubble with the weight of numbers pressing against the structure's integrity. She could see the dome wall flexing under the pressure of bodies as more joined, creating an even higher wall of bodies. More and more climbed over others until three rows of shadow spirits were pressed against the clear dome. In effect, the moonlight was being blocked from them, changing the atmosphere within the dome to a darker, colder place.

Rosa knew that everyone depended upon her.

When all was said and done, it was her idea to take the fight to the jinni. She had to strengthen their resolve and, at the same time, show leadership, before the transparent dome, now flexing beyond what she thought was normal, began to fade away. With the wand raised, Rosa, the white witch, chanted a protection spell.

"By the power of the moon at night. Let all negativity be cast from site – the energies of protective light. Protect me now with energies bright. Brink, henceforth to me. So mote it be."

Within seconds, the dome shimmered with luminous strength. The flexing under the weight of shadow spirits stopped. Rosa felt ecstatic about the positive change, albeit small. However, it was uncertain how long the status quo would continue. She shouted encouragement to the others.

"It's working! They can't get to us!" Her mood was buoyant. A sense of hope had encouraged her to use the protection spell, and all seemed well, certainly for the moment. "We are safe here in the dome. Praise be to the Lord."

No sooner had Rosa said that than she saw long, sharp fingernails from one of the shadow people sticking under a small portion of the protective dome where it joined the driveway. The thing seemed to have realised where the dome sat, and there was the finest gap to lever it upwards. For the time being, there was only one set of fingernails; however, disaster could strike if all the shadow people did the same. Moreover, the soldier Rosa knew to be the jinni was still a significant threat – a powerful force to reckon with in the final conflict. According to Tariq in past conversations, his persona as a mighty soldier was one that the malevolence liked to portray when confronting people. A psychological ploy adopted that nobody ever challenged except for Nana, the priest, Alicia, and Carl.

How could she stop the attempted lifting of the dome? As she considered the problem, Father Bernardo saw the worrying concern on her face. He let go of their hands and asked them to join to complete the circle. Taking out his silver altar cross, he walked over to the evil shadow's fingernails sticking under the dome and touched them with the religious cross. An unearthly squeal thronged the air. With satisfaction that his innovative idea had worked, he held the cross up and began to recite the Lord's Prayer. The dark spirits transformed from solid black to fuzzy, human-like shapes. They all felt the pain simultaneously that one shadow spirit felt because they were inexplicably linked.

Displaying rage with the dome and the people inside became the mighty soldier's nemeses. He would not allow the situation to play out any further. Action was needed. He held his sword on high as if in exaltation to its extreme power and moved forward, swinging the weapon from right to left in a rhythmical motion as he stomped the short distance to his sworn enemies. One of the shadow spirits got in his way, only to be sliced in half at the torso. There was no blood, merely two halves of a black body wriggling around on the ground. Both parts tried to join together, but they failed. The sight was gross and disturbing to all in the cupola.

From within, everyone who saw the soldier's formidable physique knew the situation was grave. They would die unless something happened – but what? The soldier's combined determination and strength were alarming. His power was greater than that of the four combined.

Spells, prayers and a belief in God had helped keep the group of four out of harm's way. Now, the jinni was upon them and intent on their destruction. He was single-minded in clearing the lowlife out of his way and intended a bloodbath, slicing them into pieces; such was his vicious, ruthless, evil nature. The dome's hitherto sanctuary would fall, leaving Carl, Alicia, Rosa, and the father exposed to slaughter.

"Be ready!" shouted Rosa. "If he gets through the dome, run to the front door of the Finca, get inside, and slam the door shut!"

As she said that, one, two, and then three rats ran through the lower part of the dome near the seam of the transparent wall. Rosa knew, as a white witch, that animals and children could breach the dome's defence and walk straight through unimpeded. Nonetheless, she had not considered that it would happen. The rats appeared to be in attack mode, making straight for Alicia. She screamed and ran to the back of the dome near the front door. Carl and the father rushed to her aid, stomping on the rats and rendering them lifeless. However, three more rats entered on the other side of the dome. This time, they leapt at Carl, Rosa and Father Bernardo. They were intent on going for the throat. Even though the first rat had jumped for the father's throat, his plastic white collar stopped the rat from sinking its teeth into his flesh. He ripped it away from his throat, collar and all, threw it to the floor, and stomped on it repeatedly. Carl was too quick for the flying rat; he grabbed it midair and threw it to the ground, where it scurried back through the dome wall. Rosa jumped back, throwing a handful of witch herbs from the altar table at the rat. It fell to the ground, blinded. Just as quickly, Carl kicked it out of the dome. A head's turn to look at the soldier placed him just outside the dome, swinging his mighty sword. Each time it sliced through the transparent dome, the slit resealed itself. However, everyone except Carl was anxious about the killer steel, which was too close for comfort. Mysteriously, a bizarre out-of-body connection took place in Carl's mind. His fear abated as a strange force rose within his very being.

The soldier moved closer to the clear wall of their protection and tried pressing against the domed barrier, but any effort to damage or distort the structure was in vain. His rage intensified. Not to be outdone, he started swinging his sword again, hoping to cut a piece out of the clear wall. Rosa knew that the dome would soon cease to exist. Nevertheless, they were ready and prepared to leave the dome's destruction and run to the front door for safety when and if something grave happened, and now it appeared inevitable that it would.

THIRTY-SEVEN

The sound of a horse's hooves over rocky ground pierced the night. A huge stallion in pale-green livery appeared at a gallop, moving out of the darkness and entering the Finca's driveway. Astride the magnificent beast sat Tariq, upright, focused, menacing – ready to do battle to save the four human beings from the wrath of the jinni. Instantly, the brute of a soldier reacted to the unwelcome intrusion. He turned to face Tariq and raised his sword, ready to slice into the horse or Tariq, whichever was unfortunate enough to come into contact with the brutal sword. Tariq held a spear in his one remaining hand, nestled under his arm, and pointed at the aggressor as if it were a lance.

At that point, the dome faded, and the shimmering circle disappeared. Tariq pulled on the reins; the horse reared just in time to avoid a sword slash from the brutish soldier. Shadow beings saw their chance; now, the dome had gone, in its place stood an empty driveway. All protection from Rosa's remarkable power had gone, leaving the humans exposed.

Purposely backing the horse away from the soldier, Tariq guided the horse in a wide circle, treading and mutilating even more shadow beings. Not to be outdone and obsessed with killing, black shadow figures raced towards the humans near the Finca doorway to smother them by sheer weight of numbers.

"Quickly, inside," cried Carl.

There was no need to be told twice. Rosa had already collected her box, and the priest grabbed his religious regalia. Alicia was already ahead and in the doorway, hyperventilating, making disturbing, discordant noises akin to trauma-induced asthma, which Rosa and the father realised was serious and needed immediate attention. They sprinted through the front door and slammed it shut just in time as black bodies gathered in significant numbers around the door and the windows of their home. However, unbeknown to them in the confusion, an arm and a foot of one of the shadow beings were chopped off by the closing door and left writhing about the hallway, inducing a feeling of revulsion, adding to Alicia's asthmatic attack. The sight of wriggling limb parts was overwhelming, and it became essential to remove them quickly. But they could not open the front door to throw the body parts out. With great ingenuity, as Father Bernado calmed Alicia, Rosa opened the study door. Finding a brush in the kitchen, she brushed the body parts into the study, then closed the door.

Meanwhile, Tariq seemed to be having fun guiding his horse, trampling more and more black figures, prompting the soldier to quickly reassess his tactics. Many black spirit individuals had been sliced, chopped, and trampled in the melee – black body parts lay on the ground, wriggling and writhing. More undead shadow spirits appeared and joined the skirmish, adding to the confusion in what was intended to be a simple killing spree for the soldier and thwarting its tactical plan.

Inside the finca, staring out at the driveway, Carl switched on the outdoor light, startling the black shadow figures. They immediately backed off from the Finca. Yet, the aggressive soldier remained steadfast, looking from Tariq to those inside the building. He was unsure who to tear into first. The soldier regarded the one-armed arab and the horse as a nuisance. His attention was focused on breaking into the Finca to destroy the humans while the black hoards kept Tariq busy. As he headed to the Finca, the shadow spirits bore down on the horse, surrounding him, spooking the stallion, frustrating any aggression and impetus.

One almighty kick from the soldier, and the front door flew open. He took a roundhouse swipe at the priest with his sword, which came to grief as his sword embedded itself in the framework of the door. The missed blow enraged him all the more. He had brute force on his side, yet lacked finesse and technique in close combat.

Tariq realised that the spirit people were no match for him or his mighty steed, even when present in significant numbers. Cleverly, he guided the stallion in circles again to trample the black spirits, making a pathway to the Finca's front door. Now, the odds were more than even, and the soldier saw the change of events. He turned to face Tariq, sat astride his horse, wanting to protect his friends from the evil abomination. The soldier raised his sword; this time, he appeared to be timing his engagement. However, being battle-savvy, the horse reared. His front hooves came down to administer a searing blow to the soldier's arm, knocking the sword from his hand. Instantly, the fighter reacted with anger, pain, and humiliation, but then quickly reached for his sword. Tariq leapt from the saddle, holding the spear out in a threatening stance. Now, he could confront the evil without any distraction. The soldier realised he needed more room to wield his sword and stepped sideways away from the front door for maximum space. The clash began in earnest with a swinging sword and deadly thrusts of the sharp, jagged spear.

Like two gladiators fighting in an arena, both looked for the optimum moment to deliver the killer blow. Because of its length and deadly, pointed, serrated blade, the spear allowed Tariq a safe distance from the soldier to prod and taunt, looking to bring about an end to his foe. The plan to bury the sharp and jagged point of the spear in the soldier's throat above the breastplate proved to be like swatting a fly that kept moving. However, when he came within range, the soldier's sword hacked at the wooden shaft. They moved, harassing each other backwards and forwards – prodding, poking and harrying, each waiting for the other to make a mistake. On one such swing of the sword, the jagged spear's end fell to the ground, thanks to a sharp blade. Tariq was left vulnerable and on the back foot. All he could do was try to hold the soldier back with the remains of the wooden spear. Tables had turned, and the soldier took the initiative. Tariq was pushed back with every swing of the sword, dodging to evade the deadly cutting edge as if it were the most lethal snake on Earth that could kill with just one bite. Soon, he would be out of space and out of luck.

Watching fearfully from inside the Finca, Carl felt helpless; he could not stand by and watch his friend fight alone. He had to help, but what could he do? Then, it occurred to him in a flash of inspiration. He ran through the back door, around the Finca, onto the patio, where he picked up a long-handled axe for chopping logs. Instead of running back through their home, Carl deliberately ran around the Finca, arriving at the front and surprising the soldier. Carlos the Brave made for Tariq's side. They took a brief moment to look at each other, smiled an all-knowing smile and fought as a combined front, ready to bring it to the out-of-control jinni in the guise of a soldier.

The unity of the two seemed to embolden Tariq, who took the fight up with renewed vigour. Seeing the battle unfold on the driveway, Alicia screamed Carl's name, but he was oblivious to her concern – caught up in a moment of courage, boldness, and comradeship. A swing of the axe made contact with the mighty sword, emitting a loud metallic clang. The soldier half-turned to face Carl, who posed a serious threat. Tariq's spear, minus its pointed blade, lunged forward, jabbing the soldier on the side of the ribs behind the breastplate. Although not tearing open the skin, breaching the soldier's defence was humiliating and annoying. The duo were formidable in fighting the jinni, but Carl needed to move to Tariq's left side for maximum effect and the duo's protection. As the wooden shaft of the spear lunged forward, the soldier stepped back, enraged and affronted, allowing Carl to change position. He stepped behind and to the other side of Tariq. Now, the duo was complete and able to fight with formidable force. Both shone in that moment of togetherness, feeding off each other's strength, daring, and courage.

By now, the shadow spirits had accumulated quickly and were back in the fight. They surrounded and supported the soldier by confusing and confounding the opposition. It became evident that they were changing the odds by sheer numbers. The black shadow spirits showed no concern whether they were mutilated or not. More and more spirits entered the fray – their strategy – to get in the way, to confuse and confound. At times, neither Carl nor Tariq could see the mighty soldier because of the blackness, yet they kept swinging, chopping, and flattening black figures. Tariq had dropped the spear shaft in preference for his Jambiya, slicing at the shadow spirits right and left as fast as his right arm could work. Yet, as the two warriors fought, eliminating spirits, even more took their places. Sheer numbers were winning as Carl and Tariq stepped back to the Finca's front door. Soon, they would be pinned with their backs to the front entrance, which could only mean one thing – their demise, especially if the soldier saw the opportunity and broke through the black spirit bodies, wielding his sword. He could easily slaughter Carlos the Brave and Tariq with determination and strength. Yet the duo showed no fear, as they did in their final battle with the Spanish troops hundreds of years ago. They knew that the outcome was not good, yet they continued to fight like two superhuman warriors.

Rosa had always lived her life with purity and goodness, which fitted well with the white witch ideology. Yet, as she watched the devastating fight on the Finca's driveway, she could not stand by any longer without doing something, but what? For her, the evil had to be stopped for the very last time. At that moment, she decided to use an extremely potent spell; however, it was a spell not within her coven of white witches. For all of her years as a white witch, Rosa was aware of the perils of using black magic. It was an aspect of witchcraft she had always rejected until now. She was anxious to help and knew this was the only course of action to save Carl, Alicia, Father Bernardo, and her very good friend Tariq. Desperate times required desperate measures. Her mind was made up; she had worked it out in a quick calculation and went for it, fearless yet believing in the Lord's protection.

Running to the living room, Rosa opened her box and took out a pewter bowl. She wrote 'jinni' on a piece of paper and lit it. Simultaneously, she dropped a dried bay leaf and a dried red apple peel into the pewter bowl with the paper; it flamed blue like a brandy-lit Christmas pudding. Running to the front door at Rosa speed, she lifted the bowl and blew the ashes into the night breeze. White witch Rosa recited a heartfelt sentiment.

"By all the power and good in me. I refute your evilness. I send you away to another dimension, never to return.

Red and green banishing grace. Cast all evil out of this place."

The furore came to a dramatic halt. The black shadow spirits sloped away, revealing an empty driveway. The cessation of aggression, noise, and intense fear was instantaneous. All stood motionless, looking around. Feelings of terror diminished. Carl looked at Tariq with a curious, what happened look. Then the realisation dawned, and everyone turned to look at Rosa.

"Nana, are you alright?" said Alicia.

Before she could answer, Ralph bounded across the driveway, bypassing everyone, making for Rosa.

"Nooo!" shouted Tariq, with a cry of great concern. Even so, it was too late. The dog leapt at Rosa, viciously attacking, biting her leg and then her arm as she tried to defend herself. Carl took two significant steps to reach Nana: he picked up the spearhead lying on the driveway and plunged it deep into the dog's ribs, puncturing its lung. With the intensity of the moment, grappling and gnashing of teeth from the rabid dog, blood drenching the driveway, Carl and the dog rolled around, battling for the upper hand, and then the struggle ceased.

THIRTY-EIGHT

Tariq did not come near the Finca – Casa Azahar for many months. Winter came and went; spring bloomed, and temperatures improved, creating optimism for the year ahead. Tariq knew that this was Rosa's favourite time of the year, so it seemed appropriate that he paid a visit to the Finca. Although mildly subdued, his demeanour was self-effacing, gracious, and polite. However, it became clear he was on a mission, and he explained why he was calling.

"Carlos, Alicia. It is good to see you again. My apologies for disturbing you."

"No, please don't apologise, my friend," said Carl, sporting a significant scar across his face, and minus three fingers to his left hand. "It is so good to see you again after so long. Alicia and I have often spoken about you since our encounter with the dark forces. We hoped to see you again one day, and here you are."

Tariq's half-smile barely registered on his rugged face. His demeanour was in keeping with his sadness. Everybody had found it hard to come to terms with such a terrible loss, but comforted themselves, believing that Rosa, who died that awful night with the deadly attack of the dog, would be at rest and with her dearly departed Ernesto once more.

"First, thank you for coming to my aid, Carlos the

Brave; our combined strength was extraordinary. We fought the evil jinni with enormous strength and courage. I felt our special connection come to the fore once more, like hundreds of years ago when we fought the enemy." He looked straight at Carl. "However, I am and will eternally be so sorry for how it all ended. It was a joyous reunion, but a sad occasion for us all. Regrettably, that night, we lost a wonderful lady. If I could, I would dearly have given up my soul instead of hers, but it wasn't to be. As you know, I am not a person in the true sense of the word. I am here on Earth in my spiritual form, yet for all those hundreds of years, as I roamed our country, all I wanted was to see you again. Befriending Rosa here in Murla, I found you, and I can't thank that dear lady enough."

Tears streamed down Carl's face; all self-control had gone; a minute passed as he calmed his emotions. In part, they were for the loss of Rosa, of course, but equally, his deep strength of feeling for Tariq.

Carl took a breath and spoke. "I don't know what to say, Tariq. I feel extremely sorry for the tragic loss, but I am bursting with a huge fondness for you that words can't explain. It is like losing somebody you knew and then meeting that self-same person many years later, bringing back memories and reigniting your love for them."

"Yes, I feel the same," said Tariq, appearing a bit more relaxed in the presence of his good friends. "In war, soldiers form a special bond. It is because they share so much of life and death, and experience trauma and pain together. As soldiers, we look after each other and lay down our lives for our comrades. I had then, and do now, have this strong bond with you." He placed his hand on his heart in a gesture of sentiment and compelling respect. "I look upon you as my brother, but more than that, you and I have the same soul that transcends time, space and all of life. I have never known anybody like you and never will again."

With that, Tariq stepped forward, wrapped his right arm around Carl, pulled him in and patted him on the back in a rare display of emotion. Carl was shocked by the action, not only because of the rare and genuine feelings between two men, but also because he had always believed his very good friend to be spiritual and incapable of a physical connection, as he had just shown. Despite that, he embraced Tariq with equal enthusiasm, which felt so good. Carl had to ask a question as they stepped back from their union.

"I know you are spiritual and don't possess a body as such in this world."

"Correct."

"So how did this just happen? We embraced."

"Carlos, my inquiring friend. I will tell you as much as you can understand. Yes, I am spiritual and not of human form. Nevertheless, in the hundreds of years I have wandered this Earth, I have practised and learned to focus my mind. So I can maintain my body's solidity for short periods. Yet, the difficult action takes a lot of strength from me, just like the night of my encounter with the jinni, where I maintained my bodily presence and fought the evilness. I only use this in exceptional circumstances. Now, I need to tell you something to ease your mind. Carlos the Brave and Alicia, please take a seat. I will explain."

They sat agog listening to their good friend, wondering what was next.

"When we first met in Valencia, I was the son of a merchant trader and trained as a knight of my country. My family lived and worked in Valencia; we imported goods from all over the world to the harbour and distributed them across the region. Although we were of different religions, you, a Roman Catholic and I, belonging to the Muslim faith, we were work colleagues and later became very good friends."

"Hold on a minute. Why was I working for you if I was of a different religion?"

"That is easy. Even though we were Muslims in our business, we did not exclude people from our circle because of their religion, race or creed. On the contrary, we believed we could and should all work together in the common interest for the sake of humanity. It was and still is our philosophy of life."

"Wow, you believed that then in the seventeenth century and maybe even before?"

"Yes, it was our belief," said Tariq, unapologetic for his people's inspiring belief. "Much later, we heard of King Phillip's decree to remove all Muslims from Spain, and along with my family, we became very concerned about what the future had in store for us. Talk filtered down to street level from other parts of Spain about soldiers enacting the decree, but we couldn't believe something so monumental as ridding the country of Muslims could have occurred. Yet, it did. This signalled serious times ahead, and we heard many rumours. Following the decree, barbarity broke out in many parts of Spain. The king's troop in the region of Valencia made their way from village to village, killing, torturing and ejecting Muslims from their homes and businesses – effectively brutalising our people. My family were killed, and I, very nearly. It was mere good fortune that you and I were working outside, storing produce in an outbuilding, when we heard screams and shouts and saw, for ourselves, the inhumane acts taking place around us. However, seeing people who worked for us turn against my family surprised me more than anything else. I recall running out into the courtyard towards my father, who tried to remonstrate with the workers. The scene turned ugly, and work colleagues and friends were now against us. Because I was outnumbered, I remember backing off and bumping into you, Carlos. You were standing behind me, trying to make sense of all the horrible things that were unfolding around us. Without a thought, you stepped forward in front of me and tried to calm the agitated workers in the courtyard. Even so, it was no good; your voice was lost amongst all the noise and terror. You tried to reason with them, but they wouldn't listen. The next thing I knew, somebody came towards me with a sword, swung it and severed my left arm just below the shoulder. As I fell to the ground, everything became black. I only knew what happened later when you explained it to me, Carlos the Brave. As I lay motionless on the ground with blood all over me and my arm lying mere feet away, you convinced the crowd that I was dead; because of that, they moved on. The only thing that saved your life from the crowd was that you were then, as now, of Spanish blood and a Roman Catholic.

You pulled the material off my severed arm, bound the open shoulder wound tightly, and dragged me into the outbuilding for safety. We stayed there the rest of the day until nighttime. It seems I clung to life, but I survived only because of your help. I was in extreme pain. You gave me fluids, kept me warm and went to find fellow Moors who moved me to the countryside away from the city and nursed me back to health. Had it not been for you, I would have died. And we wouldn't be having this conversation now."

Carl wiped his eyes, cleared his throat, and spoke. "I had no idea, Tariq. Of course, I can't remember all of that, but I'm so glad I could help you, my friend. It seems so inconceivable what truly happened and all that we went through together."

"Exactly."

"Even so, what I can't come to terms with is why I was fighting by your side, a Muslim, and then, we both died here on Caballo Verde?" The mystery had featured strongly in his mind since the first time he met Tariq, who spoke of standing side by side and fighting the Spanish troops.

"You never gave up your religion."

"I didn't?"

"No, not at all. What you did was rail against the injustices of the King's decree and your fellow Spaniards, who turned against the Moorish people and their way of life. You demonstrated exceptional bravery and fortitude in speaking out for my people and addressing injustice. Then, when you realised that no one was listening and that your people had turned against you, you took the unusual step of joining me and my homeless friends, eventually fighting on my side against oppression and tyranny, trying to help our cause and my people. You are no different now. What impressed me was always your sense of fairness, even when it put you at odds with the Spanish people and threatened your life. Fairness meant everything to you. And so, my friend, now you know why I have such deep feelings for you. Carlos the Brave, you helped my fellow Muslims and me for no reason other than a sense of doing the right thing in life."

A phone call disturbed the meaningful get-together. Carl's dad was on the phone, reminding him about his mum's birthday. As they chatted, Alicia conversed with Tariq.

"Thank you for the kind sentiment about Nana. You're right; she was lovely, and I miss her dearly. However, I still find it hard to believe that the jinni, as you say, could turn into the image of Ralph and attack her."

"I know. Many people don't accept that it can change into an animal or anything it pleases. It cleverly used the element of surprise and bounded across the driveway as Ralph; in reality, it was the shapeshifting jinni."

Alicia still suffered from feelings of guilt when she

thought of the dreadful scene.

On that fateful night, Rosa immediately knew what it meant when she saw the dog bounding through the clutter of black bodies on the driveway, heading towards Carl. She had put her hand out to protect Carl, and in so doing, the jinni in the form of Ralph savagely attacked Rosa, biting her arm and hand and pulling her down to the ground.

"I can still see it now, Tariq, black shadow people milling around, body parts on the ground and a state of confusion. The jinni, in the form of a soldier, had disappeared. So, because of this, Nana left the security of the Finca and moved onto the driveway to help."

"She was very intuitive and saw the danger immediately," said Tariq. "I suppose you could say she sacrificed herself to save us all. And, it was only the swift action of Carlos the Brave picking the spearhead up and stabbing the dog dead that brought an end to the terrible scene."

"She was a fearless lady, Tariq. And you are right when you say she paid the ultimate price." Alicia took out one of Nana's lace handkerchiefs and wiped her tears away.

Carl had finished his phone conversation and entered the living room, aware that Alicia was distressed and tearful.

"Is everything alright?" he asked, concerned.

"It's just me having a sad moment thinking about Nana. We were saying how courageous she was when she confronted the mad dog, which was the jinni. Lord, how I hate that evil, vile thing."

"I know. I feel the same, but the outcome could not have changed. Nana was so badly injured, and because of her age and the severity of the injury, she could not pull through. All her strength had gone. Vengeance isn't good, but I'm glad I stabbed that horrible thing to death. I would have given my life to save her; nevertheless, she could see what was happening, and being the amazing tower of strength that she was, offered herself up to that mad dog in a split second without any thought for herself."

"Strange how we haven't talked about that terrible night very much," said Alicia, "but seeing as we are, I must say I've never seen such an incredible transformation when you became Carlos the Brave." She looked deeply into his eyes and smiled the most loving, admiring smile.

As before, Tariq refused all offers of refreshment from Alicia. Strange to say, after some time talking with their friend, they witnessed an odd phenomenon. Tariq's image began to fade at the edges, as if it were a poor-quality video that wouldn't play correctly. Tariq realised he was losing his strength and began to wilt visibly. He apologised and confirmed that, as he had said earlier, it had taken a great deal out of him when he entered a brief state of solidity. His final words were short and to the point. In two days, he arranged to meet Carl and Alicia on the open land adjacent to the cave's entrance, close to the Devil's Chair.

The meeting plan was confirmed, as Alicia was able

to get a day off from work. Likewise, Carl could take the day off with the time owed. Yet, mystery dominated their minds. The only exacting thing about Tariq's request was that they both brought powerful hand torches. There was no mention of why they should meet again on the mountain. Nevertheless, it was organised and done in the inimitable Tariq way, and that was all to be said.

Tariq strolled out of the front door, turned to say goodbye and disappeared. Even having seen the same disappearing act before, it still left them feeling quite strange, and it took a few minutes for them to come to terms with his departure. Tariq's revelation about Valencia, his knowledge of Carl, and the events of that fateful day were earth-shattering. However, one thing that kept coming back was the extraordinary relationship he had had with Tariq. In the coming days, they would discuss the revelations in more detail, likely generating additional questions for Tariq, which he may or may not answer depending on how he felt.

THIRTY-NINE

Climbing Caballo Verde mid-morning to meet up with Tariq was a pleasant enough experience. It was a Friday, and they arrived at the destination a little after 11:30. Both looked forward to seeing their good friend again; such were their feelings for him. The view from that height was spectacular. The valley in spring was a mass of green, and the sunshine, which lent a pleasant warmth to the atmosphere, gladdened the heart. Above all, the smell of pine trees, shrubs, and wild rosemary infused the air with a unique, pleasing, earthy fragrance.

However, the area held a great deal of sadness for Carl and Alicia ever since their conversation with Tariq when they talked about the horrific, vile, cruel treatment that took place on the mountain and, ultimately, the cave and its entrance hundreds of years ago. It was hard to imagine that such a beautiful, green, and verdant mountain with all its glory was a theatre of war.

"You made it then," said Tariq, appearing from nowhere. Carl could not help thinking that his very good friend had fantastic knowledge of the mountain and knew it like the back of his hand. No wonder he was able to move around unobserved, able to appear and disappear whenever and wherever. In reality, he seemed lifelike to humans and could travel anywhere, thanks to his unique, otherworldly life force. His capacity for such enabled him to move between the present and maybe anywhere in history. Whatever it was, he had never divulged anything to anybody of his sentience–his path of life, which made him unique. Nevertheless, because of his unassuming personality, he was extremely likeable.

"Yes, we made it. I must confess, though, we're quite intrigued why you wanted to meet us here. But, as I said to Alicia, you would have a sound reason for making such a request."

"Precisely. Follow me." He said, heading off between shrubs and trees towards a rocky backdrop. Looking back to ensure his friends were right behind him, he climbed a rock that appeared to have steps or step holes on its surface. He rose the rocky steps to a height of about fifteen feet and stepped inwards across a flat surface, out of sight. "Follow me!" he shouted.

Carl and Alicia looked at each other, smiled, and shrugged their shoulders as if to say, 'Oh well,' and followed his example. Then, like mountain goats, they scrambled up the rocky steps. Before long, they had reached the top, where Tariq awaited them in anticipation of something very unusual.

"This, my friends, is the devil's chair." Holding his hand out, he indicated a flattened rocky area with a most unusual ten-foot-high rock face behind it. Now, they were confused. Had he brought them all this way merely to point out a rock formation? A little bemused, they looked around and back at Tariq.

"You don't know why I've brought you here, do you?"

"No, my friend, we don't."

"I am going to show you something; however, I must have your word that you never speak of what you are about to see to anybody. That includes friends and relatives. No one at all."

Although surprised and intrigued, Carl and Alicia gave their word; at the same time, they felt a burning desire to learn everything about the secret they had just agreed to keep. Still, they knew that if Tariq, their friend and someone they greatly respected, asked them to keep a secret, it was crucial to do so.

Tariq cleared away some shrub growth and leaves from the rock formation, gripped the edge of the flat rock known as the seat of the Devil's Chair, and lifted it upward until it stood vertically, leaning against the main upright rock. Effectively, he had exposed an entrance down into the cavernous beyond. However, the effort exerted in lifting the seat caused a few seconds of Tariq's image to fade and then come back. Even so, it was amazing that as a spirit, he could perform such a physical act.

"You can follow me, but be very careful and grip the rock face, putting your feet on the rocky ledges as you descend."

Once he had descended into the cavern, Tariq shouted for Carl to come next. The climb inside was like a rock-climbing wall, with handholds and footholds. All three, having descended, stood momentarily to adjust to the low light conditions.

"Did you bring the torches as I requested?"

"Yes, they are in our backpacks," said Carl.

"Good, you will need them as we walk down the cave's passageway," he said with even more mystery unfolding.

As he led the way, Tariq pointed out family etchings on the cave's walls. Names and inscriptions had been carved into the rock face; some were ornate, others plain and simple. The resultant etchings were a record of the Muslim people's lives and deaths, of those confined to the cave from 1609 till 1723. Their names were easily distinguished. Tariq's idea of torches became essential as they carefully walked along the rough, underfoot passageway. Now and then, they stopped, looked and wondered what sort of people they were reading about, what they were like, and how they would have lived had the royal decree never been issued. Surprisingly, Tariq knew them all by name and was happy to offer information about them if they stopped and showed interest. Although the monikers represented original families, relatives, or friends who had lived and died in the cave, Carl and Alicia noticed that the number of names on the walls had dwindled over the years. Over time, some of the residents had given birth. However, after many years of incarceration in the cave, the population declined through ageing or illness to the point that they ceased to exist.

While the Moors lived inside the cave, Tariq was present and did his best to make their lives more comfortable. Realistically, they knew they could never leave the cave and be united with their people. (If any had survived.) Fear was a basic emotion for the Moors and a great reinforcer, convincing them to stay on the mountain and in the cave. However, in their lifetime, some ventured out of the Devil's Chair for a quick look-see and then quickly returned to safety. Others wholeheartedly agreed never to go out; the violent past was still very fresh in their minds.

Given that Tariq was a spirit, seen to the Moors as he was to most people, he was able to advise on matters such as food and water to be found in the area or things he had seen on the mountain that had been discarded but were valuable for the internees. He helped them live as close to a normal life as possible, but more than that, in comfort and ease.

At the end of the passageway in the cave's entrance, Tariq stopped and pointed out a time-honoured etching on the massive boulder that had blocked the entrance. It was an epitaph. Carl shone his torch across the few words that read.

1609 Tariq — Carlos the Brave

Tariq pointed to the inscription. "This has been here since my people began living in the cave. The engraving was their way of showing appreciation and a lasting memorial to the two final soldiers who gave up their lives so that the remaining Moors could survive." He pointed to the inscription with great pride.

"That, my friend, was you."

Carl tried to control the heartrending emotion, yet

strange, unfamiliar, deep-seated feelings came to the fore, upsetting his composure. In the distant canyons of his mind, minute flashes of recollection teased him and then faded. Of course, he could not remember the final battle with the Spanish troops, where he died alongside Tariq. However, he now knew it was all accurate and true. Surprisingly, when he first met Tariq, he doubted the account of 1609. But now, there was tangible proof linking him to the past. No one spoke for a while until Tariq broke the silence.

"The cave people always hoped that you, Carlos the Brave, would see this many years on, and here you are..."

A moment passed before anyone spoke, and then Tariq filled the cave's entrance with private thoughts. "I feel so emotional, my friend. Every time I am here, I read it aloud, and I'm transported back in time to that day when we stood side by side on the hillside, surrounded by dead and dying brave soldiers, defending the fleeing people whose final sanctuary was to be this cave. Standing by you, a non-Muslim, fighting for our lives and our cause, was the proudest day of my life. You were prepared to take up the fight because of the fundamental principle that life was sacred and no man should ever take what rightfully belonged to someone else. So, Carlos the Brave, I honour and salute you." He put his hand on his heart and bowed his head in reverence.

Carl shook his head in disbelief at the tribute his good friend paid him.

"My friend, Tariq, until my dying day, I will never

forget this moment. I have so much love and feeling for you, unlike anybody I have ever known before in my life."

Tariq looked at his two friends and smiled in one of those rare moments. "There is just one more surprise I have for you."

"Surprise," said Alicia.

"Please wait here." Tariq walked off into the dark passageway without a torch and seemingly in good humour, which was surprising in itself.

As he left them, Carl and Alicia stood side by side, their arms around each other, shining their torches and gazing at the epigraph in a moment of great pride, yet one that seemed illusory, as if part of a dream.

Alicia was the first to speak. "It's as if this incredible experience was meant to be, Carl, as if we were brought together just for this."

Little did she know that her words appeared otherworldly, as if voiced by a divine being unable to keep a secret.

FORTY

After many years of incarceration, the cave's dark, foreboding surroundings slowly changed and became tolerable. With ingenuity, life became more manageable. Many people living together, being inventive enough to come up with clever ideas, positively changed their lives for the better. They pooled resources for a common cause, benefiting the small mountain community. Yet, the one resounding collective thought from all imprisoned in the cave was that they would never leave their confinement. Their sanctuary, with a constant, dark temperature of 17-20 degrees Celsius year-round, was comfortable. By ingenuity and a determination to survive, they had made it their forever home. As such, it was a haven from the brutal, oppressive regime they and their loved ones had experienced firsthand by the royal troops and, surprisingly, by many Spanish people in the area and beyond.

It would have taken months, maybe even years, to deal with the trauma they had all experienced. Although in some cases, suppressing the appalling terror was by far the best way of dealing with all the horrors that constantly surfaced in their minds.

The war to expel the Moors from Spain was fought in sporadic stages. However, by 1619, most displaced

Moors had gone from Iberia. Most ended up as refugees in North and West Africa or were forced into slavery and transported worldwide.

Spanish people, in general, did their best to forget about the brutality and injustice to the Moors that beset the whole country. Returning to everyday life and seemingly a cessation of violence in the country after such turbulent times gave Spain credibility in the world. Moorish mosques were converted into Roman Catholic Churches or Cathedrals, which in part signalled the emergence of a new Spain.

Carl and Alicia looked around the cave. Low-level light bathed the area, streaming in from gaps between the large boulder that blocked the entrance. The domed ceiling added a sense of height and space. On the large chamber floor, worn rugs made of sheep's wool and goat hair, collected by the young boys on their ventures around the mountain, instigated rug-making within the cave. The tufts of wool and hair were found snagged on shrubs, bushes, and rocks in the area.

Additionally, tapestries were created to instil a sense of comfort and home, lovingly crafted in various dyed colours from fruits, berries, and sap. Homemade, rudimentary furniture, in the form of stools and chairs, showed ingenuity in their making. Makeshift paintings adorned the rocky walls, and ornaments spread around gave a feeling of homeliness in an otherwise basic existence.

Their torches lit up the cave as Carl and Alicia

familiarised themselves with the rudimentary surroundings. Thanks to Tariq, the discovery provided a first-hand experience of the Moorish history of 1609.

Finally, Tariq returned to the cavern with somebody else.

Alicia shone her torch and called out, "Nana!"

"Hello, Alicia and Carl," said Rosa in a subdued, strained voice. "Yes, it is me, or maybe should I say a form of me here to see you lovely people."

Alicia motioned to throw her arms around Nana in sheer delight, but was stopped by Tariq.

"You must control yourself, Señora Alicia."

"Sorry. I was just overcome. I'm so excited to see our lovely Nana after such a horrible departure." She felt compelled to give an account of their feelings, "Before we knew it, you had been taken to the hospital and... " she faltered, "...died without us saying goodbye or anything."

Carl said nothing. He was dumbfounded, knowing that Nana had died in the hospital due to injuries sustained by the jinni in the form of Ralph, and now here she was.

"Rosa is just like me in spirit form, so you can't touch her like a normal person," said Tariq. "You should also know she is very weak, so you must not put her through undue stress."

"But why and how did it all happen?"

Although he was not at the hospital in her dying moments, Tariq sensed her passing. He also sensed that she was troubled. Attacked by the dog and leaving

Earth's realm heavily played on her mind. Rosa had unfinished business and felt compelled to see her granddaughter and Carl one final time to ensure they were alright after the horrific events of that night, and to establish once and for all that the jinni had been defeated, so no ill could ever prevail upon their two lives again.

At Rosa's suggestion, Alicia and Carl sat, and Nana stood nearby as Tariq watched the proceedings. They talked at length about the violent encounter at Casa Azahar with the soldier and the black shadow people. Their togetherness was opportune for Rosa to speak with Carl and Alicia, bringing closure to all that had transpired before her passing. Rosa asked about her daughter, son-in-law, and friends in Pamplona. Yet, she spoke more about the sad and troubling events that led to her demise. Although she knew her passing had left a considerable hole in their lives, Rosa was determined to ease any remaining worries. Doing this would help them accept and adjust to the reality of the situation and gain a deeper understanding of the afterlife.

"So are you here just in spirit, Nana?" said Alicia. She found her presence challenging to accept, even though Tariq had already confirmed that she was. Alicia had to hear Rosa's account for herself.

"Darling Alicia, yes, that is correct. When I died, I remembered floating out of my body. It seemed so very strange and yet comforting, as I no longer experienced pain or discomfort from my injuries or aches and pains from the old, decrepit body I was carrying around." She managed a brief smile. "I recall being weightless –

floating on high, looking down upon my body on the hospital bed, seeing nurses and doctors around me. I had no desire to return to my body with its Earthly limitations, so I waited for a while, wondering what to do. Then, as if out of my control, I drifted through the ceiling to a place I did not know. However, it was truly amazing. An all-encompassing pure white light enveloped me. That was when I experienced the blissful feelings of overwhelming love and warmth. Nothing mattered anymore because I was enveloped in a loving, compassionate light. I remember thinking life on Earth was rudimentary and, at times, futile compared to the divine afterlife. All I wanted to do was remain in the light, travelling through what seemed to be time. Then, as if that wasn't enough, I met the love of my life, Ernesto. It was so joyous to see him again. Although we didn't seem to talk, we communicated."

At that point, Rosa's demeanour changed. She appeared brighter, smiling radiantly at Alicia and Carl, who sat spellbound, captivated by the beautiful account of Nana's journey in the afterlife.

"Then I realised that Tariq was with us. It was such a nice surprise. He communicated with me spiritually to make sure I was alright. Responding to him and other family members who had joined us was unbelievably fulfilling. But then, something troubled me. I was happy and content beyond anything I had ever experienced before, yet it was incomplete. I knew I had to return to see you again and let you know I was happy in the afterlife. Tariq realised my concern." She looked over to him and nodded appreciatively. "He helped me to understand that it was possible to return, but with limitations."

Although silent and staggered by Nana's account, neither Alicia nor Carl were troubled by Rosa's incredible tale. More than that, they felt hugely comforted by her explanation of heaven and knew they would never be concerned or frightened of dying.

"So here I am now, thanks to Tariq," she smiled again, "to see you two lovely people and make sure you don't mourn my passing. I am so happy being with my beloved Ernesto, and meeting other family members has made it complete for me. Even better, I feel no pain or discomfort in the light, and my weakness of old age does not feature at all. We are all as one, loving, happy, and whole. So, fear not, heaven is a lovely place. Time here on Earth is just a stage in life's cycle. Once you move on, you will understand what I'm saying, and I'll be there to greet you."

"Thank you, Nana," said Carl, feeling comforted. We have missed you so much, and seeing you again is more than we could ever have imagined." He looked at Alicia and back at Nana. We love you and are so happy for you."

"Yes, we feel so happy to see you again, and after recovering from the shock, we realise it is such a precious moment. I love you, Nana, so very much," said Alicia, overjoyed with the unique, never-to-be-repeated experience.

"And I love you too, dear Alicia. The strange thing is that you haven't lost me. I am merely in another dimension, and although I can feel your presence around me in the afterlife, it's as if I understand life more innately."

Alicia took hold of Carl's hand. "I can't say that we understand life fully, but I do know that our life together is so amazing and joyous, and we love being together so much that we can't wait to return home after a day's work and embrace each other. Ours is a unique kind of love, and we know it will continue forever."

Rosa felt pleased that she had played a part in their first meeting in Pamplona, yet she still did not admit to orchestrating the union.

"Now, there is just one final thing I would like to do before I return to that beautiful place with my family. I want to embrace you, but I'm unable to do so physically. So, I've already asked for assistance from Tariq, who has helped me find a way to give you one final hug here in this mortal world."

"Really," said Alicia, beside herself with surprise and joy, yet unsure how it would work. Hugging Nana would help them say a final goodbye in peace and love, communicating their affection for each other in a truly unique and precious way.

"If you stand up and put an arm around each other's waists, standing side by side, I will walk towards you. Then, place your hand near where you see my shoulder, and we will be able to connect spiritually. However, Tariq tells me this is only possible with Carl's telepathy, which allows him to sense feelings from objects and people. So, by linking with you, we will complete a circle of love, life, and togetherness. I am not a person in the true sense with a physical body; even so, I know this will work."

With excitement and trepidation, Carl and Alicia did as asked. Nana moved towards them, close enough for Carl's right hand and Alicia's left hand to reach her shoulders. Then it happened. All the joy and love throughout eternity flowed through them. Nothing mattered anymore. Their joyous, loving circle of togetherness as one was overwhelming; they just wanted it to continue forever. Alicia saw members of her family who had passed over. Carl saw his grandparents for the first time. There were no bright colours in that realm, no sound or movement, simply love, warmth, and a sense of well-being. Alicia wanted that feeling to last. She had made contact with Nana but wanted more. The feeling was all-consuming, beautiful, and inexplicable. Carl felt all that Alicia was experiencing and more. Thoughts, emotions, and sensations rushed through his mind like never before. He willed the sensation to continue forever. Then, Tariq stepped in behind Rosa to support her.

"My friends, we must leave it there. Your nana has put so much energy into meeting you, and we must end it now."

Slowly, the experience came to a close, and they faced each other one final time on Earth's realm.

"Just like you, I will never forget this moment," said Rosa. "I am so sorry, but I must go to be with my loved ones and recover from this bliss." Joy and yet weakness showed on her fragile face.

"I'm sorry, she is fading, and I don't want to ask any more of her," said Tariq. He seemed to support Rosa even more, giving her the strength to maintain her equilibrium.

"No, of course not, Tariq," said Alicia, now feeling emotional yet holding back tears for the sake of Nana.

"We should go," Nana confirmed. Now that I know you two lovebirds are okay, I can rest easy and rejoin Ernesto and the family." She smiled lovingly and looked to her friend and confidant, Tariq.

"Well, shall we?"

With that, they walked back the way they came down the meandering passageway, but not before Rosa turned and blew them a kiss.

"Goodbye, my children . . . Goodbye."

EPILOGUE

The basket of persimmons mysteriously left at the Finca's door was left by a local lady who was unaware that Rosa had been in an accident and had ultimately moved to Pamplona to live with her daughter. The friend had left the fruit as a token of respect and thanks for the help she had received for her sick (now deceased) husband. Unfortunately, shortly after the fruit event, the local lady could not cope with life anymore and had to be admitted into an elderly person's home because of a depressive illness, which led to an inability to look after herself.

The priest continued to serve the church in his parish. However, he hit a bad spot where the drink took hold and affected his working life, stopping him from performing his duties as a parish priest. Because of alcohol addiction, he was admitted to a special hospital run by nuns. After two months and ten days, he had recovered sufficiently well enough to be discharged home; following his recovery, he took a short sabbatical. Enjoying life so much in Brindisi, Southern Italy, he gave up his position in the Catholic Church in Jalon and took up a post at a Catholic home for children in Italy. Carl and Alicia kept in constant touch with him and planned to fly out to see him soon.

The mystery of Carl's missing Persimmon fruit at the top of Caballo Verde, where they sat and ate a snack, was a strange affair. Although deceased, some spirits of the Moors remained on the mountain, not wanting to leave. One in particular, Dekel, had struck up a pleasing relationship with Tariq. He reminded him of himself as a lad full of life, vitality, and hope for the future.

Even though Tariq tried to persuade him otherwise, that his family was long gone, Dekel always believed he would meet his grandparents again. On one of those days, when he roamed Caballo Verde, attracted by the voices of Carl, Alicia, and the priest, who were taking a break, he saw the fruit and took it. Unable to eat it, he left the fruit for a young boy living with his parents in a lowly hovel further down the mountain.

Neither the jinni nor the shadow people ever appeared around the Finca, Murla, or Caballo Verde ever again. According to Tariq, there was no guarantee that the evil one had been vanquished completely. It's death by Carl driving the spearhead into the dog's chest, saw it off, but it was never the end. He believed that the secretive, sly ways of the entity were challenging to predict, and so he cautioned Carl and Alicia to keep a lookout for odd happenings. Nevertheless, after many months of nothing unusual occurring in the area, they presumed the jinni to be defunct and gone.

Tariq, their very good friend, manifested from time to time. On walks up the mountain, they occasionally saw him in passing and stopped to chat. Then, for many months, the sightings stopped. One morning, they found a message on their doorstep, written on parchment, explaining that his life on Earth was at an end. His work was complete, and it was time for him to depart and enter the afterlife (Jannah). He could not bear to say goodbye to Alicia and Carlos in person, but he felt sure they would understand. Tariq asked them not to think badly of how he left and was sure they would meet again, where he would say hello and tell them all the amazing stories of his time spent in Spain.

The final line of his deeply moving message expressed his profound love and devotion to Carl, Alicia, and Rosa, and he thanked them all for enriching his life.

Wadaeaan al' an. (Farewell for now).

A MESSAGE FROM THE AUTHOR.

Thank you for purchasing my historical mystery thriller. The story is based on historical fact (The Spanish Inquisition) from the reign of King Phillip III of Spain, 1578 – 1621. It covers a mere part of the turmoil in the region of Valencia, which raged on for years with the brutal expulsion of the Moriscos.

I hope you enjoyed the story as much as I did in writing it. If it immersed you in the history of Spain and transported you to that era, and you found the characters engaging, maybe even believable, then I have done my job.

Would you consider posting a review on Amazon? If so, head over to Amazon Books, type in the novel's name and author, and click the button at the bottom of my page to leave a review.

Alternatively, use "Your Rating" on the Kindle's last page.

Your feedback (I read them all) helps me continue writing intriguing books that help potential buyers make informed choices.

Stuart.